"You ran o

"I'm sorry," she said, her eyes glued to the stage curtains.

"If you didn't like crepes, I could have made you something else."

"It's not that." She gripped the arm rest between them. "I had to get to work—"

"Shhh," he whispered, his hand closing over hers. "We'll talk later."

Victoria was vaguely aware that the lights had dimmed, and the curtain was beginning to rise. All she could think about was Sebastian holding her hand. His four fingers were curled under her palm, and his thumb caressed the top of her fingers in an occasional slow, gentle stroke as though it was the most natural thing in the world.

She felt her body temperature rise, the awareness of his touch coursing through every nerve in her body. The fluttering in her stomach melted into a hot pit of need in her core.

She pulled her hand away from his grasp. "I forgot to put my phone on silent mode," she whispered as she fumbled with her purse.

The Billionaire's PRICE

a steamy romance

ANSELA CORSINO

QUEEN'S KISS BOOKS
Philippines

Copyright © 2016 Ansela Corsino
All rights reserved.

This is a work of fiction. Names, characters, places and incidents either are products of the author's imagination or are used fictitiously. Any resemblance to actual events or locales or persons, living or dead, is entirely coincidental.

For inquiries and orders, please contact the author at author@anselacorsino.com .

ISBN: 153-0-199-174
ISBN--13: 978-153-0-199-174

CONTENTS

1 — Into the Chocolate Box	1
2 — Scent	6
3 — The Foxhole	11
4 — Chance	14
5 — Late Night	19
6 — Drive	25
7 — Moonlight	30
8 — Distractions	34
9 — Champagne Afternoon	38
10 — No Reservations	43
11 — Delivery	49
12 — Getting Comfortable	53
13 — Bargaining	58
14 — Key Six	63
15 — Fire	68
16 — Heading for the Hills	72
17 — Rendezvous	77
18 — Air	83
19 — Gossip	89
20 — A Very Long Walk	95
21 — Losing Control	101
22 — All Night	109
23 — Waiting	114
24 — Study Habits	120
25 — Sleep Over	126
26 — Play	133

27 — A Fear of Flying		139
28 — Market Day		144
29 — Blue Bird		150
30 — Taking Flight		156
31 — Making Friends		163
32 — Distances		170
33 — Family		178
34 — Trust		185
35 — Decisions		192
36 — Moving On		197
37 — On the Street Where You Live		202
38 — Confessions		207

About the Author

The Billionaire's Price

CHAPTER 1

Into the Chocolate Box

"I'm so sorry I'm late, Vic," said Mabel Jones. She was flushed and a little sweaty as she tied her apron on, having just rushed over five blocks.

"Don't worry about it, Bel. I'm happy to do it," said Victoria Slade. She began to untie her own apron, the same brown one that had the name of the coffee shop "The Foxhole" printed on it in white. Her eyes were soft with concern. "Is Jenni going to be okay?"

"Yes, she's better now. I'll have to take her back to the doctor tomorrow for another checkup, but at least her wheezing had stopped. Thank you so much for taking over my shift." Mabel gave Victoria a tight hug. "I've had too many absences this month, I'd probably have gotten fired if you hadn't covered for me."

Victoria could see the faintest sign of tears in her friend's eyes. Clearly her daughter Jenni's latest asthma attack had been pretty bad, and had left her shaken. "Are you sure *you're* going to be okay? Because I'm happy to work your whole shift if you need to be home."

"No, no, I'll be fine. You better get going, you have that job interview this afternoon. Oh dear, can you still make it?"

"I think so." Victoria looked up at the wall clock behind them. Three thirty. She had half an hour to her interview, which meant she had no time to go home and get dressed.

Five minutes later, in the locker room, she was trying to smooth the wrinkles on her grey skirt. Her black top was of a soft lightweight wool that didn't need pressing, however, it was old and a little shabby. Not the ideal attire to a job interview, but it would have to do. Her long wavy auburn hair hadn't been properly washed since yesterday, and it smelled like turnovers, so she had hurriedly tied it up in a bun. She still had a chance to make the interview, and for that she was thankful. When Mabel called her at noon to ask if she would take over her shift for a couple of hours, she didn't hesitate. Victoria needed to get the job she was interviewing for, but Mabel needed the café job even more. She had a sickly six-year-old daughter at home whom she was raising by herself: there was no one else to take her to to the hospital whenever she had one of her asthma attacks.

When she got to Third Street, Victoria's eyes scanned the high rise buildings above her. She wasn't familiar with L.A.'s financial district, and she would have looked up the map online if she had the time. She looked at her watch for the third time in the past minute: three fifty-five. She looked up again and after a moment, she finally spotted the address.

The Mattheson Building loomed tall and stately, all gleaming glass and steel in the L.A. sunshine. Victoria's misgivings about her clothes increased as soon as she walked into the elegant and richly appointed lobby. It was like stepping into a box of expensive French chocolates, except the place may have smelled even better. Her pace slowed down, every step an apology to the pale cream marble floor with gold flecks which her cheap flat shoes had no business touching.

As she pressed the elevator button for the 55th floor, it suddenly dawned on her that it had to be a mistake, this job interview. People who had offices on the 55th floor didn't hire tutors who advertised on community newspapers and questionable online ad websites, which was the only places she could afford to post ads for her services as a tutor. She did try an agency, but they wouldn't take her for her lack of experience. She was fresh out of graduate school, and trying to make ends meet with freelance magazine writing jobs and her stint at the coffee shop.

The 55th was even more luxurious than the lobby. A chandelier graced the high ceilings, and sofas in rich leather rested on thick-piled carpeting around the round receptionist desk where a man and a woman sat, both on the telephone, as she walked towards them. Whoever it was she was interviewing with, they could definitely afford her rates.

The man saw her approach, and she gave him a nervous smile. While he nodded in return, he continued his phone conversation.

Victoria waited, but a minute passed before the man finally hung up.

"Hi. I'm Victoria Slade," she said. "I have an interview for the tutor position at four." She grimaced. "I'm so sorry I'm late."

The man smiled pleasantly. "Unfortunately, Ms. Slade, it's ten minutes past four," he said. "Mr. Chase is no longer available to see you."

Her heart sank. "I can wait. Or perhaps we could reschedule? I'm willing to come back anytime that's convenient." Who did he say it was? "Anytime it's convenient for Mr. Chase," she added.

He smiled at her sympathetically. "I'll see what I can do. However, Mr. Chase is extremely busy, and I highly doubt he would be willing to schedule another appointment."

"Is that him?" She pointed to a tall man in a suit emerging from a door on their left. He was followed by a lanky, younger man carrying a briefcase and some folders.

"Yes, but—"

"Mr. Chase!" she called out, walking toward the man as fast as she could without running.

"Ms. Slade, please—" the receptionist started to say, but she didn't hear the rest of it.

When Chase met her gaze, Victoria nearly froze.

She had fully expected him to be some middle-aged man, since the job she had applied for was as a tutor for a fifth grader. So it was a bit of a shock to find a man who couldn't possibly be older than thirty-five or thirty-six.

Nothing prepared her for the intensity of his blue eyes or the perfection of the rest of his face. His light gray suit looked like it had been molded on to his trim figure by one of the renaissance sculptors. Michelangelo, maybe. Her knees turned to jelly under her, but something about him kept her moving inexorably forward. It was almost like gravity.

"Yes?" he said.

"I, uh," she stammered.

He raised an eyebrow, but didn't break a stride.

"Hi, I'm Victoria Slade," she said, finding her voice. "Your four o'clock? I know I'm late but—"

"Punctuality doesn't seem to be a priority for you, Ms. Slade." He brushed past her.

"I apologize," she said, walking beside him. It was hard to keep up with him and his long legs, but she did the best she could. "I thought perhaps we could reschedule. I'll come back anytime—"

"Your resume says you work at a coffee shop," he said, interrupting her again. "Is that the best you could do with your masters degree?"

"No. I mean, I've stated in my resume that I also write for magazines."

As they walked past the reception desk, the man behind it gaped at her silently.

"You do freelance writing," Mr. Chase said. "And you don't make enough that you have to wait tables at a coffee shop, and now do tutoring work?"

"I have to make ends meet, Mr. Chase. Writers don't exactly get paid as much as hedge fund managers."

"No, but surely a woman of your intelligence and credentials should be able to manage her career and finances better."

"I don't understand. What does that have to do with the tutor position?"

They were walking toward an elevator. It had wider doors than the others, and was positioned farther away from the other. A personal lift, perhaps? His assistant rushed ahead of them and tapped a card on a panel on the side, and the doors opened silently.

"I'm looking for someone to entrust my child's educational care. I cannot give it to someone who can't seem to take care of their own financial well-being. Or," he said, looking at her pointedly, "can't seem to show up for a job interview on time."

She opened her mouth to argue, and realized she had nothing to say to that.

He got inside the elevator with his assistant, leaving her standing outside.

Victoria wasn't sure what possessed her, but in a moment of impulse, she dashed inside the elevator before the doors closed.

"Ms. Slade, what are you doing?"

I don't know, she thought. It was as though she was compelled by forces beyond her control.

"I, uh …" she stammered. *Great going, Slade. Really articulate.* She cleared her throat. "Mr. Chase, I completely understand how you feel."

"Do you?" He nodded to his assistant. "Let's go, Frank."

His assistant pressed a button for one of the basement floors. The elevator doors closed and they began their descent.

"I'm not an economics or finance major," Victoria continued, seeing as he made no move to kick her out of the lift. "I'm pretty good with numbers but horrible with money. As a matter of fact, I only like money as much as it can pay for my groceries or my car insurance. But I don't think your child needs a financial advisor right now. What he needs is someone who believes in the importance of learning, someone well-rounded who can make him see how different areas of knowledge are connected. Help him see how education is relevant to real life."

Chase didn't look at her as she spoke. He kept his eyes on the doors of the elevator, his face expressionless. Was he bored? Was he even listening to her?

"I think you want this for him," she added. "This is why you asked me to come for this interview despite the fact that I've had no experience. The reason you considered hiring me was because of my educational background in English and Literature, and the fact that I write for science magazines."

She studied his face, waiting for a response. Nothing.

"You didn't hire an experienced tutor because he probably already goes to school run by highly paid teaching professionals," she said. "But you want him to acquire an imagination, which is why you want to hire me."

"Anything more, Ms. Slade?" he said, still not looking at her.

"Uhm, no. That's it."

"I see. Frank, we'll be dropping Ms. Slade off at the first floor."

"Yes, sir."

She watched Frank push the first floor button, and her heart sank.

"My apologies, Ms. Slade, if you were under the wrong impression about this job," Chase said. "I'm looking for someone to take responsibility for my son's education outside of school. His school demands much from him, and I want to make sure he is able to keep up with these demands. I don't believe you and he will make a good fit. Thank you for your time."

"Oh. I see." She had hoped he would at least tell her he would think about it and get back to her, but this was clearly a man who didn't like to waste time. Disappointment felt like a physical lump in her throat, but she straightened her back, looked him in the eye and forced herself to smile.

"I understand. Thank you for your time, Mr. Chase."

When the elevator opened at the first floor, she walked out. But a sudden thought made her stop and turn. "You seem to care for your son very much," she said. "I hope you find what you're looking for."

Victoria turned and walked away just as the elevator doors began to close.

Well, that was that. She did her best, at least. She was still surprised at how she had jumped into that elevator without a thought in her head. They could have thrown her out the building for that.

What were you thinking, Slade?

CHAPTER 2

Scent

*C*innamon.

The smell of spice lingered long after she had left the elevator. It was oddly mesmerizing, breathing in her scent as she stood close to him in the elevator. Sebastian could still picture the lights glinting on her dark red hair as she walked away. His gaze had lingered on the pale skin on the back of her neck, making him wonder what it would be like to touch it.

"Sir, don't forget your check," Frank said, pulling him out of his reverie. His assistant took out a cream-colored envelope from a folder he carried. "It's the one you signed yesterday, made out to the children's foundation. I know you hate bringing your checkbook with you."

"Thank you Frank," Sebastian said, putting the envelope in his jacket pocket. The elevator doors opened and they stepped out into the basement parking lot where a large grey limousine was waiting for them. "I suppose I can't just drop this off at the reception, can I?"

"You could. But if people see you getting chummy with the hospital board and personally handing them a check, they're more likely to give a donation of their own. You'll have plenty of time after your meeting to get to the fundraiser. Are you sure you don't want me at the meeting?"

"It's really more of an informal chat with the British ambassador, Frank. I'll need you here to help Callie prep for the meeting next week for the Beijing deal. Her new assistant can barely keep up with her."

"Yes, sir."

One of Sebastian's bodyguards, Selene, opened the limousine door for him. "Mr. Chase," she greeted him as he got inside.

"How is your mother, Selene?" he said as she sat down across from him.

"She's fine, sir. Thank you."

They rode in silence, and Sebastian's mind went to the impromptu interview with the latest applicant for the tutoring job. It was a pity Ms. Slade did not pass muster. Her resume wasn't bad. Cum laude graduate of English at a respectable university. A master's degree in Comparative Literature. Bylines in the local papers. Nothing too grand, but her essays were thoughtful and sharp. He had read an article of hers published two years ago titled "Are we raising our sons to be boys or men?" and this was what prompted him to shortlist her among the applicants for the job. In the piece, she described how society has been teaching toxic values of masculinity, producing boys unprepared for a modern, more progressive age of gender equality.

He'd been raised that way, and he hated it. His father, a patriarch — in every sense of the word — of an old Texas banking dynasty did his best to mold Sebastian into his image.

Benson deserved better.

When Benson's father — Sebastian's brother Eric — passed away five years ago, and his mother permitted Sebastian to adopt the boy, Sebastian swore he would do good by his nephew. He had made sure to raise him with better values than what he himself had been forced to live by growing up.

Now his adopted son was ten years old, and while he seemed happy and healthy, Sebastian worried about the lack of a female role model in his life. Sebastian had no other siblings, and doubted he would be getting married any day soon. He thought the best solution was to hire a female tutor and companion for him. His son was enrolled in the best private school, and the curriculum was challenging enough that most of their students had tutors.

There was no question about whether or not to hire Ms. Slade. He could never abide by tardiness. When a person acted with discipline, it was a reflection of a disciplined mind. Which was what he needed in a tutor for his son Benson.

Sebastian had three other interviews lined up for the job. He was sure Ms. Slade would find a position elsewhere that would make the most of her talents, but for now that position wasn't that of tutor to his son.

"You seem to care for your son very much. I hope you find what you're looking for."

He felt an emotion nearly overwhelm him, and he realized it was regret.

It was something he hadn't felt for a very long time.

***

"Tell me again why you aren't trying acting? Lots of aspiring screenwriters try to get a break that way," Victoria said. "I mean, look how well it worked for Matt Damon and Ben Affleck. And Sylvester Stallone."

Her best friend and roommate Nicolette rolled her eyes delicately, in a way that very few girls are able to. "Are you kidding me? Can you imagine the really horrible lines I'd have to work with until I get to work in a decent production?"

"Most actors just have to go through it at the start, I think."

"Most actors have the patience for it," said Nicolette.

She had a point, Victoria thought. Nicolette wasn't the kind of person to do anything she wasn't crazy about. She was either all in or not at all. This explained much of her career trajectory: make mad money working as an escort while (in her words) her ass was still pointed the right way, until she got her scripts on theater screens across the country.

She and Nicolette were hanging out in Nicolette's bedroom watching movies. It was their favorite thing to do together. They didn't get a lot of time together because Nicolette worked mostly at night and Victoria worked during the day, so on the rare occasions they were both free, they made sure to schedule some quality girl-bonding time. Tonight, they were having quiche from the corner bakery, and watching *Old Boy*, one of Nicolette's all-time favorite films. As they'd already seen it together about fifty times, they were having a light discussion about Nicolette's writing career.

"Plus," Nicolette added, "do you know how my clients like to talk about their lives?"

"Yeah, you mentioned that." Victoria laughed, recalling the stories Nicolette would tell her about the men she'd go out with at her job, ranging from hilarious to creepy to just plain sad. One of them had her over to cook him Thanksgiving dinner because he couldn't celebrate it with his ex-wife and estranged children. A terrible cook who prided herself in this particular non-talent, Nicolette ended up serving burnt turkey and soggy mashed potatoes, but the 45-year-old investment banker was so happy he cried.

"I get a glimpse into the lives of the rich, powerful, and sometimes sad men and women of L.A.," said Nicolette. "It's the stuff great movies are made of."

"I love that I get to talk to you about these things," Victoria said. "I never get to meet anyone rich and powerful. Well, hardly ever." She suddenly remembered blue eyes and dark hair. "Hey, actually I did meet someone like that today."

"At the coffee shop?"

Victoria shook her head. "Job interview."

"I didn't know you had a job interview today. How did it go?"

"Not well. Disastrous." Victoria sighed.

"I'm sorry, sweetie," Nicolette said. "I'm sure you'll find something soon. So, this guy interviewed you?"

"Yeah. Some big brass over at Mattheson Bank downtown, the corporate office. I was late."

Nicolette frowned. "Must have been really big brass — a VP or CEO or something — if he gets to interview his kid's tutor at work."

"I'm pretty sure his tie costs more than what I make in a year. Anyway, I had to practically run after him and try to convince him he should hire me." She winced. "That was probably not the best move."

"You didn't try to sit on his lap, did you?"

"What? No!" Victoria laughed. "I jumped in his private elevator with him. The receptionist looked like he was about to get a heart attack."

"That's not something I would ever imagine you'd do, Vic." Nicolette eyed her suspiciously. "Was he hot?"

Victoria bit her lip and nodded. "Oh my god, is that why I ran after him?"

Nicolette burst out laughing. Victoria groaned, fell backwards on the bed and covered her face with a pillow.

"You know, if you find yourself running down hot bankers in hallways, it may be a sign you really need to get laid. Like, soon," Nicolette said.

"I know!" Victoria's voice was muffled from the pillow over her face.

"It's been two months, babe." Nicolette grabbed the pillow and her face hovered over Victoria's. "You're not still hung up over Jason, are you?"

"What? No!" Victoria tried to grab the pillow from Nicolette, who pulled it away from her reach.

"Oh really? Have you seen anyone since then?"

Victoria gave up trying to get the pillow back. "I've been busy. I'm job-hunting, remember?"

"Fine," Nicolette said. "But once you get a proper job, I'm setting you up with some guys I know."

"I thought you said a girl doesn't need a boyfriend."

"What is this, the 19th century? I didn't say anything about a boyfriend. All I'm saying is sex will do you some good."

"Is that why you're always so bright and cheerful?" Victoria teased. She picked up a mushroom and artichoke quiche. "Because of all the sex you're having?" She grinned evilly.

"Damn right it is. And I'm going to make sure you're getting some soon, even if I have to pay for it."

Victoria nearly dropped the quiche she was in the process of biting into. "Really, you'd do that?"

"How about we see if anyone will do you for free first." Nicolette pretended to look her friend over with a critical eye.

"I don't know. I think I smell like doughnuts. Is that a thing men like?" Victoria sniffed the front of her shirt. When she first started work at the Foxhole, she enjoyed the aroma of coffee and pastries. After a couple of weeks, however, it started to get old. And stick to her clothes and hair.

Nicolette sighed. "You seriously need a new job."

CHAPTER 3

The Foxhole

Sebastian Chase was restless.

It didn't help that his car had been stuck in a rush hour traffic jam for the past twenty minutes. Usually, he would be on his phone, or reading the business news on his tablet, but today he felt like a caged animal inside his large Lincoln town car.

He was on his way to a dinner. However, it was more of a business function than a social one. Unless he was dining a beautiful woman, he preferred his social interactions to have purpose, specifically one that would further his business goals. More business meant more work for more people.

Business. The well-oiled machine of commerce. That's what he thought about most days.

Today was different. Instead, he wondered when was the last time he took a walk out in the sun. Golf games didn't count — if you played with clients, technically that was still work. And Sebastian only ever played with clients, or business partners.

It was the same with all the parties he'd ever gone to. The Mattheson Bank was his family empire, so even family gatherings were business-related. At least, that's how he'd come to think of them. His relationship with his father was not the most cordial, and neither was he particularly fond of his father's siblings or their children. The only people he thought of as his family, other than his son Benson, were his mother and his brother Eric, and they were both gone.

It was at that moment that Sebastian realized what the date was.

"Connor, I'm going for a walk," he told his driver.

"Sir?" If Connor Mills was surprised, he didn't show it. It was part of his job. If Sebastian had suddenly asked him to wait outside a jewelry store while he robbed it, Connor would merely ask if Mr. Chase wanted him to keep the engine running.

"Please give my regrets to the Chapmans, and charge their dinner check to me."

"Certainly, sir."

Sebastian opened the door and stepped out the car. He didn't know where he was going, not really, but that didn't matter.

He consciously walked away from where everyone seemed to be heading, walking past restaurants, flower shops and banks. He remembered his brother Eric once told him he wanted to open up a small shop that sold nothing but socks. "Wouldn't Dad throw a fit?" he'd said, laughing.

"Probably," Sebastian had replied. "Then he'd come back after a month to check if your sales were improving."

"Sadly, it seems you're the only businessman in the family, Sebastian. I don't think I'll be good at anything. Maybe I should find me a nice hardworking wife, and I could stay home and cook for our kids."

"So long as she doesn't plan on selling socks, you should be fine."

Eric and their mother passed away in a plane crash on this day five years ago. Eric had left a son, and a wife he'd been separated from a mere two years after they were married. Their mother only had him and Eric, having been divorced from Sebastian's father since Eric was born. Sebastian was the only one who ever remembered she was in that plane crash too.

There would be no phone call from his father. No dinner on the anniversary of his mother and brother's deaths. No words of consolation for each other. They didn't do that sort of thing. They didn't have a personal relationship, just a business one. All George Mattheson expected from him was a healthy growth in the family corporation, and a healthy heir to that corporation to take over after Sebastian retired.

It would just be another day for his father.

The streets were both familiar and unfamiliar to him. He may have passed through the area once or a hundred times, he wouldn't know. Sebastian didn't take walks, not really. He barely glanced outside when being chauffeured from place to place. He wasn't hungry, but a sign on a coffee shop window caught his eye for some reason he couldn't put his finger on. On impulse, he went inside.

It was not a fashionable coffee shop by any means. The décor was simple and old fashioned. The first thing that hit him was the familiar smell of cinnamon and bread. He took a seat at a table farthest from the door.

"What can I get you, hon?" said the waitress who appeared almost immediately after he sat down. She was thin and pale, and looked about forty. Her brown hair was pulled up in a bun. "The doughnuts are freshly made. They're real good with coffee."

"I'll have one then," Sebastian said. "And coffee."

"I'll be right back." She looked tired, but her smile was warm.

According to her nameplate, she was Mabel. Sebastian didn't even need to read it — customers called her by her name. She chatted up a couple of them on her way to the counter, asking how they were and if they wanted a refill on their coffee.

It didn't take long before she was back with Sebastian's coffee and doughnut. He nodded his thanks. As she moved away, an elderly man from the next table called out to her.

"Hey Mabel. How's Jenni?" he said. "I heard you had to rush her to the hospital yesterday."

"She's fine, Cal. Spent two hours in the emergency room, and I was near out of my mind with worry. But the doctor changed her meds and she's been fine since then. Thanks for asking," Mabel said. "Thank goodness Victoria offered to take my shift yesterday."

It was then that Sebastian realized why the name of the place seemed so familiar. He'd seen it on a resumé recently. The Foxhole. Current employer of one Victoria Slade.

"That was right sweet of of her, Mabel," the elderly customer said.

"That girl is some kind of angel, I tell you," Mabel said. "She had an appointment that same afternoon too. A job interview I think. Now that I think about it, I hope I didn't make her miss it." She shook her head and picked up an empty dish from the elderly man's table. "More water, Cal?"

CHAPTER 4

Chance

Victoria was in a good mood.

She was sleepy as hell, however. She'd finished four thousand words on the manuscript of her novel last night, and ended up going to bed at five a.m. It barely gave her a few hours of sleep, and enough time to do her laundry that had been piling up since the week before.

Four thousand words! She was rarely that productive. She'd been writing that novel for a year now, but things have been going at such a slow pace. There was always something more urgent to attend to. But something had inspired her yesterday. Maybe the fact that the interview had been an utter disappointment, and, afterwards, spending some quality best friend time with Nicolette and forcing her to come to terms with the lack of excitement in her life. Whatever it was, she hoped it was the start of a new writing streak. Before last night, she hadn't touched her manuscript in two weeks.

That should be enough doughnuts for today, she thought, putting the last one in the cake display case. It wasn't her job to cook, but making the doughnuts was a special task she liked doing. She had spent the past two hours frying them and dipping them in sugar, it now was time for her to work the tables. "I'm heading out front, Mack. You can handle things here, right?"

Ellis McClay was frying something on the stove with his back to her. He waved to say it was ok. The short-order cook didn't like to talk much. Victoria smiled to herself and headed to the back to change her apron before going out front.

It startled her considerably, seeing Sebastian Chase. It wasn't that he looked out of place — the Foxhole was a popular spot for corporate types who worked within a five-block radius — but seeing him there felt like something out of a dream.

In a perfectly-tailored grey suit, he looked entirely like the busy businessman that he was, but not exactly. He looked out of place, but perhaps it was because she could only remember him among the gleaming steel and concrete of a place entirely different from the warm confines of the Foxhole. Seeing him sitting at one of the shop's tables like it was something he did every day was somewhat jarring.

"Do you have any more doughnuts, lady?" asked one of the teenagers at a table near where she stood, and she realized she'd been practically gawking at Chase.

"Of course, yes, sorry. How many?"

"Two," said the teenager.

"Anything else?" Her mind was racing. What should she do? Come over and say hi? She was at work, and it wasn't as though he was a friend.

"Nah. Just the doughnuts."

"Be right back."

Chase wasn't in her assigned section. That meant she wouldn't have to serve him. He'd still see her, though. Should she smile? Nod?

Victoria sighed. If it were anyone else, she wouldn't be overthinking all this.

She went to fetch the doughnuts. She picked up a coffee pot and refilled customers' cups. She took two more orders. All the time she kept surreptitiously glancing over at Chase trying to ascertain if he'd seen her.

If he had, he didn't give any indication so far that he recognized her. He sat there and drank his coffee and looked at his doughnut like it was some kind of alien artifact.

"You know, if you stared at him any harder, your eyes might pop out of their sockets," said a voice behind her. Victoria nearly jumped out of her skin.

"Oh. Hi, Rach," said Victoria, trying not to blush. Rach was a fellow waitress working that afternoon shift. She didn't speak much, and in fact looked sullen most of the time.

"I didn't mean to stare, really," Victoria said. "I kinda ... know him."

"Well, he doesn't seem to know you," Rach said, and left.

No he doesn't, Victoria thought.

Fair enough. The man was a CEO of a large bank, he would have too much on his mind to remember a single interview of a woman he didn't give the job to.

Now, if only Victoria could focus on her own work, maybe she wouldn't lose this job as well.

She couldn't help wonder, though, what brought him to the coffee shop. She'd never seen him there before. Chase was a good-looking, imposing figure of a man — she was sure to remember him. After all, she remembered every married couple who lived within a two-block radius who'd come by for a quick breakfast on their way to work. And the assistants who worked from the buildings across the street who picked up coffee and pastry for meetings in the afternoon.

Men like Chase didn't go for a coffee and doughnut at five in the afternoon on a weekday and just sit there without so much as a tablet or cellphone in hand. And even if he did, there must have been about a hundred other coffee shops near his office. Did something terrible happen and he needed some time alone? Someplace far from his usual haunts, maybe an old coffee shop with good old-fashioned homemade doughnuts?

Well, if he did, he didn't seem too eager to eat it. The doughnut sat there in front of him, getting cold.

Her doughnut. Why wouldn't he eat it?

After fulfilling orders of two other tables, Victoria glanced at Chase one more time while refilling coffee cups. Mabel was chatting with him while she served him what looked like his second refill. The doughnut still sat there, uneaten.

She couldn't take it anymore.

She waited until after Mabel had left, and walked over to his table. Chase looked up at her but showed no sign he recognized her.

"You know, it may not look very fancy," she said, trying not to lose her nerve. "But that's a really good doughnut."

"Really." He glanced down at the doughnut, looked up at her and raised his eyebrows.

"Yes. I made it myself. It's my dad's recipe. At the end of a hard work day, it's just the thing to give you a little comfort. And it's not too sweet, so —" She stopped when Chase picked up the doughnut and took a bite.

He chewed thoughtfully for a second. He didn't look like he liked it, but he didn't look like he hated it either.

"Well?" She looked at him expectantly.

"It's a good doughnut. Thank you, Victoria."

She felt her face flush hearing him say her first name. "Uh, y-y-you're welcome," she blurted out. She was about to head back to the counter but he spoke to her again.

"Do you have any other clothes?"

"Excuse me?"

"Do you have any clothes more ... decent-looking than that outfit you wore to the interview yesterday?"

"I'm not sure what you mean by ... decent—" Victoria started to say.

"I mean, do you own any clothes that don't look as though they should be donated to Goodwill?" He looked at her from head to foot, taking in her slightly faded flower print dress and light sneakers. "Although from what you're wearing now, I'm afraid I know the answer to that."

Stunned, she could only stare at him, unable to say a word.

"Well?"

"Well." She swallowed, trying to keep her anger from making her voice shake. "No, Mr. Chase. Unfortunately, I can't afford to buy a lot of new clothes. Although I'm not quite sure why I'm telling you this, seeing as it's really none of your business what I wear."

"It is, if you're working for me."

Was he crazy? Victoria thought. "I'm not —"

"Is something wrong here?" Mabel asked behind her. The woman smiled pleasantly at Chase, and looked questioningly at Victoria.

"No!" Victoria said. "I mean, we were just talking about the doughnuts," she added hastily.

Chase smiled back at Mabel. "Mabel, would you mind terribly if Victoria join me for a minute?" he asked.

"*Victoria*, is unable to join you, Mr. Chase," Victoria said, trying to keep her temper down. "She has to wait tables." It was hard to ignore the way his blue eyes sparkled as he smiled at the now flustered Mabel, and it only made Victoria angrier.

"Of course, uh..." Mabel started to say.

"Call me Sebastian," he said.

"Of course, Sebastian." She turned to Victoria. "Oh don't worry, Vic, I'm happy to take care of your tables for a couple of minutes. Rachel will help me." She winked at Victoria before leaving her alone with Chase.

"But .." *Rach never does anyone any favors,* Victoria was about to say to Mabel when Sebastian Chase interrupted her.

"Sit down please, Ms. Slade." He was no longer smiling.

Victoria hardly knew this man, and yet he was ordering her around and expecting her to comply. But she didn't want to cause a scene, so she sat down opposite him at the table.

"May I have your notepad, please?" he said, holding his hand out.

Now more puzzled than annoyed, she took her notepad out of her apron pocket and handed it to him.

He took out a fountain pen. "When you go here," he said, writing something on the pad, "look for a Ms. Deborah Williams. She'll know what to do." He tore off the piece of paper and handed it to her.

Victoria stared at the paper. It was the address of Barneys on Wilshire. And a floor in the building. "I don't understand."

Chase was writing on the notepad again. "It's a store, Ms. Slade," he said, not looking up. "They sell clothes."

"I know what Barneys is," she said, exasperated. "I don't understand why I'll be going there."

"I will not have you enter my home in rags. You'll need new clothes before you start on Monday. Deborah will send me the bill."

"Start ... But I thought you didn't want —" Victoria stopped. She was about to say, *I thought you didn't want me.* "I thought you didn't think I was right for the job."

Chase put his pen in his pocket and handed her the notepad. "Perhaps I had been a bit hasty," he said. "My assistant will set an appointment for you at the office before Friday to submit a few documents and sign a few papers."

"What's this?" Victoria said, reading the notes on the top of her notepad.

"That's a few of the subjects Benson is taking this semester. My assistant will email you the full curriculum, but you can start reading up on what's on that list tonight."

CHAPTER 5

Late Night

"So basically Christopher Columbus was a horrible person," Benson said. The 10-year-old sat across the table from Victoria. His posture was straight as an arrow, and had been that way since they started their first tutoring session two hours ago.

Which was why Victoria consciously sat up straight too, even if it was exhausting. She felt ashamed to slouch when her student was sitting with such perfect posture.

"Yes," Victoria said. "They don't teach you that in school, do they?"

Benson shook his head.

"Well, history never tells the whole truth," she said. She wondered if maybe contradicting Benson's school teachers on her first day of work was a particularly bad idea.

"So why do we study it then?"

"That's...a very good question." Victoria smiled inwardly. The boy was smart. She was not going to hate this job. "I think we study history so we can find out the truth about us. Even lies tell us something."

It was uncanny how Benson looked so much like Chase. The young boy had blond hair, but he and his uncle had the same blue eyes.

She couldn't quite figure out the funny feeling she had when she found out that Benson was Chase's nephew, not his son. Until Chase's assistant mentioned it, she'd assumed he was Chase's son. And that there was a Mrs. Chase in the picture.

"I wonder what Mr. Everett would say if I ask him about it," Benson said, glancing down at his book.

"Well, let me know."

He looked up and frowned. "You think I should bring it up?"

"I think...you should never be afraid to ask questions. If they're sincere." Asking too many questions has gotten Victoria in trouble at school more than a few times. But she didn't remember ever regretting it.

Benson shrugged, and closed his book. "I think that's the last of this week's material," he said. "Do you want to go over next week's?"

"Oh no. I think we've had enough for tonight. You can get dinner. Your homework's all done, so I think you can hit the Playstation or something."

"I don't play games."

"You don't like them?"

"I've never had a Playstation. Or an Xbox."

"Does your uncle not want you to play games?"

"No. It just never came up."

Victoria helped him put his books and notebooks away. "I have a Playstation myself," she said. "Games are fun, and a great way to relax."

"Aren't you a bit old for gaming?" Benson grinned.

She smiled back at him. "No one's ever too old for fun, kid." She paused, thinking. "You know, I could bring it over sometime. The new Tomb Raider is pretty cool, we could go a few rounds on that."

"Okay."

Victoria eyed him suspiciously. "Just like that? You're not going to ask your uncle first if it's okay?"

"What for? He hired you as my tutor, didn't he?"

"Yes?"

"Well, that means he trusts you not to teach me anything bad. And besides," he added. "If I don't like games, I can stop playing."

"That's true." Victoria couldn't stop smiling. Benson was so precocious, she had to restrain herself from pinching his cheeks.

To think she almost didn't get this job.

It was still all very strange to her. Chase interviewed her, but said she wasn't what he was looking for. And then one day he shows up at the Foxhole with a job offer.

Benson may not be into games, but maybe his uncle was.

There was a knock in the study, and the housekeeper, Mrs. Sellers came in. "It's time for dinner. Victoria, won't you join us?"

Victoria hesitated. Was Chase home? She wasn't expecting to be having dinner with the family. "Would that be all right?" she asked.

"Oh, yes, please eat with us," Benson said. "Uncle Sebastian always comes home late. It's just me and Mrs. Sellers."

"Oh." So she wasn't having dinner with her boss. "All right then."

Victoria wasn't used to eating with people she just met, or other people's kids, but dinner wasn't as awkward as she thought it would be. Mrs. Sellers, who was in her sixties, didn't speak much, and neither did Benson. But he was always glancing at Victoria, as though he expected her to make conversation. Which she did. They talked about his favorite subjects at school and sports he was into. He was polite, and she found herself enjoying the boy's company.

After dinner, Benson excused himself to read before bed. Mrs. Sellers asked Victoria if she could wait for Mr. Chase to get home, as he wanted to speak to her before she left.

"Shall I wait in the study?" she asked the elderly woman.

"Maybe you'd prefer the living room?" Mrs. Sellers said. "The one on this floor has a television, so you won't get bored."

"Oh, right. Yes, that would be great, thank you."

Sebastian Chase's house was incredibly large. It had three floors and was divided into two wings. She was almost sure each floor could fit about a dozen rooms. It definitely had more than one living room, but Mrs. Sellers said only the one on the first floor of the main wing had a TV.

Victoria found the channel that showed old movies, and luckily, it was playing one of her favorite Humphrey Bogart films. She settled down on the couch with some tiny cakes and a soda the housekeeper brought her.

The cakes were delicious. Mrs. Sellers mentioned they were madeleines, and she'd just made them that afternoon. Victoria couldn't remember ever having them in her life, and she sighed contentedly as she bit into the buttery goodness. She could definitely get used to this.

What was it like being so rich you had servants bake you tiny French cakes anytime you wanted, she wondered. If she didn't have to make her own dinner or do laundry, she'd probably be able to finish her novel in a month or two. It was way too late for her to have been born to wealthy parents, and she doubted she had a long-lost aunt somewhere out there who needed an heir to leave their fortune to. She had no illusions about hitting it rich by herself someday. There were very few millionaire authors out there.

But she loved writing. There wasn't anything else she could think of doing for the rest of her life. And she was used to not being rich. She knew life could still offer you happiness and good friends and love, even if you didn't have a lot of money.

Key Largo ended around 10pm, and Mr. Chase still hadn't arrived.

Victoria was getting sleepy, but she had assured Mrs. Sellers, who popped in fifteen minutes earlier to tell her Mr. Chase was still at the office but he would be getting home shortly, that she was all right to wait for him. After all, the man was paying her more than what she made for a full day at the coffee shop for only a couple of hours tutoring Benson. She could wait up for him this once.

***

It was midnight when Sebastian let himself in the front door. He was tired. The conference call with China didn't end until an hour ago. But it had been an extremely productive call, and his company's directors were going to be very pleased at the board meeting next month.

He took his jacket off, and tossed it on the chair beside the door. His day wasn't over. There was another important meeting he had to go to before he could call it a day: he needed to speak to Benson's new tutor. He wasn't at all sure if she had left already, as he was about three hours late getting home.

The housekeeper would have gone to bed an hour ago, so most of the lights were turned off. There was just enough light to allow him to walk down the hall to the first floor living room. It was dimly lit, but the television was turned on. He could see the back of the couch but there was no one sitting there that he could see. Puzzled, he moved closer to look for the remote control to turn off the television, and found Victoria lying on the couch, fast asleep.

He caught his breath.

While he was aware that he found Victoria enticing, he had no plans of pursuing the matter. It was out of the question, and he was prepared to give no hint of his attraction until it went away. Which it would, he was sure of it.

But he was unprepared to see her in such a vulnerable position — in his house, in his living room, lying on his couch. It gave him a slight tinge of possessiveness, along with the strong urge to kiss her awake.

Her white blouse looked well worn, and it seemed a size too small. It was so tight it accentuated her breasts — which heaved whenever she inhaled. And it was so short, every breath she took lifted its hem enough to show him a tiny bit of her skin above the waist of her jeans.

Sebastian cursed under his breath. Without taking his eyes off the sleeping woman, he unbuttoned the cuffs of his shirt angrily, and then began to undo his necktie.

Victoria felt Sebastian's presence even before she opened her eyes. The room had become warm, and the scent of him hung in the air, teasing her.

When his lips touched hers, it sent a blaze of heat from her head down to her spine. He slid his hands down her back until they rested on her hips, and she arched her back instinctively, until her breasts touched his chest. Almost immediately, she felt his body press down on hers gently, and his kiss deepened. She moaned softly. She parted her legs, and sliding each one up against his, she wrapped them around his thighs. He moved his hands up her waist until they reached her breasts. His thumbs gently caressed her nipples.

What was happening?

His tongue was persistent in its exploration of her mouth. Slowly all her inhibitions faded away, drowned out by the wild beating of her heart.

She was kissing a beautiful man, that's what she was doing. And letting him kiss her, and touch her —

"Ms. Slade," Sebastian said, his voice low.

She was about to reply, "Yes?" But his mouth was still on hers.

Wait.

If Sebastian was kissing her, who was talking?

Victoria tried to open her eyes.

"Ms. Slade!"

She woke up. Suddenly realizing where she was, she sat bolt upright...

... and found herself facing Sebastian Chase.

He was sitting on a chair a few feet in front of her, both arms on the arm rests. Staring at her. He had no jacket, and his shirt cuffs were unbuttoned. His tie was missing.

He looked angry.

"Oh god, I'm so sorry, Mr. Chase," Victoria said, standing up. She tugged at the hem of her shirt, trying to fix her clothes that fell into disarray as she slept.

"Sit down."

"Uh, yes, sir." She sat back down on the couch.

Victoria was mortified, to say the least. Her first day on her new job and she falls asleep on her boss's couch. She flushed, remembering what she had been dreaming about. Oh God, she didn't say his name out loud in her sleep, did she?

"What is that?" he asked.

"I'm sorry?"

"That ..." he pointed a finger straight at her. "What you're wearing."

"It's ... my clothes. What do you mean?"

"Did I or did I not give you specific instructions to buy new clothes before coming to work?"

"Mr. Chase, it was hardly necessary —"

"What is or isn't necessary is not for you to decide, Ms. Slade. You are in my employ and I dictate the terms by which you will dress yourself while performing your duties."

"I'm a tutor, Mr. Chase. What I wear has nothing to do with my duties. Benson ..." She took a deep breath, trying not to get too worked up over his unreasonable demand. "Benson and I had a great first session, and he was not ... disgusted at how I looked."

"My son is polite. If he *had* been disgusted, he would, of course, not have shown it."

"Unlike you?"

She regretted it the moment she said it.

What was wrong with her? Why was she trying to piss off a man who was paying her good money for a decent job? And why did he look so hot when he was angry?

Sebastian didn't say anything for what seemed like forever.

Oh God he's going to fire me.

"I was pointing out an unacceptable facet of your ... person as my employee," he said, ignoring the question.

"Forgive me, sir, but if I was so unacceptable to you, why did you hire me?"

"Are you making me regret that decision, Ms. Slade?"

Chapter 6

Drive

"I apologize," Victoria said. It was stupid to lose a job because she couldn't get over the discomfort of having her employer buy her clothes. "I will do as you ask, of course."

"I wasn't asking."

"Uh, no. Of course not. Sorry."

Sebastian sighed impatiently. "You don't have to like me, Ms. Slade —"

"I didn't say —"

"But if you deliver results, I might be able to tolerate your presence in my home."

"That's... good. I guess." She smiled wryly. "Is there anything else?"

"Mrs. Sellers said you were on time today, which is a promising start," he said. "But I'd like you to tell me what you think of Benson."

"Benson is wonderful," she said, grateful for the change of subject. "He's bright and has a lot of focus. And he seems to be open to new ideas and experiences." She wanted to gush about the boy. She wanted to tell him, "He's adorable and the kind of student most teachers probably dream about," but at this point, it may only seem like she was just trying to get on his good side.

"And just what kind of ideas and experiences did you have in mind?"

She paused, thinking. "He should widen his horizons a bit. He reads a lot, but most of the books he reads are classics written by dead white men. Not that there's anything wrong with Dickens and Twain, but I'd like him to try reading some L.M. Montgomery and Yoshiko Uchida as well. And from what we've talked about, I think he'd really enjoy Jacqueline Woodson's books."

Sebastian nodded. "I'll leave that to you, then. I suppose that will be all for now." He stood up. "Will you be able to get home all right?"

Victoria stood up quickly. "Yes, I ..." She looked at her watch. One a.m. She missed her window. There wouldn't be another bus until two, she would have to wait at the bus stop for an hour. She couldn't take a cab, it wasn't going to be cheap.

"What's wrong?"

"Nothing's wrong," Victoria assured him.

He didn't look convinced. "Shall I call you a cab?"

"No!" She winced when she realized how loudly she protested. "No, thank you." She up her purse from the coffee table. "I'm sure I can find one outside."

"It's late," he said. "It's a safe neighborhood, but I'd rather you not stand outside at one a.m. waiting for a ride."

"I'm taking the bus, actually."

"At this time of the night?" He didn't know much about public buses; he'd never actually had to take one.

"Oh, it'll be fine. Good night."

***

He caught up with her as she was halfway out the living room. "I'll drive you out to the main road," he said.

"What? Oh, no, that's really not necessary."

It made Sebastian feel guilty: the idea of her outside, waiting for a bus past midnight. She had to wait up this late for him to get home.

"I insist. The garage is this way."

He took the Bentley. He didn't often drive it, but it was the only convertible he owned, and he thought she might like a convertible, even if they were driving without the top down.

He wouldn't have been able to tell if she did, however. She looked nervous, and while he was used to people getting nervous around him, he wished she would relax a little. It was hard enough trying not to stare at her eyes or her body, without her looking like she would jump out of her skin if he so much as touched her hand.

"Do you ever drive?" he asked as they settled into their seats.

"I used to. I don't have a car anymore."

"You may have to drive Benson to school activities sometimes. Do you think you can handle this car?" He watched her as she fastened her seatbelt. She had small hands. They looked very soft.

"This is a really expensive car, Mr. Chase. I'm not sure I trust myself to drive it."

"You will be driving my son. Do you think it's the car I'd be worried about?"

She looked at him. "No, I suppose you'd be more concerned about Benson."

He maneuvered the car out of the garage and up the driveway. "Do you trust yourself to drive him?"

"Yes. I do." She knew she would be careful, and keep him safe.

"Then trust yourself to drive the car. It's just a car."

She smiled. "You're absolutely right."

"That's a first."

"First what?"

"The first time you ever agreed with me on anything."

Victoria didn't know what to say to that. Neither of them spoke during the short drive to the bus stop.

"I don't see any buses," he said, searching the road.

"There's one coming around two," she said, and began to unfasten her seatbelt.

"That won't be for another ..." He looked at his watch. "Forty minutes."

"It's fine, I can wait."

Sebastian sighed. "Put your seatbelt back on, Ms. Slade."

"Wait, where are we going?" she asked, puzzled, as the car moved forward. "The bus stop is right there."

"I'm taking you home."

"That really isn't necessary —"

"We're already on our way, Ms. Slade. Your seatbelt, please."

She buckled up again. "I ... um ... live in Calista," she said.

"34 Fenton Street. I know."

"Do you know where all your employees live?"

"The ones I entrust with my child, yes."

"Do you ... know whom I live with?"

"Why would I know that?"

"I'm thinking now that maybe you'd have run a background check on me."

"Nicolette West. You went to college together." He glanced at her. "Of course I ran a background check on you." What he didn't say was that he had hired her before he ran that check. Because he didn't expect to see her that day at the coffee shop. He didn't expect to find out why she was late to the interview.

"How much do you know?"

She didn't sound defensive, just curious. As a man who ran a banking conglomerate, he wasn't used to talking to people who weren't keeping something from him — an agenda, a deal with a rival company, a desire to take his position someday.

"I know enough."

When they stopped at a red light, he saw her look around the car appreciatively. "Do you ever drive with the top down?" she said.

He pressed a button, and the top of the convertible folded back.

The breeze felt cool and gentle as they moved forward when the traffic light turned green. They couldn't see the stars, but the nearly full moon was beautiful and cast a picturesque glow over the horizon. Sebastian breathed deeply. He felt...young. Tonight he wasn't an overworked CEO of a large bank, but a young man taking a beautiful woman out for a drive.

He glanced at Victoria.

Her eyes were closed, a small smile playing on her lips. Small strands of her hair were flying in the wind and whipping around her face, but she didn't seem to mind.

"Is this better?"

She opened her eyes. She looked surprised when she saw he was staring at her. "Uh, yes," she said, embarrassed. "But do you like it top down? I wasn't really asking you to—"

"Do you think I ever do anything I don't want to do?"

"I guess not. I really appreciate you driving me home, Mr. Chase," she said.

He nodded. "I appreciate you waiting up for me," he said, after a pause. "I had a conference call that ended late." It was strange why he felt compelled to tell her this. There were very few people to whom he ever bothered explaining himself.

"I understand. I know you must be very busy."

"Your time matters too. No one should have to waste their time waiting for other people."

"Sometimes you have to," she said, almost wistfully. "Sometimes it's worth it."

Sebastian looked at her in surprise.

She smiled. "I was afraid you'd fire me if I didn't wait for you."

"And yet you didn't think I'd fire you if you didn't get new clothes like I told you to."

"I didn't think you were that serious about it. Don't get me wrong," she added at his raised eyebrow. "I'm definitely going to do it. I said I would."

She fingered the sleeve of her blouse thoughtfully. Looking at her, Sebastian felt a sudden need to kick himself. He must have made her feel terrible. No one deserved that. He knew how fortunate he was to have what he had. Being poor was not something to be desired, but no one should be made to feel like they should be ashamed of who they were.

Back at the house, when he berated her about not doing what he'd told her, he wasn't angry about her clothes. He was furious at himself for the thoughts that ran through his mind as he watched her sleep.

He wanted to touch her face, and her hair.

Sebastian wanted to kiss her.

CHAPTER 7

Moonlight

Victoria remembered her first time in the ocean. It was on a cruise with her parents, a trip her father had won at a company raffle during a Christmas party. Her mother stayed with her as she stood on the deck, looking at the vastness of the sea with the wonder-filled eyes of a 10-year-old for the first time. There was a feeling of getting cut off from the world, losing anchor, heading to somewhere unfamiliar, strange, and exciting.

She felt that now. While she knew exactly where Sebastian was taking her, spending this moment with him — a curiously intimate moment considering they were almost strangers from different worlds — was unnerving and unreal. Reality felt like a distant memory.

She knew it would never happen again. In a moment of weakness and guilt, Sebastian offered to take her home. In a beautiful car, under a magnificent moon. She would recall this moment on the nights when she'd be alone and lonely or bored. It would be a good memory, but that's as far as this would go.

It was funny, really. She wasn't meeting any eligible men because she was desperately looking for a job. Now she's found a job, and this gorgeous man was taking her home.

He wasn't even her type. She preferred warm men. Men who smiled. Men who would look at her like she was the only woman in the room. Sebastian only acknowledged her presence when she did something to make him angry. It seemed like most of the time, her existence barely registered in his consciousness.

"Sebastian Chase seems flakey," Nicolette had said, when Victoria had told her about inexplicably getting offered the job despite being turned down the first time. "Are you sure he's the actual CEO and not some crazy Mattheson nephew they gave a VP position to because no one would hire him?"

"I looked it up right after my interview," Victoria said. "It's him, Sebastian Chase, CEO of Mattheson Bank. Apparently he's the son of old man Mattheson, the guy who founded the bank from old Texas oil money."

"Why is his last name Chase, then? Is he one of those wildly enlightened men who take their wives' last name?"

"I don't know." Victoria really couldn't find a definitive answer to that question. She did find out that Chase was Sebastian's mother's maiden name. He hadn't said anything on record, and the media speculation varied: he was adopted, he was an illegitimate son, he was disowned at a young age and accepted back when his brother died and there was no other heir left.

She couldn't bring herself to ask him. Not even when it was just the two of them driving through the quiet night together. It was an intimate space, but she feared she could break the moment with the wrong word.

"Don't fall asleep on me now," Sebastian said. His voice was almost a whisper.

"Oh no," she said. "I'm not tired." Victoria sat up even more straight, as if to prove she was wide awake.

"Really? That must have been a good long nap you had back at the house."

"Sorry. I don't usually just doze off like that."

She felt herself blush, grateful it was probably not bright enough for him to see her face turn red. She could have been drooling in her sleep. Or snoring. Or mumbling things from her dream he probably didn't want to hear.

"You could've switched channels, you know. The other channels have programs that are actually in color."

"Oh no, I watch that channel a lot. I love old movies."

"You're 25," he said. "Is that a hipster thing?"

She laughed. "Do you even know what that is?"

"I assumed it was someone who only liked things that existed before they were born." He turned to her, frowning slightly. "Am I terribly out of touch?"

"Not terribly," she assured him. "How old are you, anyway?" She regretted her words as soon as she spoke them but he didn't seem to mind the question.

"Thirty-two. Does that sound ancient to you?"

"No. But using the word 'terribly' is."

"Really now."

"Sorry." She giggled.

As she observed his profile, Victoria thought she saw a small smile play on his lips. A tiny one.

Maybe one day she'd make him laugh.

She groaned inwardly. *It's official. I'm completely crushing on my boss.*

His smile disappeared. "This isn't your place?" he asked. He looked alarmed.

"Huh?"

"This is the address. 34 Fenton Street."

It was only then that she realized they had stopped. The car was parked in front of a five-story apartment building flanked by an abandoned lot full of piles of scrap metal, and the burnt-down office building that used to hold a bunch of law offices, private investigation firms, and a pawnshop before it was destroyed by a fire a month ago.

She was home.

"Oh right. Yes, this is my place. Thank you again, Mr. Chase."

"Wait!" He put a hand on her shoulder as she opened the passenger car door. "You actually live here?"

"Well, yes." What was his deal? Her place was nowhere as nice as his, obviously, but it was a decent apartment in a not-so-terrible neighborhood.

"Is it...safe?" His hand rested lightly on her shoulder, as if it was enough to keep her from leaving.

"It's perfectly safe, Mr. Chase. I've lived here for several years now." And she'd only gotten mugged once. "Are you planning on keeping me in the car all night?"

"Of course not." He let go of her shoulder.

"Thank you again for the ride. I'll see you on Tuesday."

"Right. Good night, Ms. Slade." He still seemed unsure about dropping her off. Victoria felt something funny in her chest as she looked at him.

"Good night," she said.

She got out of the car and walked up to her building. Right before going in, she turned back to smile at him. She hoped it would reassure him that she was all right.

Sebastian felt like a complete idiot.

He could have woken up Connor and asked him to drive Victoria home. Instead, he, Sebastian Chase, CEO of Mattheson Bank, was sitting in his new Bentley, parked in front of what looked like a crack house right next to a burned-down building at two in the morning. He half-expected some thug to come out of the shadows and pull a gun on him at some point. His instincts were urging him to drive away fast before he got shot or stabbed or both.

But he couldn't.

Sebastian waited for Victoria to get herself safely inside. You'd think that if one were out at two a.m. on a street where only one streetlight in four was actually lit, one would be running to one's front door. She was practically dawdling as she walked up to her building.

He had to restrain himself from getting out to walk her to her door. But considering his current state of mind, he would probably have just pulled her back into the car. Then drive her back to *his* house.

You just want to take her home. To your home. Your bed.

Surely that was safer than this godforsaken place, he said to himself, trying to rationalize his thoughts that were turning increasingly lurid.

Thoughts that included the image of her red hair tumbling across his sheets as he covered her naked body with his. The sight of her looking up at him through half-closed lids, her mouth agape as she braced herself for the thrust of his manhood he held at bay, waiting impatiently between her thighs.

Blinking hard, Sebastian tried to clear his thoughts. Victoria had disappeared into her front door, and he was the fool sitting outside with his fantasies.

He cursed under his breath as he started the engine.

That was the end of it. It had to be. Nothing good was coming out of thinking about his son's tutor in a sexual way. Although Sebastian took it for granted he could seduce Victoria — most women fell for his charms quite easily — she was his employee. And he had a rule never to sleep with someone who worked for him. He found the idea of a romantic employer-employee relationship distasteful, even exploitative.

Sebastian had been driving for a while before he noticed his knuckles had turned pale. He had been gripping the steering wheel too hard.

Chapter 8

Distractions

"Personally, I find their demands somewhat unreasonable, considering ours is supposed to be a partnership," said the brunette to her audience in the conference room. The dim room was lit up on her side by the screen behind her. "Negotiations are taking too long," she added.

It took a few seconds for Sebastian to realize Callie Holmes's last comment was directed at him. "Any suggestions?" he asked smoothly, realizing he'd been distracted.

"I say we quit pussyfooting around," she said, crossing her arms. "I understand you wanted us to take cultural considerations in this, but I believe our friends in China can appreciate straightforwardness."

"You do."

She cocked her head. "I'll be happy to take the lead in this, if only they'd take me as seriously as they do you."

"Because you're not a man?" Elton Lowry said, grinning.

"Because I'm not the CEO," she said.

"Do it then," Sebastian said. He stood up. "I'll be there for tomorrow's conference call, but you can do the talking. Next week, you and I are flying to Beijing."

"Would they not wonder why the EVP for corporate and not the EVP for world services is negotiating for Mattheson?" Elton said, cocking an eyebrow.

"We'll see, won't we? Come along too, Elton. And make sure to pay attention to Callie in action," Sebastian said. He nodded to everyone, and they all stood up. The meeting was over.

"I'll pack a red suit," Callie said, grinning.

Quit pussyfooting around. It was as if Callie had read his mind. Images of Victoria smiling beside him as they drove through the streets of L.A. last night kept him preoccupied through his Executive Vice President's report. How she looked lying on his couch, her hair spread out like spilled wine around her face as she slept. Sebastian wondered if anyone had noticed.

Then he remembered the look Callie gave him when he looked up from his reverie.

"Something wrong?" his assistant, Frank Mallory, asked as Sebastian got to his office. "Sorry, I thought your meeting would be longer," he explained, when his boss looked at him quizzically.

"Everything was fine, Frank." He sat down at his desk. Three new documents had been laid on it since he had left for the meeting an hour ago. He barely looked at them as he scribbled his signature on each of them.

Her laugh was like the rich tones of a church bell. Deep, and a little husky.

He wondered how she would sound as he made love to her. The things he would do to her to make her moan. He imagined her voice as she cried out his name.

"I'm going out in five minutes," he said, signing the last contract. His voice sounded ragged to him, and he cleared his throat. "I'll be back at six."

***

One more day, Victoria thought.

She'd only been half an hour into her shift when she accidentally bumped into Rach who was carrying a tray of burgers and shakes. Thankfully, the younger girl had astounding balance, and the damage was limited to a little splash of chocolate milk on the tray. However, Victoria winced when she recalled the dirty look Rach gave her as she walked away.

Then there was the two instances when she poured too much coffee into a customer's cup, letting the hot liquid spill onto the table.

"What's the matter with you today, Vic?" whispered Mabel, after seeing Victoria berated by her customer, an irate woman with a toddler and an infant in tow.

"Just a little distracted, I'm sorry," Victoria said.

"Boy problems, huh?" The older woman winked.

"Not really," she lied. Victoria had been zoning out all day. But she didn't really want to talk about it, even to Mabel. "Problems at my other job," she said.

Technically, that was true.

She had kept going back to the dream she had Tuesday night. Sebastian waking her up with a kiss. Sebastian's hands all over her body as his mouth ravaged hers. Sebastian's body pressed against hers.

Victoria shivered at the memory.

Not even a memory, she corrected herself. The memory of a dream.

As she cleaned up the broken pieces of the cup that had slipped off a tray she'd been carrying, she told herself this would be the last of it.

No more thoughts about her unattainable boss. No more distractions.

If she didn't get a hold of herself, she'd lose this job. She might even lose the other job too. God only knew what kind of trouble she'd get herself into if she didn't stop panting after her boss.

One more day, she thought. Tomorrow, she'll be over it. She'll come to work and be a professional, and no one gets fired.

She tossed the broken shards of china into the trash bin behind the counter.

"Hey, Slade," Rach called out to her. "That guy who didn't know you is asking for you."

Victoria turned around, broom in hand. She blinked twice to make sure she hadn't conjured something out of her own daydream.

Sebastian stood in front of her. Dressed in a dark blue suit, he was standing so close she could smell his cologne. "Busy?" he asked.

She looked down at the broom she was holding. "You could say that," she said.

"You and I have somewhere to go."

My hair is a mess, was the first thought that came to her head. But instead she asked, "I'm sorry?"

"We have unfinished business, Ms. Slade. Remember last night?"

"You mean..." She felt her knees go weak with fear.

"Yes," Sebastian said. "You can put this off as much as you want, but I am a man who would much rather deal with work...issues as soon as possible."

"Please, Mr. Chase." Victoria kept her voice as low as possible. She didn't want Mabel or anyone else at the coffee shop to hear. "Not now."

"You're coming with me. Now. You could walk out to my car on your own or I carry you over my shoulder. Your choice."

She swallowed. "I'll walk," she said.

Victoria realized she should have known her boss wouldn't just let this go. And now he was going to do something she never dreamed he would. Something she dreaded. Something she was definitely not prepared for.

***

"Ms. Slade, one would think you were about to get a root canal," said Sebastian, noticing Victoria wiping her palms on the side of her faded jeans.

He tried not to notice the way her back curved down to her finely shaped backside. Or how her jeans hugged her curves the way well-worn clothes seemed to fit the woman who owned them. Like the shirt she wore yesterday, her blouse was a size too small, and her breasts strained against the soft material whenever she breathed.

He needed to get her something to wear that was less ... tight. Soon. Maybe then he'd be able to keep his fantasies about what she looked like underneath her clothes at bay.

Maybe a sweater. A really loose one. Or those man-sized shirts.

"Is it that obvious?" Victoria said. She smiled weakly.

They were ushered by a smiling sales woman into a plush room that looked like a cross between an office and a really large dressing room. "Ms. Williams will be with you shortly," she said, then left.

"I don't understand," he said. "Most people would be happy they were getting new clothes. I did say I'll be taking care of the bill."

"It's not that..." She seemed unsure of how to explain. "I always feel like I'm making the wrong choices when picking clothes." She laughed, embarrassed. "I'd go home and put them on, and then realize I made a mistake and the money I spent was wasted."

"It's my money to waste. And anyway," he added. "If you don't want to make the choices yourself, we'll have Deborah make them for you."

CHAPTER 9

Champagne Afternoon

The door opened and a gorgeous woman in her thirties walked in. Wearing a stylish yellow tunic and boots, she exuded confidence and elegance as she approached them.

"Sebastian, honey, it's been so long," she cooed.

He kissed her on the cheek. "Hello, Deb," he said. "You look as breathtaking as ever."

"So do you, darling," she said, looking him up and down admiringly. She turned to Victoria and smiled. "You must be Victoria."

"Uh...yes," said Victoria. She looked even more nervous when Deborah appeared.

"Ms. Slade has decided she would leave everything to you," said Sebastian. "She's completely in your hands."

"Let me take a look at you, honey," Deborah said, walking around Victoria, appraising her. "Hmmm...beautiful hair. I always love working with redheads. And you have a good figure. I don't believe we'll have any problems finding you a few things for work."

"Thanks," said Victoria. "I mean, good. I think." She smiled sheepishly.

"Sit down, honey. Sebastian, make yourself comfortable. Shall I call for coffee?"

"Okay," Victoria said.

"Maybe not coffee," said Sebastian. He sat down on a large leather chair. "How about some white wine?"

"Of course," said Deborah. "Champagne, perhaps?"

"That would be perfect, thank you," Sebastian replied.

"I didn't mind coffee," Victoria whispered to him when Deborah left. She took a seat on a white couch.

"You serve coffee all day," he said. "Aren't you sick of it yet?"

"Well, yes, but...Champagne seems a bit much—"

"Deborah will serve us a goat's head on a platter if I ask for it," Sebastian cut in, and was rewarded with a giggle from her. He suppressed a smile, and added, "Besides, you look like you need a drink. You should learn to take the good things people offer you."

"I'm just a tutor, Mr. Chase," she said. "When someone offers me champagne for buying a couple of dresses, I feel like a fraud."

"Well," he said, resting his elbow on the arm rest and leaning his forehead on the knuckles of his fingers. He cocked his head and regarded her with mild amusement. "I believe there will be a lot more than just a couple of dresses."

"Oh God," Victoria said, eyeing the rack of clothes Deborah wheeled in front of her in horror. They looked expensive. And they smelled even better than she did.

"She means they're lovely, thank you," said Sebastian.

"Oh, no," she said. "I'm sorry. It's just that..."

"Come, sweetie," Deborah said, taking her hand and helping her to her feet. "You're completely in my hands, remember? Don't think, just try these on. I'm here if you need help zipping up."

Victoria shot a panicked look at Sebastian as Deborah led her away to the fitting room. His face was devoid of expression, and he merely lifted his glass.

"I never told you my size," Victoria said.

Deborah waved her hand dismissively. "Honey, I do this for a living. Now go try this first," she said, and handed her a white suit with red trim.

It fit perfectly. Victoria buttoned up the jacket and stepped out to Deborah's critical appraisal.

"That will do nicely for PTA meetings, don't you think?" she said. "Here, this is something more comfortable for when you're going over the books with little Benson." She handed Victoria a pair of grey slacks and a dark blue top.

"Does Mr. Chase need me to show him what I'm getting?"

"Honey, this isn't *Pretty Woman*." Deborah smiled slyly at her. "Or is it?"

"Oh no! I mean, he and I aren't..." Victoria turned red. "I just thought that since he's paying for this..."

"This is barely going to make a dent in his black card, sweetie," Deborah assured her. "You're obviously a nice girl who wants to be considerate, so what you need to do is not dilly-dally around worrying about money, because what Sebastian is really losing here is time."

"Time?"

"You realize how much he's losing taking a few hours during a workday just to take you clothes shopping?" At Victoria's horrified look, Deborah added, "Now, don't worry about it. It's something he wants to do, obviously. If you know him long enough, you'll realize he's the kind of man who does what he wants for his own reasons."

As Victoria put on the blue blouse and slacks, she wondered just what those reasons were. Was Sebastian toying with her? Did she seem so pathetic to him that he decided to take it upon himself to show her charity? Or was her looking the part of his son's tutor something so important that he had to personally drag her out of her other work and take her to Barneys just to make sure she was dressed the way he wanted the next time she was at his house?

She felt dejected, even as Deborah's face lit up in approval when she saw her. "Lovely," she said. "Do you always wear neutrals, honey? That works with your coloring, but jewel tones look fantastic on you too."

"Thank you."

"What's wrong? Oh dear, was it what I said about Sebastian?"

"N-n-no. I mean—"

"Don't think about it too much," she said, and started going through the rack choosing the next outfit. "He thinks this is important, so you should trust him. And I'm confident he wouldn't be going through all this if he didn't think you were worth it."

"Worth it?"

"When Sebastian sees potential in a person, he tries to help them grow into whatever it is he thinks they should become. He can't help himself."

"So I'm a project," Victoria said, almost to herself.

"You're an investment," Deborah corrected her. "If a smart businessman like him sees value in you, that means something." She handed Victoria a white sleeveless cashmere top. "So enough with the long face and go try this on."

"Suitable," said Deborah several minutes later, as she looked over the dark violet jersey dress Victoria was wearing.

Victoria had to admit she really liked the dress. It was made of soft material, and clung to her curves effortlessly without being constricting. What she wasn't comfortable with was the lace thong and matching bra Deborah had made her wear under it.

"Honey, there's nothing wrong with your underwear," the older woman had said to her when Victoria protested wearing the thong. "But you can't wear anything with visible seams under that dress, you'll ruin it."

"But I'm only trying on the dress," said Victoria, shaking her head as Deborah held up a black box containing the delicate undergarments. "It's not like I'm going anywhere in it right now."

"Well, do you have any thongs at home you can wear under that dress?"

"Not really, no," Victoria had admitted. All her underwear was pretty but practical. She'd never even worn a thong before.

"So you might as well take this then."

With a sigh, Victoria had acquiesced. The bra was all right but the thong had felt uncomfortable, and it took all her self-control to not fidget with it.

However, now that she had put on the dress, she could appreciate how the uncomfortable underwear made the dress look better on her.

After nodding her approval, Deborah picked up a shoe box and handed it to her. "Try these."

It was a pair of black suede flats. "I suppose you don't wear heels a lot, do you?" Deborah said.

"Sometimes," Victoria said. "Like, clubbing, you know? But guys tend to get scared off when you're as tall as they are." She smiled ruefully.

"Well, then you should only go out with either tall men or really confident ones," said Deborah. "Turn around."

Sebastian is tall. And confident.

Victoria shook her head, trying to banish thoughts of her boss, almost afraid that Deborah could read her mind.

She turned obediently, and felt a slight tug behind her and heard the sound of a pair of scissors as Deborah snipped off the price tags.

"Come. Sebastian has been waiting a couple of hours," Deborah said. "I'll have the new clothes sent to your place, and the ones you were wearing when you came in."

***

Sebastian was on the phone with his VP for Marketing, and just as the latter had hung up, Deborah burst in. Behind her followed Victoria wearing a dark violet dress and an embarrassed expression.

He fought the urge to stare, letting his eyes flicker over the younger woman then wander sideways to look at the wall. "That's all right," he spoke on the phone to no one. "Send it to me first thing in the morning." He pretended to hang up.

"I hope you didn't miss us too much, honey," said Deborah. "Sorry to keep you waiting."

"Not at all, Deborah," Sebastian said, putting his phone in his pocket. He kept his expression neutral as he looked at Victoria, trying to keep his eyes on hers instead of wandering downward to the curves of her breasts and hips in the soft clingy dress. "How was the root canal, Ms. Slade?"

"It wasn't so bad," Victoria said. "I'm really sorry we took so long." She had her hands clasped together in front of her, as though she was trying to keep them from escaping.

"It's all right. Shall we?"

Victoria nodded, and grabbed her purse.

Sebastian did not, of course, expect the savvy stylist to dress his son's tutor in oversized shirts, but nothing prepared him for how stunning Victoria looked when she came back from the fitting. In a moment of panic, he pretended to still be having a conversation on the phone just so he had a little time to compose himself after the initial shock.

"Thank you, Mr. Chase," said Victoria, as they left Barneys in his car. "I really do appreciate this. I'm sorry you had to drag me there yourself."

"Maybe if you weren't so stubborn, I wouldn't have had to," he said, a little too brusquely.

He immediately regretted his words when he saw her expression change. The way she hung her head after he'd spoken, he realized he might as well have yelled at her.

I'm sorry, he wanted to say. But having spent a lifetime of never having to apologize for anything, he couldn't say it.

He swallowed hard, trying to quell the unexpected ache in his chest. Unable to think of anything more to say, he let the silence settle between them.

Perhaps it was better this way, he thought. He was thinking about her too much. He'd taken off in the middle of a workday just to see her in a dress. It was better for the both of them if he kept his emotional distance. Better for him, at least.

Once he had strengthened his resolve, he allowed himself one glance at her.

Victoria was staring out the window of her side of the car, her hands resting on the purse on her lap. Her face was expressionless.

Mentally cursing himself, Sebastian made a decision he hoped he wouldn't regret.

CHAPTER 10

No Reservations

"I guess I should have asked you where you were dropping me off," Victoria said, looking around.

Sebastian had parked in front of Al Porto Italia. A valet in a red and gold uniform was hurrying to open the door for him.

"I thought we'd get dinner first," he said, not looking at her.

"It's fine, Mr. Chase," Victoria said, forcing a smile. "I can take the bus from here."

But he had already gotten out. He walked around the car and opened the door for her. "I have something to discuss with you before you go," he said. "You can either wait in the car, or join me."

Victoria didn't say anything for a few moments, then she nodded and got out.

Inside, a stout, middle-aged man in a suit greeted them cheerfully. "Mr. Chase!" he said. "I didn't know you had a reservation with us tonight."

"No reservation, I'm afraid, Aberto," Sebastian said. "Will you be able to fit us in?"

"For you, of course!" Aberto gestured to a waiter, who nodded and left. "We will have a table ready for you and your lovely date in a few minutes."

Victoria turned red.

"This is Ms. Victoria Slade," Sebastian said. "Ms. Slade, Aberto owns Al Porto."

"Lovely to meet you," Victoria said, shaking his hand. "And I'm not his date," she added shyly.

Aberto burst out laughing. "Sebastian, did you kidnap this young lady, perhaps? She looks like she is ready to run the moment we take our eyes off her."

Sebastian smiled. "Ms. Slade is merely anticipating your seafood risotto," he said. "I told her yours is the best one can get outside Italy."

"Ah, we do our best. I am homesick most days, so I try to bring Italia to Los Angeles."

The waiter came back to inform him the table was ready. Aberto escorted them to a table by a window, and excused himself to go back to the kitchen.

Victoria looked around at the plush interiors and elegant couples sitting at the white cloth-covered tables dining on wine and exquisitely plated dishes, and wished she were home. Her boss was angry with her, and the prospect of having to sit through dinner with him was not something she was looking forward to.

She smiled at the waiter who pulled out a chair for her. The young man responded with a smile. He had dark hair and fine features, and his eyes sparkled as he looked at her. For a moment her heart lifted. "*Grazie*," she said.

"*Prego, signorina.*"

"I'll have my usual, Marco," Sebastian said. He sounded almost curt. "And the lady will have the same."

"Very good, sir," Marco said. But he looked back at Victoria, as though to confirm her order. She smiled and nodded, grateful for his consideration.

"Will you be having wine tonight, Mr. Chase?" Marco said.

"Your best chardonnay, please. Thank you."

"Are you always this friendly to everyone, Ms. Slade?" Sebastian said, after Marco had left.

"I try," Victoria said. "When you work in the service industry, you appreciate the little things."

"Are your customers rude to you at work?"

"Sometimes," she admitted. "It makes you appreciate kindness more."

As she spoke, she felt a little ashamed of herself. Sebastian had been incredibly kind to her today, and the fact that he was a little too direct with the way he spoke did not change that.

"Are you and Ms. Williams old friends?" asked Victoria. "She's amazing."

"Deborah and I have known each other several years, yes."

"Does she dress all your employees?"

"Only the really stubborn ones."

Victoria grinned. "She does have a way with people," she said. "I think I was more afraid of her than you."

"I'm not surprised. It was her idea for you not to change back into your clothes, wasn't it?"

"Yes," she said, embarrassed. "I told her I didn't have to get dressed, I was on my way home."

"She did that so I would take you out to dinner."

"Why—"

"Ms. Slade, you are not an unattractive young woman," said Sebastian. "It will be unavoidable that people will suspect you and I might be... involved."

Victoria swallowed. "I guess," she said. "But surely they don't expect you to be dating a waitress."

Sebastian looked at her amusedly. "I didn't mean 'dating,' Ms. Slade. I meant sex."

The word hung heavy in the air between them as soon as Sebastian spoke it.

Sex.

He wasn't sure why he'd brought it up. Perhaps it was the twinge of jealousy he felt when her face lit up as she smiled at the waiter Marco. Or the way her wine-red hair glinted in the dim light of the Al Porto Italia. The way her skin glowed made him ache to reach out across the table to caress her hand with his fingers.

Perhaps he wanted to unnerve her a little, the way he was bit by bit coming undone every second they were in the same room together.

The slight flush on Victoria's cheeks gratified him only a little.

"I see," she said, looking down at the place setting in front of her. She toyed with a spoon for a while, as though contemplating what to say next. "But you said I was here because you needed to discuss something with me. Was this it?"

"No." Sebastian paused as Marco arrived to pour water into their glasses.

"I'll bring your wine momentarily, Mr. Chase," said Marco. Sebastian nodded.

"However," Sebastian continued after the young man had left. "I'm bringing this up so we're clear on the limits of our... professional relationship, Ms. Slade."

"I didn't think there was any confusion about it, Mr. Chase." Victoria frowned. "If you think I've behaved inappropriately in any way —"

"No," he cut in. "I wasn't implying ... What I meant was, you're a young, unmarried woman working in my household. And as such, people may... infer a great deal more about our relationship than what it is."

She looked at him in silence for a few moments. "Then," she said. "Shouldn't you be speaking to them?"

"My concern is you, not other people."

"But as you say, I have not behaved inappropriately, so I don't understand what you're trying to tell me."

Sebastian sighed. "What I mean is you must expect people making assumptions—"

"I don't think I should be expecting anything except to be treated like a professional," said Victoria. She pressed her lips together tightly, then went on. "I expect this most of all from my employer. I haven't made a move on you, Mr. Chase. Neither have I confessed to having feelings for you. I do my job the best I could. You barge in my other place of work, drag me away to buy me clothes, and make me have dinner with you at a ridiculously romantic Italian restaurant. And yet you sit there telling me that people might see us as having a relationship outside of our professional one. Don't you think that's a bit unfair?"

She took a long drink of water, set it back on the table, and waited for his reply.

He sat in silence for a while, reeling from her words. They stung him more than he was willing to admit, and he tried to keep his face impassive as he tried to think of what to say.

"This won't happen again," he said. "If that's what you're afraid of. I don't make a habit of dining out with my staff."

Someone behind Sebastian cleared his throat. It was Marco, approaching them with their wine. He poured some for Sebastian, who took a sip and nodded his approval.

Victoria smiled and thanked the young man as he poured her wine. Marco smiled back, his eyes raking over her face appreciatively.

Sebastian was almost sure the boy did that to annoy him, and he tried not to glare at his back as he left.

"You don't understand, Mr. Chase," Victoria said. "I'm saying I don't care. I did what you wanted, I got myself clothes for work. And I'm here now because you say you need to discuss something with me.

What Deborah or Alberto or anyone thinks about what goes on between the two of us doesn't concern me. I'm only trying to do my job."

"Then we shouldn't have a problem." He took a drink of his wine to mask swallowing the sudden lump in his throat.

"We don't." She gave him a small smile, and Sebastian wondered if she did that to soften the blow of her words. "If you like," she said, "we could discuss that other thing now, so I can leave you to enjoy your dinner."

"Ms. Slade, people may think we're on a date, so the last thing I want is for them to assume I said something so terrible that you would leave me in the middle of dinner."

After a long pause, she smiled a little and nodded.

"So if you will permit me," he said. "I would like to take you home. *After* we've had dinner."

"All right."

"Do you like wine?"

"Yes, I do." Victoria ran her fingers over the base of her wine glass. "This Chardonnay smells really good." She hesitated, then asked, "What did you want to discuss?"

It was clear she wasn't going to relax until he'd finally tell her what he wanted to talk about.

"I've set up a meeting between you and Benson's homeroom teacher on Friday morning," he said. "It's standard procedure whenever a student has a new tutor. You'll go over the curriculum for the semester and discuss the areas where Benson needs to improve. Will you be available? You'll be accompanying Benson to school, and meeting his teacher after first period."

"Oh of course," she said. "What time should I be at your house?"

"You'll leave at six-thirty. I suggest you spend Thursday night at the house to save you time."

"Spend... the night?"

Sebastian winced inwardly, although it didn't show in his face. It was an awkward suggestion, considering he'd just brought up the topic of their professional relationship. Benson's previous tutor had occasionally spent nights at his house when it was needed. He shouldn't have issues requesting the same of Victoria.

Except he did. The thought of her sleeping in his home brought up images he would rather not have in his mind with her sitting across from him.

"Yes." He did his best to sound casual. "It seems a waste of time having you go home tomorrow night only to come back early the next day. I'll have Mrs. Sellers prepare a room for you. I will compensate you for your time as well."

"Thank you. That would be more convenient, I suppose. And I could use the extra pay," she said.

He nodded. "Considering the meeting was a rather late request, I'd like to make it easier for you to attend it."

Sebastian tried very hard to believe his own words.

CHAPTER 11

Delivery

"Did you go on a Rodeo Drive robbery spree or something?" Nicolette said, her hands on her hips, eyeing the piles of boxes and paper bags in the living room. Normally, she would be irked at having to receive a delivery anytime before noon, the usual time she woke up, but she sounded more puzzled than annoyed.

"Oh my God, there must be some mistake," Victoria said, coming out of her room, her eyes wide. She remembered fitting only about a dozen or so outfits. It looked like there may be about four times that number of clothes in boxes and shopping bags crowding her tiny apartment.

"Well, the delivery guy said they were for you," said Nicolette, going through the shoeboxes. "Holy crap, these are next season's Louboutins."

"Looboo-what?" Victoria checked the shopping bags. "I was expecting some clothes, but not *this* many." At her roommate's raised eyebrow, she added, "My boss thought I didn't have the proper clothes to be Benson's tutor so he's paying for these."

"He bought you Jean Yu?" Nicolette held up a light pink silk thong. "This tiny thing costs about half a grand. Are you sure he didn't hire you to be his mistress?"

"What?" Victoria grabbed the underwear and checked the tag. There was no price on it. But it felt like a light, gossamer dream in her hands. "Who pays half a grand for a pair of underpants?"

"Sebastian Chase, apparently."

Victoria frowned. "I don't think he actually picked these out. It must have been Deborah."

"Who?"

"He called her a stylist. I don't even know what a stylist is. She made me try out some of these outfits."

"I don't know who Deborah is, but I love her already. This military coat is gorgeous," Nicolette said, holding up a knee-length, green pattern, dress-like coat against her front. "Although this really is more your style than mine."

"That looks expensive," Victoria said, doubtfully.

"It's Alexander McQueen." With a sigh, Nicolette draped it carefully on the back of the couch. "I'd say that set Sebastian back around three grand at least."

"I take the bus, Nic." Victoria wanted to plop down on the couch in frustration, except it was full of shopping bags. "I can't wear a three-thousand-dollar coat on the bus."

"Oh sweetie, I know," Nicolette said. "A client gave me a huge yellow diamond ring once. I was, like, oh thanks babe, I'll just keep it in the safe in the study." She glanced around their small, humble apartment. "He had no idea I was being sarcastic. So I sold the ring and put the cash in the bank." She was planning on retiring from the escort business when she turned 28, so she saved most of the money she made.

"Well, if it was a huge diamond, you must have gotten a lot for it."

Nicolette snorted. "I got about half of what it cost originally. The diamond industry is a scam. Anyway," she said. "My point is, rich people - *really* rich people - are completely clueless about these things. They don't think about having to wear Marc Jacobs rain boots while running after the bus in rush hour because most of them have never ridden the bus." She wrinkled her nose. "Actually, no one should think of wearing Marc Jacobs anything, that brand is crap. But you get my point."

"Help me," Victoria wailed. "I can't wear my usual stuff, my boss is going to freak out if he sees me in poor people clothes again."

"Go make coffee first." Nicolette studied a white lace bra approvingly. "Then let's figure this out."

Victoria walked towards the corner of the room where the kitchen was, still slightly groggy from sleep. It all seemed surreal. Last night, she was on a non-date with a gorgeous man in a fancy restaurant, and today she was waking up to five-hundred-dollar underwear and a whole wardrobe - that cost only God knows how much - that had been delivered right to her home.

But Nicolette was right. Caffeine, and maybe some food, will help her get some perspective.

She made the coffee, and as it was brewing she checked the fridge. "You want some fried rice?" she called out. "We still have some of the Chinese from the other night."

"Sure. Do we have milk?"

Victoria took off the cap of the milk bottle and sniffed. "Ough, no, it's gone bad. Sorry."

"I'll pick some up tonight," said Nicolette. "Do you want juice?"

"Sure, but I won't be coming home tonight," Victoria said. She popped the containers of fried rice and egg rolls in the microwave and turned it on. "I forgot to tell you, they asked me to stay over tonight."

"They? You mean your boss?"

Victoria turned away so her roommate couldn't see her blush. "Yeah. I got an early morning meeting with Benson's homeroom teacher tomorrow morning, and he thought it would be easier for me to stay over so I can accompany Benson to school."

"Hmmm. Sleeping in the same house as that hunky piece of male. Maybe I was wrong to be worried about your dating prospects."

"How do you know he's hunky?" Victoria said, laughing, then stopped, her face turning serious. "Hang on. He's not a client, is he?"

"Nah. I Googled him. Always seen with a different woman every month, but never a serious girlfriend. Imagine, all those supermodels and actresses, and only *you* get to live with him."

"I'm not *living* with him, silly." Victoria took the plastic containers out of the microwave and plopped them on the dining table. "I'm staying over one night. Food's ready." She poured coffee in a mug and handed it to Nicolette.

"It's a start." Nicolette grinned at her mischievously before taking a sip of coffee. "Where will you be sleeping?"

"There are, like, two hundred rooms in his house. One of them, I guess." Probably one close to Benson's room, Victoria thought. Was she going to be his nanny, too? She didn't remember Benson or Mrs. Sellers or Sebastian mention a nanny.

"Well, if he makes a move on you, at least you have gorgeous designer underwear now," Nicolette said. "Speaking of which. You obviously don't have to worry about whatever underwear you're wearing on the bus. Unless you're planning to flash people."

"Got it. No flashing." Victoria settled on a chair and took a bite of an egg roll. "Are there any clothes in there that won't get me mugged?"

"Actually, there are a bunch of slacks here, and sensible tops. You can wear one of your ugly jackets over them."

"My jackets are not ugly." Victoria frowned. "Are they?"

"Oh, sweetie. They are, I just never had the heart to tell you. Now that you have other options, I can be honest and say you have terrible clothes. Well, you used to. You don't now." She let out a silent whistle as she pulled out a large dark blue purse out of a shopping bag. "I insist you take this gorgeous thing to work today. Don't worry, if you're taking the bus, people will think it's a fake."

"Okay. I'll need an overnight bag, though."

Nicolette looked through more bags. "Bingo. This ought to do it." She held up an oversized black bag with a familiar logo on the snap.

Victoria looked horrified. "Is that Chanel?"

"Yup. Just carry it with the logo facing you when you leave the house." Nicolette stared at the bag thoughtfully, then looked at Victoria. "Why don't you just ask your boss for a car? He probably has a fleet of them."

"I'm not asking my boss for a car. Who does that?" Victoria started on her fried rice, eating as quickly as she could. She asked for an early shift today to make up for leaving work early yesterday. "He's letting me use one of his cars for when I need to drive Benson around, but I don't think he'll let me take it home. He seems fond of that one."

"How would you know?"

"It's the car he drove... me home in the other night."

"What?"

"I had to wait up for him, and there were no buses so he drove me home. It's no big deal."

Nicolette raised an eyebrow.

"Really, it's not." Victoria put her dirty dishes in the sink. "He was just being nice." Maybe it wouldn't be a good idea to tell her best friend that Sebastian also drove her home the night before.

"Hmmm. If you say so." Nicolette winked at her. "Now hurry up so I can dress you and get back to bed. And I swear, if you get so much as a splash of coffee on that Birkin, I will kill you."

"That what?" Victoria asked, puzzled.

Nicolette shook her head. "Never mind."

Chapter 12

Getting Comfortable

It was Victoria's second time at Sebastian's house, but it still took her breath away.

Somehow, in her new clothes, she felt less like a mouse creeping in from the street into the elegant home and more like a professional going to work. She was in slacks and a silk blouse, and it did give her a little more confidence all day.

"Benson isn't in yet, Ms. Slade," said the woman who let her in. She was dressed in the grey slacks and black blouse that was the uniform of all the household staff except Mrs. Sellers. "But I can show you to your room now if you'd like to settle in first. I'm Nina, by the way."

"Thank you, Nina. But please call me Victoria."

"Certainly. This way, please."

Victoria glanced around her as she followed the woman up to the second floor. When she noticed Nina looking at her, she smiled. "Sorry, I'm just trying to familiarize myself with the place so I don't get lost," she said.

"Yes, it is quite a massive house," Nina said. "I nearly got lost in here my first week. Here we are." They had gotten to the end of a brightly lit, heavily carpeted hallway. She opened a pair of double doors and lead her into the most beautiful room Victoria had ever been in.

The floors were hardwood, and beautiful lamps lit up the high ceiling. There was a living room facing the door, with cream and gold upholstery, set upon a white carpet. On her left to the far end of the room was a large canopy bed, and a dresser beside it. On the far end at the right was a five-foot wide glass desk and a leather chair. Shelves half-filled with books lined one wall.

Where was her room? "I'm sorry," Victoria said. "Where ..." She stopped when she realized this *was* her room.

"Do you like it? Luckily Mr. Chase's interior designer was available on short notice to spruce it up a bit."

"Uhm ... yes, it's very nice. Thank you," Victoria managed to blurt out. There must be some mistake. The room was three times as big as her apartment. "Are you sure this is my room?"

"Did you want a bigger room? This is the biggest one close to Benson's study—"

"Oh no! I mean, it's huge, actually. It's a little too big. Are you sure there wasn't a mistake?"

"Mr. Chase checked on it himself this morning and he seemed satisfied," Nina said. "Oh, and the computer and tablet has been set up with the wifi." She gestured towards the desk, and Victoria only then noticed there was a Macbook and iPad on it. "Those are yours, but if there's any software you need, just let me know and I'll set that up."

"Right. Okay, thank you."

A door beside the dresser led to the bathroom, and Nina led her in to take a look. It was the size of Victoria's entire apartment. There were no tiles - the walls and floor looked to be entirely made of green and gold marble. The free-standing bathtub in front of a glass window that took up almost the entire wall was unlike anything Victoria had ever seen. It looked like a tub inside another tub.

Nina noticed her interest. "You'll really like this. It's an infinity bath. Have you ever had one?"

Victoria shook her head. "Is that like the pool?"

"Yes. It overflows to the outer tub continuously. I've never been in one, but I hear it's quite a treat."

"It all looks ... so nice," Victoria said, still overwhelmed.

"Bathrobes and towels are over there on that closet. Oh, and I nearly forgot," Nina said, leading her back to the room, where she opened another door into a smaller room. Racks lined three of the walls, on which hung some women's clothes. In the middle of the room was a tiered stand like a wedding cake, except it seemed to be made of wood, and there were shoes on it.

"Ms. Deborah sent the clothes over," Nina said.

"But... she already sent clothes over to my apartment," Victoria said. "A lot of them. Tons."

"Mr. Chase thought you should have some things here for when you need to spend the night," Nina said. "I think they should all be in your size."

"Oh," was all Victoria could say. It suddenly hit her that she was standing in the middle of her own walk-in closet.

"If there's anything else you need, I'll be glad to help you," Nina said, leading a stunned Victoria back to the room.

"I think I have everything I need, thank you," Victoria said. What was she here for again? Oh, right. "Will you please tell Benson I'll meet him at the study at five?"

"Certainly, Ms. Slade."

"Oh, and Nina? Would you know what time Mr. Chase will be coming home?" Victoria asked. "I, uh, need to speak to him about something."

"I believe Mr. Chase will be joining you and Benson for dinner, Ms. Slade."

***

The study session with Benson went well, and after they were done at seven, Victoria went to find Nina to ask her what time Sebastian was expected home.

"He's already in, Ms. Slade," Nina said. "I've told him you would like to speak with him, and he said to send you up to his study after Benson's session."

Victoria thanked her and set off to find Sebastian's study, with Nina's directions.

One of the heavy wooden double doors was ajar, but she knocked on it lightly.

"Come in."

Victoria took a deep breath and let herself in.

Sebastian was standing behind his desk, facing the windows, his back towards her. He had a drink in his hand.

"Mr. Chase, I hope I'm not bothering you," Victoria said.

"Is your room satisfactory?" he asked, turning to face her. "Nina tells me you've settled in."

She nearly caught her breath when Sebastian's face came into view. "It's ... beautiful." *My room is pretty nice too,* she thought.

He nodded. "Those are the clothes Deborah picked out, I take it?"

Victoria instinctively ran a hand down her pants. "Yes. That's what I needed to speak to you about."

"You don't like them?"

"I do! They're so beautiful," she said, then mentally kicked herself as she realized she just described both her room and her clothes as "beautiful". *You're so articulate today, Slade. Way to go.* "It's just that there seems to be a lot of them."

"I don't understand."

"I tried out a dozen outfits yesterday, but the ones sent to my place plus the ones in the room upstairs seem to be, like, five times that number."

"Ms. Slade, I think Deborah would have wanted you to fit all of them yesterday, but we would have been there all night."

"Yes. I mean, I know what you mean. I just thought I'd only be getting the ones I tried on. Not that there's anything wrong with the others," she added quickly.

"I still don't understand. I thought you liked them."

"I do. But ..." Victoria paused, wracking her brain for the right way to say what she wanted. "They're just too many clothes, Mr. Chase. I appreciate your generosity, but I'm not ... comfortable with it."

"Ms. Slade, you said you'd take the clothes. You said you understood that it was part of your job."

"I did but—"

"You didn't specify how many you would be *comfortable* with. Frankly, that's not my concern."

"I see." She reddened. He made her seem like a spoiled, whiny brat. Like she was complaining about having too many clothes. Which she was. "I'm sorry. I did say... Thank you, I guess. I mean, I do appreciate it. The clothes are quite lovely. I'd never had anything so nice."

"You're welcome." He set down his glass. "Would you like a sherry?"

"Oh." She wasn't expecting to be offered a drink. "Yes, thank you," said Victoria, although she wasn't sure if she actually wanted one.

Sebastian poured some wine in a tiny, delicate glass. "It's an Amontillado. I'm not particularly fond of the lighter stuff." He moved closer to hand it to her.

His cologne wasn't particularly strong, but the scent of him from such a close distance made her heady. "Thank you," she said, fighting the strong desire to close her eyes and lean in to breathe in more of him.

Instead, she took the glass and sniffed the contents discretely before taking a sip.

"What do you think?"

Victoria cleared her throat. "I don't really know much about wine," she said. "There are one or two I like, and I just keep buying those."

"But surely you can have an opinion on that wine you're drinking now."

"I like it." She smiled, a little embarrassed she didn't have anything more profound to say about it. "I've never had chilled red wine before."

"How was today's session with Benson?" he said, setting his glass down and sitting. He gestured for her to do the same.

"Good. I think." Victoria sat down on the nearest chair. "He seems to be paying attention in class, and takes a lot of notes. I notice he does have quite a lot of homework for a fifth grader."

"His school prides itself in challenging their students," said Sebastian.

"I would imagine so. Is there anything I need to prepare for tomorrow?"

"No. Their homeroom teacher just wants to get to know her students' tutors, maybe discuss the curriculum and the child's school activities."

"I see. You won't be needing me after that, will you?"

"I don't think so. You have plans Friday night?" He seemed mildly interested.

"No. My roommate and I usually do something together if she has the day off, but she has to work late tomorrow. We don't get to see each other so often. Her schedule is ..." Victoria paused, realizing she'd rather her boss didn't know what Nicolette did for a living. "... rather hectic."

"Yes, I imagine it would be. Escorts usually work nights, don't they?"

Chapter 13

Bargaining

Victoria should have known Sebastian already knew all about Nicolette. "That came up in my background check, didn't it?" she said.

"Naturally."

"Well..." She took a deep breath. "She's a screenwriter, actually. Nothing that's been produced, but she's written a few scripts." She realized she sounded defensive but she felt she had to explain. "The escort job isn't something she's ashamed of, but it's only for a couple of years. She sees herself mainly as a writer."

"And how do you see yourself, Victoria?"

She reddened a little. "I'm a writer too. Nothing that's been published."

"But you've written...books?"

"Nothing finished. I'm still working on my first novel."

"Working on it. You're twenty-five. Did you just decide you were going to be a novelist last year?"

"Since I was twelve," Victoria said. Perhaps it wasn't the best idea to tell him what an amazing failure she'd been as a novelist. He already thought she was a massive failure for being poor and having crappy clothes.

Sebastian took a sip of wine. He looked thoughtful, but didn't say anything.

"So you're all right with it, then?" she said. "About the person tutoring Benson living with an escort, I mean." She was hired, after all.

"It's not really my concern. People give up things for sex all the time. Sometimes it's love, sometimes it's money."

"You make it sound like you think everyone's a ..." She stopped, not sure if it was appropriate to say the word she was thinking.

"A whore?" Sebastian said without so much as blinking once. "I'm saying everyone has a price. It doesn't mean some of us can't be good people."

Victoria stared at him for a long time, uncertain what to say.

"I... that's either incredibly open-minded or incredibly cynical of you," she said, finally.

"Maybe I'm both. Obviously *you* have no qualms about what your friend does for a living."

"I don't. She's smart, and she's a kind, generous person. I respect her. She's probably the person I respect the most in the world."

"So you wouldn't mind paying a man for sex, then?"

"What?" She didn't expect that question. "I...uh, of course not. Not a problem with me."

"Have you ever done it?"

"Paid a m- no, I haven't." After a second, she added, "Not yet." The truth was, she'd never even thought about it.

"But you would."

"Of course."

Wait. What did she just say?

"So hypothetically speaking, you'd pay to have sex with me."

She swallowed hard. "Well, not you necessarily... I mean, you're not my type."

Sebastian raised an eyebrow.

Victoria sighed. Of course there was no way he'd believe she didn't think he was attractive.

"I think you're ... cute," she added.

"Cute."

"Yeah." *If by cute, you mean so hot I wet my panties at the sight of your neck, then yes.* "Of course, I couldn't possibly afford you," she added in a small voice. She avoided his eyes. How on earth did the conversation get to this?

Sebastian seemed nonplussed. "Oh I don't know," he said. "I think you and I can agree on a reasonable rate."

"I'm sorry?"

"I pay you two hundred dollars for a two-hour session, correct?"

"Y-yes." Victoria wasn't quite sure where he was going with this.

"Now since you bring your very fine college and graduate education to the work of teaching my nephew, I can't possibly charge you the same rate for work that doesn't require the same level of... academic expertise."

"No, I guess not."

"I believe twenty dollars would be a fair rate then."

"Twenty dollars. An hour." Was he serious?

"A night."

Victoria stared at him, unable to think of what to say. "Oh," she said.

"What do you think? Fair?"

"What? Oh, yes. Very fair." She wanted to laugh. This was all hypothetical, of course. It wasn't like he was actually offering her sex for money. She nodded, feeling a little relieved. "This is all hypothetical, right?"

"What do you think, Victoria?"

"But... you're my boss," she said, completely confused. What was he doing?

"Would you put money in an account at my bank?"

"Yes, but that's not—"

"Then why not pay me for any other service then? It's a transaction, nothing more."

A transaction. Like a bank deposit. Twenty dollars for an incredibly hot, incredibly wealthy man to be hers for a night. In a naked way.

Getting the obvious question out of the way, she said, "Why do you want to do this?"

"Because," he said, leaning back against his armchair and linking the fingers of his two hands, "I'm curious to know how full of shit you really are."

"You don't believe I'd do it," she said, trying not to sound as deflated as she felt. It was all a bluff. And she believed it, like the idiot she was.

"No, I don't. Like most intellectuals, you seem to live your life in the hypothetical. You say you want to be a writer, and yet you've never even finished a novel."

His words stung as though he'd slapped her. "It's not that easy."

"No. But it's not that hard, either. You won a fiction prize at the age of sixteen, if I remember your resume correctly. There are entire shelves in bookstores full of crap books written by hack novelists who can't put a proper sentence together. What's your excuse?"

Victoria sat silently, staring back at the man who, thirty seconds ago, just offered himself to her at a bargain basement rate, and was now explaining to her how much of a failure she was. Again.

Just when she thought she'd gotten used to his artless honesty and his insults, Sebastian would find a way to beat her self-confidence back down again.

And his eyes. The humor and kindness she imagined were there a few moments back were gone. His blue eyes held nothing but contempt now.

"I hired you because I believed you were gifted. Because I wanted someone to help my nephew understand why it was important to achieve more than what society expected of you." Sebastian stood up, and laid a fist on his desk heavily, but not with enough force to make a sound. Yet it betrayed his anger more than if he had thrown the desk across the room.

"It looks like I made a mistake."

They looked at each other in silence for a long time.

Victoria swallowed hard. "Are you firing me, Mr. Chase?"

"Get out."

She couldn't meet his eyes, but she nodded once before turning to leave.

***

There have been certain times in his life where Sebastian Chase fucked up, and they were few and far in between. This was definitely one of them. In fact, this may have been the worst.

That he felt like shit was an understatement.

What the hell happened?

What was supposed to have been a simple sexual proposition had turned into an awkward, blundering mess. He had no idea what fever or demon possessed him to suddenly offer to sleep with Victoria. For twenty dollars, no less.

Obviously, he was desperate. She was his employee. He needed something — anything — to justify what he used to think was one of the lowest depths a man could sink to, which was a relationship with a woman who worked for him. And all his pathetic intellectual powers could come up with was to ask her to pay him for sex.

Of course she turned him down. How disgusted was she at him at this moment? If her tone of voice was anything to go by, he'd be surprised if she hadn't run out the house already as soon as she had left the room. At the very least, he may not be able to look her in the eyes anytime soon.

Her beautiful brown eyes. Like liquid chocolate, tempered by a sweet champagne, luring him into their depths.

Sebastian took another large drink of the sherry. What he really felt like doing was smashing the glass at his head. What a monumental moron he was.

He was almost sure his fascination for Victoria would die out after a day or so. He knew beautiful women — they flocked to him like bees to honey. And while he was aware he was not exactly an ugly male specimen, he knew that it was his money that made him irresistible to women, and even some men.

Victoria was not one of these women.

She had no interest in him more than that of an employer who gave her a position that enabled her to use her education and skills, perhaps not in the way she intended, but he knew she found the work fulfilling. She was honest in her dealings with him, and unlike most of the people he'd met, didn't seem dazzled by his wealth or his power.

Was that why he could not stop thinking of her? Was she just another pretty face made special by the fact that he did not make her fall on her knees just by walking into the room?

Sebastian was sure all he needed was one night with the girl, just one encounter to make her satisfy his lust and he would be over her. After that, he would no longer dream of her dark red hair spilling like wine on his sheets as she moved in ecstasy underneath his hard body, her mouth moaning his name as he plowed his manhood firmly into her inner depths. He would stop drowning in her eyes every time they lit up like a midday sun whenever she greeted him.

Thanks to his failure today, he may be doomed to a few more weeks of the agony of his unsated desire for the girl with the wine red hair and sun-drenched smile. Because surely this hunger for one woman could not last forever.

He emptied his glass and prayed to the heavens that this was true.

Chapter 14

Key Six

There was a knock at the door.

This is it, Victoria thought. He's come here to fire me.

She walked towards the door, took a deep breath and opened it.

It was Mrs. Sellers.

"Mr. Chase regrets he cannot join you for dinner, Victoria," the elderly housekeeper said. "He had to leave. However, he's requesting that you stay over Sunday night till Tuesday morning."

"Why?" As soon as she spoke, Victoria realized she may have sounded hysterical. "I mean, does he need me for ..."

"Mr. Chase is leaving for a business trip to Beijing on Saturday. He'll be gone for a few days, and he would like it if you kept Benson company while he's gone. Could you come by on Sunday?"

"Oh, yes, I'll be happy to," Victoria said. *I'm not getting fired after all.*

"He will, of course, compensate you for your time, and you're free to attend to your other job and social activities during that time."

"I am?"

Mrs. Sellers smiled. "Of course. You don't have to be here all day. He just needs you to check on Benson - make sure he does his homework and has everything he needs for school."

"All right. I'll be here on Sunday. Is there anything else?"

"Dinner will be ready in half an hour."

"Thank you."

As she closed her bedroom door, Victoria felt like a huge weight on her shoulders disappeared. She wondered, however, why Sebastian suddenly left the house.

The memory of when he'd lashed out at her at his study still made her heart hurt. She was an adult who had never been ashamed of her life choices, and yet one word from Sebastian and her confidence was shattered. His probing questions and that judgmental look on his face made her question her self-worth, made her feel small.

And yet ... all that time she spent with him — dinner, shopping, having a quiet talk in his study — made her forget the rest of the world existed. When he wasn't criticizing her, he was kind and thoughtful and he actually listened to what she had to say.

Not to mention the fact that the way he looked at her made her knees weak.

Victoria walked across her enormous room and plopped down on the bed, burying her head on a pillow, trying to find comfort in the warm, scented sheets. She's had crap jobs before. An overbearing, judgmental boss was nothing she'd had to deal with before. Why was this one bothering her so much? He was gorgeous and smart and rich, yes, but that didn't explain why she craved his approval so much.

She wasn't stupid — she didn't harbor any hope that he could be interested in her as a woman. They didn't seem to have anything in common. She was a waitress who served coffee and doughnuts, and he could walk into any fancy restaurant without a reservation and still be seated at the best table. He had sophisticated tastes, and she couldn't recognize a three-thousand-dollar coat if it landed on her lap. He was a successful, powerful businessman, and she was a failure as a writer.

This had to stop. Victoria needed to stop thinking about him, stop wondering what he thought of her, stop caring so much about his opinion of her. She would do her job, and if he had anything else to say about her clothes or her writing, she would smile and ignore it. The way she did with all her previous employers.

If only she could just stop thinking about how good he smelled, or how her heart skipped a beat whenever she saw him. Or which one of the many, many rooms in this enormous house he would sleep in tonight.

The next day, Victoria's phone rang while she was changing after her shift at the Foxhole. "We're going out," Nicolette said without preamble.

"Tonight? Aren't you busy?" Victoria said.

"Client cancelled. He had to go out of town for business. You're not working at Chase's house tonight, are you?"

"No, I'm done for the week. I'm not sure I can afford to go out tonight, though." Victoria had just wired her paycheck to her mother, and she wouldn't be getting another one till next weekend. "I'll be getting some extra cash next week," she added, remembering the extra days Sebastian would be paying her for. "We could go out then."

"I might not get a Friday night off for some time, sweetie. I'll take care of everything tonight, and you can pay me back next week, ok?

C'mon, you have all those nice new clothes, you need to take them out for a spin."

Victoria laughed. "Okay. I'll be on my way home in a bit."

She had to admit she could use some fun. Nicolette insisted on dressing her for the evening out, even putting on her make-up and doing her hair.

"Why didn't you ever offer to do my hair before?" Victoria asked. She was sitting at the dresser, trying to keep still as Nicolette took off the curlers she had Victoria wear for half an hour. Her red locks bounced in shiny waves around her shoulders.

"Hmmm. Maybe I just don't want your nice dress ruined by your usual ponytail," Nicolette said. "There, isn't that better?"

Victoria smiled at her reflection. "Wow. I look older."

"Sophisticated, you mean. You'll have the boys drooling at the club tonight, especially in that dress."

"I don't even know why I have this." Victoria winced, looking down at her low neckline. She was wearing a black cocktail dress that showed off her cleavage and half her back. "Did Deborah think I'd be needing this for tutoring a ten-year-old boy?"

"What makes you think Chase didn't personally choose that himself?" Nicolette put her hands on Victoria's bare shoulders and leaned over, her head beside Victoria's. "Maybe he wants you to do more than just tutor his son."

"Very funny, Nic."

"Seriously, he hasn't made a move on you yet?"

"No! I mean ... not really."

"Well, either he has or he hasn't, which is it?"

Victoria took a deep breath. "He asked me — *hypothetically* — if I would pay him to sleep with me."

"I'm sorry, what?"

"We were discussing your... job," Victoria said, relieved she had someone to finally talk to about it. "Then said that if I was okay with you sleeping with men for money, then I ought to be okay with paying men for sex. Then he asked me if I'd pay *him* for sex."

Nicolette let out an exaggerated gasp. "Please tell me you said yes."

"He was bluffing, ok? He went on about how full of crap I was, how I never seemed to follow through with what I want."

"I don't understand." Nicolette frowned. "Was he hitting on you or giving you a lecture?"

"Giving me a lecture." Victoria sighed. "He made me seem like a stupid kid who wasn't doing anything with her life."

"Jesus, your boss is weird."

"He's not as weird as you think, I'm probably just explaining it wrong," Victoria said. "Mostly because I don't understand him myself."

"He's weird, Vic. Does he not have anything else to do with his time than lecture you about your life choices?"

"Actually he's really busy. I barely see him when I'm over there."

"Yeah, well, forget him. Let's go. Time for you to have fun."

There was a long queue outside Key Six but Nicolette confidently walked directly up to the entrance, with Victoria following nervously. As soon as he saw Nicolette, the bouncer grinned and unhooked the velvet rope to let them through. "Cute date, Ms. West," he said.

"Thanks, Sam," Nicolette said. "This is my roommate, Victoria."

"Nice to meet you," Victoria said, smiling. When they were inside, she whispered to her friend's ear, trying to be heard over the loud music, "You come here a lot?"

"A couple of my clients like it here," Nicolette said. "I always make sure they tip the staff generously. They love me for it."

Key Six was one of the more expensive clubs in the area. Even Victoria could see how posh the interior was, and how well-heeled the clientele looked. A tall, beautiful blonde African-American woman in a manager's suit approached them, a smile on her face. "Ms. West, how lovely to see you tonight. Did you reserve a table?"

"Clara, hi," Nicolette said. "I'm afraid a table reservation is too steep for us. My friend and I were just going to hang out at the bar tonight."

"If you like, I could give you table twelve. Compliments of the house. It's a little small, but if it's just the two of you..."

"Thank you! We'll take it."

"Wow," Victoria said as they sat down. The table was for two, with one couch that was only big enough to fit three people. "They really do love you here."

"It's just so nice to be here with a girlfriend for a change," Nicolette said. "Do you like it?"

"Yes!" Victoria could barely hear her over the music. She didn't go to clubs often, but with the energy of the people around her and the hypnotic beat of the music, she was starting to relax and enjoy herself.

"Two martinis, please," Nicolette said to the waiter, a tall, cute, blond who eyed her appreciatively.

"Are all the waiters here this gorgeous?" Victoria asked, her eyes following another tall waiter walking past their table. He was black and had a shaved, perfectly-shaped head and amazing arms.

Nicolette laughed. "You're drooling, girl. And the wait staff aren't the only pretty ones here. Check out the guys over there."

Turning toward where Nicolette was looking, Victoria saw three men at a table staring at them, smiling. She turned away quickly.

"Cute, right?"

Victoria nodded. "Wait, are we here to pick up boys?"

"We're here to do whatever you want, Vic."

The waiter arrived with a bottle of champagne. He set down an ice bucket by their table, and two flute glasses in front of them. "Compliments of Mr. Kirkconnell," he said, pouring the bubbly wine into their glasses.

"Who?" Victoria said.

"Ardan!" Nicolette leaned forward, resting her elbow on her knee crossed over her other leg. "Fancy seeing you here. I thought you'd be at Fire tonight."

A tall, dark-haired man in a black shirt and tie appeared in front of them. He bent down and gave Nicolette a kiss on the cheek. "Not in the mood for it, gorgeous," he said.

"Really?" Nicolette said, looking at him suspiciously.

"Seriously!" he said. He turned to Victoria and smiled. "Somehow, I'm even more glad I came here."

The first thing Victoria noticed was his dark eyes, framed by incredibly long eyelashes. Then her eyes fell on the sensual curve of his lips.

"Victoria, this is Ardan," Nicolette said. "You here with anyone, Ardan?"

"A couple of guys from work," he said to Nicolette, but his eyes stayed on Victoria. "But I'm sure they won't mind if I ditch them for you."

Chapter 15

Fire

Fire was L.A.'s biggest fashion showcase of the season.

While Sebastian wasn't a fan of public parties, the company that was putting on the show was one of Mattheson Banking Corporation's biggest clients — the global fashion house Safira. Although it was work that brought him there, it didn't hurt that it was a brand of luxury lingerie, or that the hottest supermodels of the world were headlining the show.

An usher appeared at his side the moment he entered the club, which had been transformed into a luxurious, brightly-lit space. He wasn't sure he recognized the theme of the decor — he saw gleaming brass installations. The ushers were dressed in what looked like Victorian-inspired clothes, except there was a lot more exposed skin. His own usher was a buxom blonde in a dark dress which had a skirt that was so long it trailed the floor when she walked and was separated in the front, giving him a view of long, stocking-encased legs. The front of her dress was covered in nothing more than sheer white lace through which one could clearly see her lavender bra.

As she led him to his seat, a petite woman in her forties dressed in red silk came up to him. "Sebastian, darling," Sophie Ledeoux greeted him, then pulled him close into a warm hug.

"Hello, gorgeous." He smiled at her fondly. "This all looks amazing. Although, I'm not quite familiar... "

"Thank you, Sebastian." Sophie smiled. "It's called 'steampunk'. It looks wonderful, doesn't it? " Her accent was French tempered with a bit of her native Texan drawl, from having been born in the south of the US and moving to Paris when she was ten.

"It does, yes." Of course. The male ushers were also in Victorian costume, only their shirts were worn unbuttoned to the middle of the torso. Trust Sophie to come up with something so irreverent and unexpected. She was a brilliant artist and businesswoman. He recognized her talent when she started out in the industry four years ago and took a chance on her when no bank would give her a loan. They had been good friends ever since. There were few businessmen he admired, and she was one of them.

"Now, *cheri*, I will have to leave you to attend to matters backstage, " Sophie said. "But Lydia here will bring you champagne and anything else you need. " She nodded to his usher.

"What about a date?" He winked at Sophie, who feigned regret.

"Unfortunately, as much as I'm sure Lydia would be happy to sit with you during the show, she will be busy serving drinks."

"I meant you, of course," said Sebastian. He held Sophie's hand in both of his.

She laughed. "*Mon cher*, as much as I adore you, I prefer my men untroubled by work and always ready to attend to my needs." Sophie's boyfriends were usually aspiring models and actors in their early twenties, whom she supported financially so they had all the time to spend with her between auditions.

"Well, when you're tired of playing the field, you know my number," he said.

Sophie winked at him and left.

Lydia, who had stepped back a few paces while Sophie and Sebastian made their greetings, was once again by his side. Like all ushers with the guests they were assisting, she kept her body close to his and smiled at him flirtatiously while they walked. Sebastian found himself glancing at her breasts as they heaved every time she breathed. Every time she took a step, the creamy skin of her thighs glinted as they brushed past the gap in her skirt.

"So, it seems I can't have you all to myself tonight," he whispered.

"Well, you could have me all to yourself after the show, Mr. Chase." She spoke close to his ear while laying her hand lightly on his arm.

"That sounds very tempting. Maybe I'll come find you later."

She showed him to his seat in the front row. "Maybe I'll let you find me," she said. She smiled at him before leaving.

The show was as spectacular as Sebastian expected. He knew a few of the supermodels who sauntered down the catwalk, as he had attended nearly all of Safira's fashion showcases. And two of them he'd actually dated before — Tammi Taylor, the Canadian brunette with the spectacularly long legs, and Min Hye Kwon, who was Korean and had the most unnervingly beautiful eyes.

They were brief affairs, and they ended with neither heartbreak nor complications. He caught Min Hye wink at him during a turn at the end of the runway, and he smiled back. If he remembered correctly, she was dating a Japanese rock star these days.

This was just what he needed. A night to relax and enjoy the sight of beautiful women. It had been a while since he was with a woman, he realized. Since the negotiations with the bank in Beijing had begun a few weeks ago, he hadn't had the time to meet anyone.

No, that wasn't entirely true. His assistants could have called any number of the women he knew and set up a date. Actresses, models, executives who worked in the same industry he did — he had several of them in his personal phone book. For the past several days, for some reason, it had not occured to him that he needed to see a woman.

That need was certainly making itself known to him now.

He blinked his eyes and tried to focus on the the dark beauty who was walking down the stage at the moment, wearing nothing but flesh-colored thongs and a bra that made her look almost entirely nude if not for the jewels around her cleavage. Indira, he thought, trying to remember her name from the time they had been introduced a year or two ago. He had wanted to ask for her number, but he may have been with another woman at the time.

Perhaps she would be interested now. Maybe Lydia wouldn't mind if the three of them got into bed together. If not her, Min Hye definitely would— if he remembered correctly, she had been more than happy to do a threesome, although he was sure he wouldn't be able to tempt her to cheat on her boyfriend now.

The lights dimmed. After a few beats, a redheaded girl in black lace and silk lingerie began her walk down the runway.

He froze for a second, taken aback by her long red hair, the familiar unconsciously sexy sway of her hips. It couldn't possibly be ... No. It took him a few moments, but he noticed she wasn't very tall and her breasts were a little bigger.

Jesus, it could almost be her, he thought. Despite himself, the image of Victoria in a black lace thong and a tiny black silk bra sprung, unbidden, in his mind. Victoria walking towards him, unconscious of her near nakedness, her pale breasts gleaming with a slight sheen of sweat, softly rising and falling as she breathed. As she moved closer to him, she lifted a hand to her shoulder and slowly pulled down a strap of her bra.

His pants felt tight. Cursing silently, Sebastian adjusted his jacket, trying to find a way to hide the stiffness in his crotch. However he couldn't tear his eyes away from the woman on stage.

She walked with her hands on her hips now, her eyes dark and teasing. When she stopped in the front of the runway, her eyes found him.

She held his gaze confidently, and her eyes lingered on him while she turned to walk back to the back of the stage.

Don't go, he thought, feeling a sudden hollowness in his chest.

"That Erika Daniels is really something, isn't she?"

It was the man seated to Sebastian's left who had spoken. He looked to be in his forties, but fit enough to be ten years younger.

"Not really my type," he added, with a grin. "But doesn't she just grab your attention?"

"She does, yes." Sebastian nodded. The stage was empty but the lights were pulsating. In a few seconds, every model would be back for the finale.

"I'm Burke, by the way." They shook hands cordially.

"Sebastian. She's not a model, is she?" The girl didn't seem to be more than five foot five, by his estimate.

"Erika Daniels is a country singer," Burke said. "She's pretty hot right now. I don't usually come to these things, but Erika is in this show and I'm pretty nuts about her music. I take it you don't listen to the radio much?"

"I'm afraid not."

At that moment Erika appeared again, this time in a green lace thong and a white satin bra with a large sparkling emerald embedded in the fabric between her breasts. Her red hair was piled up high on her head, with a few tendrils of hair loose, curling gently around her face.

Before she turned to walk to the back of the stage, her eyes found his again.

"You should take a listen to her new CD," Burk said. "She's an amazing singer, she really is."

"I believe I will," Sebastian said.

Chapter 16

Heading for the Hills

"Why have we never met before?" Ardan said. "Has your roommate been keeping you locked up?"

Victoria laughed. "I don't really go out much," she said. "This place is a bit above my pay grade."

"Where do you like to party then?"

"The library, I guess."

He frowned. "Is that the new club over on Sunset?"

"Oh no! I meant the place with books and—" She stopped and laughed when she noticed Ardan grinning. "You're funny."

"I'm really not. You should see girls fleeing after my first couple of bad jokes."

"So I just have low standards, then?"

"Maybe you're just really kind."

"Well you did buy us this champagne," Victoria said, raising her glass. "So I've decided to be nice to you."

Ardan laughed. He put a hand on his chest. "I appreciate that."

The club was so loud they had to put their heads together when they spoke just so they could hear each other. She wasn't sure if it was the champagne or the way his eyes sparkled when he laughed or his masculine scent, but she felt quite giddy.

"So, why the library?" he said. "Are you a part-time researcher?"

"Writer," she said. She found books and magazines were better resource materials than the internet for most of the science articles she wrote.

"Really?" He pulled out his phone and tapped it a few times. "What's your full name? I'd like to read a book of yours."

"I write science articles mostly," she said. "For print magazines. I haven't written a book yet."

"But you will someday, right? I should just get your full name, just in case. And your number too," he added.

"You don't even know what kind of book I'm writing," she said.

"Not science books?"

"No, I'm working on a novel. With robots." She tried to keep a straight face.

"I love robots."

Victoria was pretty sure Ardan could have said "I love chicken entrails", and he would still have sounded drop dead sexy. "Victoria Slade," she said, finally relenting. She gave him her mobile number.

Nicolette came back from the dance floor, a dark-haired man in tow. "You guys are getting acquainted, I see," she said, sitting down next to Victoria. Her companion signaled for a waiter before sitting down next to her.

"Who's your friend, Nic?" Ardan asked, nodding amicably at the other man.

"Julian Lucas," he said, reaching over to shake Ardan's hand.

"Ardan Kirkconnell, hi. Hey, you're the actor!" Ardan said. "I knew you looked familiar."

"I'm surprised you recognize me." He shook his head. "Even my landlady has no idea."

"Hey, you know, I think you're pretty good in those episodes of *Over Easy* I've seen you in," Ardan said. *Over Easy* was a popular sitcom about three chefs who were best friends.

Victoria's face lit up. "Oh yeah, you played Janet's boyfriend!" she said. "You were really funny. I was kind of bummed you left."

"Well, Janet broke up with me. I mean, my character."

"Well, you were too nice for her. I always thought you and Isabel would have made a better couple."

"See? Your character sticks to people's memory." Ardan said. "You'll go places, my friend, trust me."

"Thank you. I hope that happens soon. Don't get me wrong, all this partying is fun, but I'd really rather get more work."

"I told Julian maybe he and I will get to work together someday," Nicolette said. "I have a whole bunch of hot Hispanic characters in my scripts."

"I'm all yours, baby," Julian said.

"God he's adorable," Nicolette whispered to Victoria when Julian excused himself to go to the bathroom.

"You think all Hispanic guys are adorable," Victoria said, giggling. "You're mixing business with pleasure?"

"I'm having my pleasure *before* business, that's what I'm doing. I've got no plans of sleeping with actors I work with, trust me. Speaking of pleasure... " She cocked her head, looking at Ardan. "Hey buddy, you gonna dance with my friend here or what?"

"Nic!" Victoria said, blushing.

Ardan hesitated. "I am a terrible dancer," he said apologetically.

"It's fine," Nicolette said. "So is Victoria. Go have fun." She added, ignoring the dirty look her best friend shot her.

Ardan grinned. He emptied his glass, then got up and straightened his suit jacket. "My lady, may I have this dance?" he said, holding out his hand.

No longer smiling, his eyes met Victoria's. For a second, the music and the noise of the crowd all faded away.

All she could hear was the beating of her own heart.

***

"Erika Daniels asked to meet you," Sophia said.

"Did she?" Sebastian said. He took the scotch a male usher served him, and nodded his thanks.

The show was over and he had come by to offer her his congratulations on a successful show. They were sitting in one of the VIP lounges in the balcony of the club.

"She asked me to make sure you'd be at the afterparty," Sophia said. "She's a nice girl, so don't break her heart, okay?" She wagged an index finger at him in mock scolding.

He took a sip of his drink. "Sophia, you know I never break women's hearts."

"You don't, do you? You approach all your affairs like a bank transaction. Mutual benefit for a specific period of time. I'm surprised you don't make each of them sign a contract swearing to never fall in love with you."

"Well, that wouldn't look very romantic would it."

"So the semblance of romance is all you try for."

"Yes. That's why no one gets disappointed." Sebastian cocked his head slightly, his eyes mischievous . "I would think you would approve. All your relationships come with an expiration date too, if I'm not mistaken."

"Ah, they do. But unlike you, I let myself fall in love."

"Doesn't it hurt?"

"Exquisitely, my dear. You should try it."

***

"Look, do you guys wanna go to a party?" Julian said.

Victoria pointed at what had to be her fifth glass of champagne, a quizzical expression on her face. "Aren't we already partying?" she said. She and Ardan had spent a total of five minutes on the dance floor before they both broke down laughing at their miserable attempts to bust some moves.

"It's an afterparty," Julian said. "For a fashion show or something. Lana said I should come by, there'll be lots of showbiz people there." He turned to Nicolette, grinning. "Unless you don't like that sort of people?"

"Oh, honey, I am that sort of people," Nicolette said, patting his cheek. "Well, I will be someday."

"After that party last month for a film release, didn't you say you thought showbiz people were pretentious?" Ardan said.

"Those were indie folks, Ardan, dear," Nicolette said. "These will be Hollywood types. Just as pretentious, but prettier and with more money. Shall we?"

"I'll call for the check," Victoria said, signaling one of the wait staff.

She and Nicolette spent the next next twenty minutes watching with amusement as Ardan and Julian fought over who got to pay the bill. Ardan won, but only because Julian found out how much the two bottles of Cristal cost.

They drove to Beverly Hills in Ardan's car, with Victoria sitting up front and Nicolette and Julian at the back.

"It's inside Summit," Julian said, and gave Ardan the house number. "It's probably easy to find, there are only, like, 80 other houses over there."

Nicolette gave a low whistle. "I heard Cate Blanchett used to live there," she said.

"That was Priscilla Presley's house, she used to rent it out to celebrities a lot," Ardan said. "I think my mom stayed there for a while."

"Is she an actress?" Victoria said. It wasn't much of a stretch — Ardan was handsome enough to be an actor himself.

"She was a producer, actually. She's retired now."

"You're not in showbiz, are you?"

"Nah. Nothing that exciting. I'm a lawyer. Probably the most boring kind — I do real estate and tax law."

"Well, you know. If it makes you happy." Victoria leaned back in her seat, enjoying the luxurious feel of leather.

"It does! It's not fair, really. People always assume people who are writers are doing what they love. They never think that of accountants."

"That's not even true about writers, you know."

"You don't love writing?"

"I do love it," she said. "But that has less to do with me being a writer than the fact that I'm pretty terrible at everything else."

"Okay, there is no way you're a terrible… uhm, escort," he said. He suddenly looked angry. "Did some jerk client tell you that?"

"What?" Victoria's eyes were wide with shock. "I'm n-n-not…"

"You're not?" Ardan looked confused. "But I thought…you and Nic worked together."

"No! I mean, I can't even kiss a guy on a first date." Victoria was mortified. Did he think she was a working girl this whole time? She turned to see if Nicolette and Julian were listening, and found the two of them kissing, oblivious to the conversation in the front of the car.

She sighed with relief. Turning to Ardan, she asked, "Did you think this was a … paid engagement?"

"No, I swear," Ardan said. "I … I thought you liked me."

"So, you were really going to call me, then?" she said. "Most guys don't want to have anything to do with escorts."

"I'm going to call," he said. "Look, this was clearly just a misunderstanding." He smiled. "So what exactly are these things you're so terrible at, Victoria Slade?"

"I'm a tutor. And I work as a waitress at a coffee shop."

He looked at her. "I love coffee," he said.

"As much as you love robots?" she teased him.

"Not as much as robots, no. I mean, obviously."

"Obviously."

CHAPTER 17

Rendezvous

"What's a girl got to do to get a drink around here?"

Sebastian looked up. It was Erika Daniels, now dressed in a white two-piece midriff dress. The glitter and sequins of her costumes at the show was all gone, and her hair was now tamed down and it fell in soft waves on her shoulders.

He had been deep in conversation with Terrence Sykes and Kalisha Wilson. They were a power couple in the music industry, being producers behind some of the most popular rap artists today. They were sitting on a deep purple leather couch in the corner of the enormous hall of Sophia Ledeaux's home, the afterparty in full swing around them.

"Honey, the bar's over there, I think," Kalisha nodded to the side. "Unless there's something special you wanted."

"There is," Erika said, sliding her backside on the couch between Sebastian and Kalisha. She looked at his drink. "I'd like that one, please."

He looked at her with amusement for a few moments, then handed her his half-empty glass of vodka tonic. Their eyes held each other's gaze as she slowly sipped his drink.

Putting down the empty glass, Erika turned reluctantly to Kalisha. "Ms. Wilson, I believe we met at the Grammys," she said. With her East Texas drawl, she sounded warm and friendly.

"We did." The older woman smiled and nodded to Terrence. "Do you know my husband?".

"We haven't met, no." Erika reached over to shake his hand. "Mr. Sykes, it's a great honor. I'm a super fan of you and your wife."

"Well, I'm a super fan of my wife, too," Terrence said. "Aight, it's been great catching up, my man." He stood up, and Kalisha took his cue and stood as well. He reached down and shook Sebastian's hand. "I'll see you next week."

"I'll have my assistant make the appointment," Sebastian said.

"Erika, you take good care of my man, Sebastian, aight?" he said, a sly grin on his face. Kalisha smiled at them indulgently.

"Do you always talk business at parties?" Erika said, after the couple left. She rested her elbow on the back of the couch, her hand on her neck as she fixed her gaze at Sebastian.

"Yes, but only with people I like," he said.

"That's too bad. I was hoping you'd like me, but I'd rather we talk about something fun." She smiled uncertainly. "Did...Sophie say anything about me?"

The girl was sitting close enough that he could recognize the Chanel perfume she was wearing, but she moved even closer until her leg was pressed against his.

"She did. That was a stunning performance tonight, Ms. Daniels."

"Thank you." She crossed her leg, rubbing up her thigh against his in the process. The slit of her dress fell apart to reveal her bare leg. "I hope I did justice to the Cat's Eye. It's so pretty, I was really sad to have to give it back."

"The emerald you wore in the finale." He nodded. "Sophie let me have it for the night." She caught her breath in surprise as he traced his thumb on her delicate jawline. His fingers curled around her chin, and he pulled her face close to whisper in her ear. "I had it sent up to your room."

Erika shivered visibly when his breath caressed her ear. "Sebastian, what —"

"I'd like to see it." His hand dropped to her chest and he grazed her exposed cleavage with the back of his fingers. "In private."

Sebastian could almost feel the pounding of her heart as his hand brushed her chest. She was almost breathless with excitement. "Give me five minutes?" she whispered.

"Go."

***

A mob of mainstream media and tabloid paparazzi surrounded the entrance of the Ledeaux mansion.

"Who's your date, Julian?" a reporter asked as the actor posed for photos, his arm around Nicolette's waist.

"Nicolette West," Julian said. "Hollywood's most brilliant new screenwriter."

"Ms. West, aren't you and Mr. Reitman in talks with Tom Cruise for a movie after *Reacher 2*?" another reporter asked.

"Only if he drops the *Top Gun* sequel," Nicolette shot back smoothly. "We'll have to see." She smiled dazzlingly at the cameras.

"That girl is nuts," Victoria murmured as she watched them walk down the rest of the red carpet.

"Completely," Ardan said. "I mean, there's no way he's dropping *Top Gun 2*."

"Shhh. Shut up, people will think we're being serious." But she couldn't help laughing.

"Here, take my hand."

Victoria slid her hand in his. She felt brazen, but she was so comfortable with Ardan despite knowing him for only a few hours. She let him lead her through the throng of reporters.

The flash of a thousand cameras nearly blinded her. "Why are they taking our picture?" she whispered.

"I think they just take photos of everyone passing through," Ardan said.

"I'm pretty sure they just think you're famous. 'Cause you're hot and all." She kicked herself mentally as soon as she realized what she'd just said.

He grinned. "Why, Ms. Slade. You think I'm hot?"

"Could we just go in now?" Victoria said, trying not to blush. "I'm not really comfortable with strangers taking my picture."

"Sorry about that. If it helps, you look beautiful."

The inside of the mansion had been transformed into a nightclub. Lights strobed the walls and floors, and aerial silk dancers glided up and down red fabric hung from the high ceilings. The dance floor was packed with women in tight clothes and men in evening suits, their bodies swaying and bouncing against one another in hypnotic rhythm.

"There's Nic," Victoria said, waving back at her friend who was at a table with some people across the room. Nicolette was standing up and waving at them, trying to get their attention. "Go on ahead," she said to Ardan. "I just need to use the ladies' room."

***

It was all too familiar to him. The unlocked room. The beautiful woman waiting behind the door in whatever state of dress - or undress - he chose. They would sate each other's hunger, and he would not linger more than necessary. If, after a night, he found himself still aching for the taste of her, he might request another rendezvous.

But that did not happen often.

The knob of the ornate oak door turned easily in his grip, and he stepped into a dimly-lit room.

She sat on a gold and white chaise lounge, her bare legs stretched out, her arms draped over the arm rests. Her short purple silk robe was unfastened and fell open in front to reveal the jeweled lingerie he had seen her in earlier that evening, as did everyone in her rapt, adoring audience.

His eyes raked over her as he closed the distance between them in unhurried strides.

"Well?" she asked breathlessly. "It looks much better up-close, doesn't it?"

He stared down at her silently as he took off his jacket and tossed it on the bed nearby. He rested one knee on the chaise lounge between her thighs. Leaning over, he put a hand on the back of the chair behind her, and his other hand moved down her neck to gently slide her robe off one shoulder.

"Beautiful," he murmured, before he bent down to kiss her neck.

She moaned as his lips touched her skin. "Sebastian ..." she gasped, her fingers tugging on the buttons of his shirt. He pushed her hand aside and unbuttoned his shirt himself. He did not take it off. Instead, he took off her robe, pulling it up over her head. It dropped silently on the carpeted floor behind her.

Giggling, she put her arms around his neck and pulled his face down to hers. He put a finger on her lips before she could kiss him. "I'm here for something else, Erika," he said. He slid his fingers around the back of her neck and, with his thumb, pushed her chin upward until her head was thrown back.

"Anything you want," she moaned as he kissed her throat. "I'm yours, baby."

Her back arched in pleasure as he moved his mouth down her breasts.

***

Victoria couldn't find the bathroom. She'd tried a few rooms on the first floor, all of which were locked, and she realized she was now in a different wing of the enormous house. "Excuse me, miss," Victoria said to one housemaid who passed by. "Where's the ladies' room?"

"There's a couple right by the entrance to the ballroom where the party is," the maid said. "You didn't see it?"

Victoria shook her head. "I really need to go soon. Is there one in this wing of the house?"

"Second floor." The maid pointed down the hallway. "Go up those stairs, turn left. It's the door at the end of the hall."

"Thank you," she said, but she'd only gone a few steps towards the stairs when she felt someone come up behind her.

"You're not, by any chance ditching me to meet with some guy upstairs, are you?"

Ardan spoke close to her ear, and his nearness sent a delicious tingle up her spine. "I was," Victoria said. "I didn't know it would be this hard to get rid of you."

"I'm not sure why I can't seem to stay away from you," he said. "I mean, you're a terrible dancer—"

"So are you."

"I was pretending, so you wouldn't look bad."

"Well, you fooled me." She laughed.

"C'mon," he said, taking her hand. "The maid said the ladies' room was in the second floor, right?"

They found the bathroom easily.

When she was done, she found Ardan outside where he said he'd wait for her.

"Something wrong?" she asked.

He was staring at her with an odd look in his face.

"Nothing."

It happened slowly. Ardan moving toward her. Victoria walking backward until she felt the cool, hard wall on her back. His hands cupping her face, his mouth taking hers gently in a kiss.

For a few moments, she forgot to breathe. She closed her eyes as his lips played on hers, nibbling and licking in the most deliberately slow strokes. "Victoria ..." he whispered between kisses. "You're so beautiful."

He nibbled her lower lip, and a moan escaped her throat. Ardan lowered his arms to encircle her waist, pressing her harder against him and the wall. When he finally slipped his tongue between her lips, her grip on his shoulders tightened involuntarily.

While his mouth pressed hard on her, his tongue stroked hers languidly, teasing her senses until she felt dizzy with need. *More*, Victoria begged silently, wrapping her arms around his neck.

She gave a low whimper in protest when Ardan pulled away slowly. His forehead brushed hers, and he kept looking into her eyes. "Would you like to get out of here?" he asked, his breathing uneven.

"Ardan ..."

"No pressure, Vic. We can just talk if you like." He kissed her forehead. "I just don't want to be around anyone else but you tonight."

Before Victoria could answer, she saw him turn to his right, as though he'd seen something in the corner of his eye.

She turned to look. The door to one of the rooms a few feet down the hall was open, and to her horror, in front of it stood Sebastian.

His shirt was open, his belt unbuckled. But despite his state of undress, he had his unflinching gaze fixed on Victoria.

She wanted to run away, but Ardan's arms were still around her.

Calm down, Victoria commanded herself desperately. *You didn't do anything wrong.*

She couldn't explain the guilt she felt, standing there with Ardan's arms around her.

Did Sebastian see them kissing? How long had he been watching them?

"Oh, hey, " Ardan said amicably. "I hope we didn't disturb you?"

It seemed almost like an eternity before Sebastian finally spoke. "No," he said.

A red-haired young woman in a very short robe emerged from the room, and, unaware of Victoria and Ardan down the hall, slid her arms around Sebastian's waist. "Come back inside, baby," she purred in a Southern accent. "I'm not nearly done with you yet."

CHAPTER 18

Air

He slid the left strap of her bra down her shoulder, exposing her breast. He took it into his mouth, sucking her creamy white flesh gently.

She whimpered in pleasure, her hands caressing his back, encouraging him to further explore her body with his lips.

His hand moved behind her to unfasten the clasp of her bra. She shrugged it off and tossed it aside. He fastened his lips on her other breast, teasing her nipple gently with his tongue as he slid his hand down her back.

"Sebastian ..." She trembled at his touch. "Take me now. I want you."

That's not her voice.

He paused, his mouth still on her heaving bosom. Slowly, he lifted his head to stare at her face.

It's not her.

She leaned forward and tried to kiss him again.

"Stop," he said. He looked at her face curiously, as though for the first time.

What was he doing here? he wondered. Why wasn't he with the woman he wanted, instead of trying to relieve his sexual frustration on a stranger?

"What's wrong, sugar?" She reached down the front of his pants, her eyes growing wide as she felt the size and stiffness of his erection. "Nothing wrong down there," she said, giggling.

"Erika..."

She pulled up her legs to kneel in front of him. He held still as she pushed his shirt open and kissed his lean, muscular chest. "I'm going to be so good to you, Sebastian," she whispered, her lips on his skin. "I'll let you do anything you want to me."

"I'm sorry." He got off the chaise lounge, pushing her away gently.

She stood up and grabbed his arm as he tried to turn away. "Did I do something wrong?"

"No—"

She wrapped her arms around his waist, pressing her nearly naked body against his. "Fuck me, then," she said. "I know you want to."

He looked down at her face, her small, sensual mouth parted slightly, her eyes heavy-lidded with desire. Her large pert breasts gleamed in the moonlight streaming through the windows.

God, she was beautiful.

It would be so easy to give her what she wanted. To throw her down on the bed and take his pleasure with her — the way he had done so many times before, with so many other women. She was willing and hungry for him. The raging erection in his pants throbbed against her bare stomach, demanding release.

"I need air," he said, pulling away from her embrace. He started buttoning up his shirt as he walked across the room to the door.

"You'll be back, won't you?" she asked.

He didn't reply.

Sebastian stepped outside the room, and froze in his steps. He could hear a female voice moaning from down the hallway. He turned to see a woman with her back against the wall, and a man kissing her.

It was as though he had stumbled onto the wrong fantasy.

Victoria breathless with desire as his mouth ravished hers. His hands gripping her waist, her ass. She clinging to him desperately, begging him to make love to her.

Except someone else was kissing her, holding her. And Sebastian could only watch helplessly from a distance.

For once in his life, he had no idea what to do.

He knew he should leave. But his legs refused to move. He watched them silently, as though he could will them to stop their passionate embrace from where he stood.

Sebastian couldn't make out Victoria's expression when she finally noticed he was there. She just looked at him without a word.

The young man was nonplussed. "Oh, hey, " he called out to Sebastian. "I hope we didn't disturb you?"

There was a great deal Sebastian wanted to say to him. And even more he wanted to do with the man's handsome face — most of them involving his fist. He clenched his jaw. "No," he replied.

He felt a woman's arms encircle his waist. Erika smiled up at him and asked him something. He wasn't sure what it was. He could barely hear her over the pounding of his heart.

Erika's robe fell open, her bare breasts exposed. Instinctively, he wrapped his arms around her. "Let's go back inside," he muttered.

Once in the room, Sebastian slammed the door shut. He was angry. He had no right to be, yet he was furious.

Victoria had a boyfriend. Of course she did. He was too wrapped up in his own infatuation he never gave a thought as to whom *she* might be in love with. Who was kissing her. Who was keeping her warm in bed at night.

He was a goddamn fool.

He turned around to find Erika taking off her robe, leaving her once again naked except for her small, barely existent thong.

"Now," she said, unbuckling his belt. "Where were we?"

Sebastian grabbed her wrists and pulled her hands away. "We're done here," he said.

"Was it something I said?"

"No," he said, buttoning up his shirt.

"I thought you liked me." She sounded hurt.

"I'm sorry." He picked up his jacket. "I just ... need to be somewhere else right now."

What exactly he was going to say to Victoria, he had no idea. He owed her no explanation, no apology. But he'd be damned if he was going to let some other man keep him from her.

When Sebastian opened the door into the hallway, Victoria and the man she was with were gone.

***

Victoria nearly stumbled as she half-ran down the stairs.

"Are you okay?" Ardan said. He grabbed her shoulders, trying to keep her from pitching forward after nearly missing a step.

"I need air," she muttered under her breath.

"Let's go outside." He kept his arm on her shoulders and guided her down the rest of the stairs. "I'm sorry, I didn't think," he said.

"What do you mean?"

"Kissing you up there. I thought we were alone and —"

"It's all right," she said, forcing a smile.

They found a door that led out to a garden at the back. They stepped out into the crisp night air, the faint sound of the party music thumping from a distance.

Victoria felt sick. She blinked back tears, and reminded herself she had no right to this jealously that was gnawing at her insides. Of course Sebastian was seeing someone, why wouldn't he? But having the painful truth laid out in front of her felt like a blow to the gut.

Did she have feelings for him? How stupid was she to think that the kindness and attention he'd shown her meant anything more than what it was. She let him dress her up in fine clothes, and let herself believe she was special. Even beautiful.

Christ, she was an idiot.

"This may be a stupid question," Ardan said, "but do you know them?"

No, Victoria wanted to say. But she hated lying. "Yes."

"Oh." He looked puzzled. "Why didn't you say anything?"

"I was...embarrassed." She smiled, hoping to mask the hurt in her eyes. "He's my boss."

"Oh, God, I'm sorry."

"Don't worry about it," she said. "Can we get back to the party?"

"Just promise me Nicolette won't make us dance."

She laughed, feeling a little better. "I promise."

When they got back to the party, Nicolette and Julian were sitting with several people Victoria didn't know. "Hey, look who decided to join us," Nicolette said, grinning slyly.

"Sorry, I got lost," Victoria said, sitting down beside her. "You got any champagne left?"

Julian handed her a glass of the bubbly drink. She gulped it down in seconds, then held out her glass for a refill.

"Hey, Vic, am I going to have to carry you home tonight?" Nicolette asked ten minutes later as she watched Victoria throw back her third glass of champagne.

"Whaddya mean?" Victoria said, then realized she was slurring her words. "I mean, no, I'm fine," she added, enunciating each syllable carefully.

"Liar," Nicolette whispered. "Don't worry, I think we can get Ardan to carry you in case you get too sloshed." She looked over at Ardan, who was sitting on Victoria's other side. "Hey buddy, you okay to drive?"

"At your service ma'am," Ardan said. "Are we leaving?"

"Oh no," Victoria said. She smiled dreamily. The alcohol was making her oddly cheerful. "I'm having fun." Maybe if she drank enough champagne, she'd erase the memory of seeing Sebastian with that half-dressed woman.

"We'll stay as long as you want," he said.

"Your eyes are pretty," she said, then blinked. "I'm sorry, did I say that out loud?"

"Yes." His eyes searched her face. "And don't be."

"Huh?"

"Don't be sorry."

"Okay." She lifted her face up to his and kissed him.

***

She was doing this on purpose, Sebastian thought, watching Victoria and her boyfriend lock lips across the room. It was almost like she knew he was there to see them.

"Mr. Chase?"

He turned. The young man looked familiar.

"Yes," he said, trying not to show his irritation.

"Sophie was wondering if you'd join her if you were no longer...busy."

"Phillip, is it?" Sebastian said, recognizing Sophie's current boyfriend. "Please tell Sophie I'm sorry, but I'll be leaving now."

"Certainly, Mr. Chase. I'll tell her," Phillip said.

After he left, Sebastian took out his phone and called his chauffeur. "Connor, get the car ready."

"Yes, Mr. Chase. Leaving early, sir?" Connor said.

"Yes," Sebastian said, looking over at Victoria. She was laughing at something her date was whispering into her ear. "It's time to call it a night."

***

Victoria felt giddy. All the alcohol she drank tonight had definitely gotten to her head. In fact it was sloshing around in her brain, making her lose her balance.

She giggled as Ardan caught her waist, keeping her from toppling over on the sidewalk of her apartment building.

"Easy now," he said. "I'll help you up to your apartment, all right?"

"I'll be fine." She put her arms around his neck and leaned into him. "But you're welcome to come upstairs with me."

"Victoria..." He bent his head down until his forehead brushed hers.

"Yes?"

"Are you seeing anyone?"

Her smile faded as her mind flashed back to earlier in the evening. Sebastian coming out of the bedroom, his unbuttoned shirt practically falling off him; the way he dismissed her with his eyes before dragging his lover back with him into the bedroom.

She had tried so hard not to think about it. God knows how much champagne and highballs she'd drunk trying to drown out the thoughts of Sebastian and his girlfriend making love in that room. Even now, through a haze of alcohol, her heart caught in her throat when she remembered the way his arms tightened around the woman's delicate shoulders.

"No," she said. "Does it matter?"

"I'm going to ask you out," he said. "It matters to me."

His arms felt strong and comforting around her waist, and Victoria was not in a hurry to go anywhere. "Well, in case you're curious to know," she said, "I'm going to say yes."

The elevators of her building had been out of service for a year now, so they had to take the stairs. While she managed to walk up the steps without incident, she was grateful she had someone whose arm she could hold on to. When they dropped Julian off where he'd parked his car outside Key Six, Nicolette had gone with him after discretely reminding her roommate where they kept the condoms.

When they got to Victoria's front door, Ardan took her hand. "I'll call you, all right?" he said.

"Don't you want to come in?"

"There's nothing I'd like more." He cupped her face gently, caressing her cheek with his thumb. "But you've had a little bit to drink tonight, Vic. I don't want to be something you'll regret in the morning."

Victoria closed her eyes for a moment, and rested her cheek his hand. "Haven't you ever done something you know you'll regret?" she whispered.

"A few times. But I don't want that with you." He kissed her forehead. "I'll call you tomorrow."

CHAPTER 19

Gossip

Victoria woke up to a blistering headache and the sound of Stevie Nicks blaring from outside her bedroom door. She crawled under her blanket, trying to hide from the morning sunshine streaming through her window that seemed to burn through her eyeballs.

I'm never drinking again.

The headache wasn't going away, so after a minute she grudgingly got up to get coffee.

She found Nicolette in the kitchen frying bacon. "'Morning, Vic," she said, and looked at her slyly. "Ardan's still asleep?"

"No idea," Victoria mumbled, pouring coffee into a mug. "He brought me home last night and left."

"Oh." Nicolette plopped a plate of bacon and scrambled eggs in front of her.

"Thanks. Why are you making breakfast?" Victoria asked, eyeing her friend suspiciously. Most mornings, they usually just ate whatever leftovers they had in the fridge.

"We're celebrating," Nicolette said. "Well, we were *supposed* to be celebrating you taking a guy home for the first time in God knows how long." She sighed. "Pancakes?"

Victoria saw the stack of pancakes beside the stove. Instant pancakes, fried bacon and scrambled eggs made up the entirety of her roommate's kitchen repertoire, and she had made all three. "Oh, Nic. Sorry, I don't think I have much of an appetite today."

"It's fine. I thought you guys really hit it off, though."

"We did. I think we did." Victoria picked on her bacon. "He said he'd call."

"He will." Nicolette settled down with her own plate on the other side of the table. She picked up her iPad from the table and pulled up a website. "By the way, did you run into your boss last night?"

"What?"

Nicolette handed the tablet to her roommate. "Looks like he got caught cozying up with that country singer at the after party. Erika, I think her name was. You didn't see him there?"

Victoria looked at the website, a lump in her throat. There was a photo of Sebastian and the woman he was with. They were sitting quite close together on a couch, and Sebastian was touching her face. She swallowed. "I did," she said, her eyes fixed on the photo. "We didn't really talk."

The article said a close friend of Erika Daniels told the media that she and billionaire CEO Sebastian Chase had met at the Fire after party, and that he was "quite crazy about her." Erika's PR reps would only say that they were "just good friends," but the singer's close friend disclosed that Sebastian had bought her the jeweled bra she wore at the show as a gift.

"That bra with the emerald is worth a cool two million dollars," Nicolette said. "And I thought that designer underwear he got you was already a bit much."

"Two million," Victoria echoed numbly. She put down the tablet. "That's ... Good for them, I guess."

Quite crazy about her.

From what she had seen of them at the party, it looked like the feeling was mutual. It was almost like something out of a movie: two perfect people finding each other one night, and falling in love almost immediately.

They did look good together, she had to admit. And Erika was probably a lot more suited to Sebastian than she could ever be. Not that Victoria had been holding on to the hope of him actually being interested in her that way.

Hadn't she?

Sebastian was handsome, intelligent, and insanely rich. And he paid her more attention than a man ought to give someone who tutored his child twice a week. He made her feel special. Victoria thought it was a crush, nothing more. A simple attraction no one could blame her for.

Until last night when the sight of him with another woman in his arms nearly knocked the wind out of her.

Nicolette took a bite of bacon and chewed thoughtfully. "Hey, maybe you'll run into her at his house. Too bad neither of us listens to country."

"If he starts dating Rihanna, I'll let you know," Victoria mumbled under her breath.

***

"You and your girlfriend are in the news."

Sebastian pinched the bridge of his nose in an attempt to quell the headache that had been plaguing him since he woke up that morning. Or rather, since he got out of bed. He'd barely slept all night.

"Callie, Page Six is hardly news," he said, signaling the flight attendant. "An aspirin, please," he said to the tall young man.

"It's on TMZ, actually," said Callie Holmes. "But I'm guessing you already know about it." She was sitting across him, reading the last two week's Asian stock reports on her Macbook.

They were on one of Sebastian's Bombardier Global private jets, heading to Beijing. Elton Lowry, Matthesons's World Services EVP, was behind Callie, chowing down a late lunch of lobster and quiche. Three accountants and four lawyers were on that same flight, currently busy going over the contracts and numbers. Callie's, Sebastian's and Elton's personal assistants were in another cabin, fielding their bosses' emails.

Sebastian took the aspirin and washed it down with a glass of sparkling water. It was his third aspirin that day, and he only felt slightly better than he did at breakfast.

Callie bringing up the issue with Erika wasn't helping either. The PR department had informed him of the "news" report on a couple of gossip websites, and they had all decided to not give any official comments on it.

It was not the first time Sebastian had been involved with a celebrity, but his past lovers have all been discrete, respectful of his desire to retain his privacy. There was no doubt Erika was behind this media mess. Her PR company would officially deny a relationship between her and Sebastian, and then feed misinformation to whatever gossip rag was willing to print it.

He got a text message from her that morning.

Thank you for the lovely evening. Enjoy China. Dinner when you get back? P.S. I won't be wearing anything under my dress next time.

How Erika knew about his trip, Sebastian had no idea. He'd already had one of his assistants look into it. However, he did allow himself a begrudging admiration for the girl. While he abhorred her dishonesty, he couldn't help acknowledge her tenacity to get what she wanted.

He wasn't quite sure why he was resisting the woman's charms. She was beautiful, sexy, and accomplished. And from what she'd told him last night, she was willing to do anything for him — sexually, at least.

It was sheer stubbornness on his part, holding out for Victoria. He was torturing himself trying to find a way to have what he couldn't. She was an employee, a woman he shouldn't even be thinking about outside of work. Especially since she was apparently also seeing somebody else.

Sebastian's jaw clenched. The image of Victoria surrendered and pliant in her boyfriend's arms was burned into his memory. He had spent the entire night before sleepless, bothered by alternate thoughts of what she and her boyfriend might be doing at that very moment, and what Sebastian longed to do to *her*.

In Sebastian's waking dreams, it was Victoria telling him she would let him do anything he wanted to her. It was Victoria who was desperately trying to undress him and begging him to fuck her.

He never replied to the other woman's message. If Erika Daniels wanted him, she would have to try a lot harder.

***

Victoria had that Saturday off, so she had set herself a goal that day to finish writing at least one chapter of her novel, after she was done with laundry and housecleaning. So when 7 p.m. rolled around, she was justifiably horrified to realize all she'd done since five o'clock was Google Erika Daniels on her iPad, and read everything she could about the singer.

Cursing, she immediately deleted her search history and closed her browser.

"Where've you been?" Nicolette said. She'd just come back from yoga to find her roommate on the couch, furiously typing on her laptop. "I've been texting you since six. "

"I didn't hear my phone," Victoria said. She got up to look for her cellphone, and found it lying on top of the fridge, where she put it before doing the dishes. "Oh crap, the battery's dead. I forgot to plug it in, sorry. Was it urgent?"

"Damn right it was." Nicolette put down the paper bags she was carrying on the table behind Victoria's laptop. "I was getting Mexican, and I didn't know if you wanted a burrito or a taco."

"Please tell me you got both." Victoria plugged in her phone, and went over to open the paper bag. She was starving. She hadn't eaten anything since breakfast, having forgotten lunch altogether.

"Of course I did. What are you doing tonight?" Nicolette disappeared into her room.

"Nothing," Victoria replied, her mouth full of beans and rice. "What about you?"

"I have work," her roommate said, speaking loudly so Victoria could hear her from outside the bedroom. "That was in one of the text messages I sent you."

Still eating, Victoria turned on her phone. It was still plugged in its charger but there would be enough juice in it that she could turn it on.

There were a few text messages from Nicolette. And one from a number not in her phonebook, timestamped at two p.m.

Busy? — *Ardan*

Victoria checked her missed calls, panicking slightly. She had two from the same number, one at three p.m., and another at six. From Ardan.

She was trying to decide whether she should call back right away or wait till he called again, when she got another message.

Look, I have this work thing in Santa Monica, and I have to drive over there tonight. But if I could see you for a few minutes, I'm parked on the street outside your apartment right now. If you can't or don't want to come down, just ignore this message and I'll be gone in five minutes. — Ardan

Victoria hit the call button.

Ardan answered on the first ring. "Victoria—"

"I'm coming down."

Victoria was breathless as she stepped out of the building a minute later. He was waiting for her below the front steps, his hands in his jeans pockets, a hopeful smile on his face.

They both started speaking at the same time.

"I'm sorry I didn't answer—"

"Did you get my messages—"

After a moment's silence, they burst out laughing.

"I'm sorry, you go first," he said.

"My battery died," she said. "My phone battery, I mean. I wasn't ignoring your calls."

He looked relieved. "I was afraid you'd think I was stalking you."

"Come to think of it," Victoria said, frowning, "calling me up while standing outside my building is kind of creepy."

"I was hoping I was cute enough that you'd overlook that."

She pretended to look him over. "Hmmmm... It's possible. So I think I'll let that slide for now."

"Thank you." He grinned.

God, his smile could bring any woman to her knees, Victoria thought. She looked down nervously, and blushed as she realized she was wearing her housecleaning clothes — an old shirt with a tear in one of the sleeves, and tiny denim shorts with frayed edges.

"I'm sorry," she said. "If I'd known you were coming, I would've gotten dressed."

The way Ardan's eyes raked over her legs and her torso before they settled back on her face made her whole body warm. "So that outfit wasn't for my benefit then?"

"No!" she said. "I mean ... I was cleaning." Way to go, Slade. Because bringing up the topic of chores with a guy is really sexy.

"Would you like to come up for a bite?" she said, trying to change the topic. "We have Mexican."

"I don't have a lot of time right now, I'm sorry."

"Oh." She tried not to sound too disappointed.

"But I'll be back on Wednesday," he said softly, taking a step closer. "May I take you out to dinner on Wednesday, Victoria?"

A smile slowly spread across her face. "I would love that."

Chapter 20

A Very Long Walk

Victoria tried to remember where she put her cellphone.

It wasn't in her room. It wasn't in the living room downstairs where she spent the hour before Benson's lessons watching TV. It wasn't with her during dinner.

She tried to recall if she brought it with her during the tutoring session, which they had outside at the gazebo on the massive grounds behind the mansion. It was a nice change of scenery, having the lessons outdoors instead of in Benson's study. There was a copse of trees surrounding the gazebo, and a fountain a few feet away. She imagined this would be a great place to hold a party.

If she couldn't find her phone anywhere in the house, she had to go back out there to look for it.

"It's all right, Mrs. Sellers," she said to the housekeeper who was on her own phone calling Victoria's so they might be able to figure out where it was if they heard it ring. "I think I left it out in the gazebo."

"Oh dear," Mrs. Sellers said. "I'll have one of the guards get it for you." She reached for the kitchen intercom.

"There's no need, really," Victoria said. "I'll go and get it myself."

"Are you sure, dear? It's a long walk."

"It's lovely outside. I don't really mind."

"Well, don't stay out too long. It smells like rain tonight."

***

It took Victoria a while to find her phone. It was lying on the grass outside the gazebo. She guessed it must have fallen from her pocket. She checked her messages and found one from Nicolette that was reminding her to get milk and sugar from the store on her way home the next day. As she typed her reply, she remembered Ardan sent her a message earlier that day that she hadn't replied to yet.

Do you like sushi? I know a great Japanese place.

She smiled as she read it again. He'd been sending her messages every day since Sunday. One to greet her good morning, and one to bid her goodnight. Their date was the next day, Wednesday, and it was the first time he'd brought it up. She sent her reply.

I love sushi.

A drop of water fell on the screen of her phone just as she hit the send button. She looked up at the sky. It had started to rain.

Cursing under her breath, she started running back to the house. She had gone a few feet when she realized her phone was getting wet. But as she hurriedly tried to slip it into the pocket of her slacks while running, she lost her balance and fell forward.

Her knees hit the ground first, and she skinned her palms when she used her hands to break the rest of her fall.

She struggled to get up, but her feet slipped on the muddy grass and she fell once more, this time on her front. Laughing at her clumsiness, she rolled onto her back. She lay still for a while, eyes closed, as she let the rain fall on her face.

Come on, Slade. Just a few more feet and you're back inside the big warm house.

She tried to get up again, wincing as she pressed her wounded hands on the ground to push herself up. But before she could get back on her feet, a pair of strong arms swooped her off the ground.

"Hey!" she shouted in panic, her arms flailing.

"Damn it, Victoria," Sebastian growled, cradling her more tightly in his arms. "Do you want us both to fall?"

"What?" She froze, looking up at his face in shock. "Mr. Chase, what are you doing?"

"Trying to keep you from drowning," he said.

"I can walk," she begged, mortified. One of his arms was lifting her legs, the other was under her back, pulling her hard against his chest. His face was inches away from hers. "Really. Just let me down—"

"Ms. Slade, I'm already soaked to the skin, so you might as well accept my help," he said, then his voice softened. "Do you really think this is the best time for us to get into an argument again, Victoria?"

"I'm sorry." She felt she was going to melt from the heat from his body. His closeness made her dizzy. She crossed her arms over her chest, desperately trying to hide the pounding of her heart.

"Hang on to me."

She hesitated a bit, before finally uncurling her arms to wrap them around his neck. The scent of his skin engulfed her senses, and she wondered if she could want any man as much as she wanted him now.

It felt like a mile, that walk in the rain. She wanted to run away, far away from Sebastian and these feelings she was tired of fighting. But she couldn't do anything but lie there helplessly in his arms, wounded and vulnerable. Like her heart.

His long legs covered the distance in steady strides as he carried her toward the house. One of the guards was waiting, and he opened the door for them. "The first aid kit is over there, sir," he said.

She heard the door close behind them. "You can put me down now," she said.

Sebastian didn't reply, and he did not put her down until he had brought her to the couch near a large pair of windows. Outside, the storm was bearing down in angry torrents.

He laid her down sideways on the couch, her back against an arm rest. He sat down facing her, and gently pulled up the hem of her slacks until they bunched up over her knees. He inspected her legs, cursing under his breath. Her right knee was bleeding, and both knees were bruised.

"It doesn't hurt so much now," she said. "Please don't worry about it."

"You'll need antiseptic," he said. He reached for a small grey bag on the coffee table. "This won't hurt."

"I can do it, really." She leaned forward and tried to take the kit from him.

Sebastian's hand caught hers, and she nearly gasped at the sudden skin contact. "Do you always put up a fight every time someone wants to help you?" he asked. "Or only if it's me?"

She opened her mouth to protest, but the look he gave her made her heart stop. "I'm sorry."

He was silent as he wiped the blood off her knee and palms with a wet tissue.

"We didn't mean to intrude on you and your girlfriend," she said. At his raised eyebrow, she added, "At the party."

He took some iodine out of the first aid bag. "You didn't," he said. "I take it you saw the gossip blogs?"

"Yes." She smiled faintly. "I don't usually read them, but it's not every day you get to read about your boss on TMZ."

He took each of her hands to put iodine on the broken skin. "It's all gossip, Ms. Slade," he said.

"But... Erika Daniels is —"

"Erika is a lovely girl," he said, cutting her off. He turned his focus on her knee as he applied iodine on the wound.

Victoria felt the air leave her lungs.

"But it was a mistake," he went on, after a long silence. He pulled the hem of her slacks back down. He looked up, meeting her eyes. "Don't be afraid of making mistakes, Victoria. Life is short."

She nodded, casting her eyes down. Erika was just one woman that she knew of. How many more of his mistakes would she have to live with? And if knowledge of his casual lovers made her chest ache this badly, what of the woman he would ultimately fall in love with?

"You'll need a shower."

"Huh?"

He stood up. "Or a hot bath. Get all that mud off you."

"You too," she said. He wasn't wearing a jacket, and it was the first time she noticed how his wet shirt clung to his torso. She averted her eyes almost immediately, the sight of his muscular chest stubbornly burned in her mind.

"Yes. Well." He shrugged. "Can you walk?"

The pain of her banged-up knees had subsided quite a bit. She stood up. It was uncomfortable, but she knew she could manage. "I'll be fine." She forced herself to smile. "Thank you, Mr. Chase."

"You're welcome, Ms. Slade."

***

The marble infinity tub was incredibly luxurious and comforting, if only Victoria could enjoy it. She would have to spend the entire evening in the hot bath just to recover from -well, everything that happened tonight. The memory of Sebastian's hands on her legs. His hard, warm chest against her shoulder as he carried her. His strong arms around her body.

Her entire body ached with a longing she never knew was possible.

She had meant to make a quick call to Nicolette, then turn in early to be up in time for her morning shift at the Foxhole. But that was before Sebastian showed up. Now she didn't know what to do with herself; she was almost sure sleep would not come easy.

Was she a coward? Perhaps she was just being realistic. Sebastian Chase was out of her league, that much was obvious to everyone. But when he wasn't criticizing her lack of ambition or her clothes, he was surprisingly kind to her. Whatever friendship he offered her, she had kept at arm's length because she was afraid of the feelings he stirred up inside her. And then there was that ridiculous offer of sex for pay.

She bit her lip. Why did she suddenly remember that now? He had the privilege of offering up hypothetical scenarios, while she was the poor waitress he was so ashamed to be seen with until he had dressed her properly in clothes whose brands she didn't know how to pronounce.

Sebastian may have dared her to buy him for a night, but it was doubtful he even gave it another thought afterwards.

Don't be afraid of making mistakes, Victoria.

She closed her eyes, thinking about her life choices. She was not an incredibly successful woman, by any means. Her choices may have been unusual, but safe. She finished college and graduate school. She made sure to make enough money to support her mother in the nice retirement home in Florida. She tried to make it as a writer. Well, she was still trying.

Life is short.

Victoria clenched her jaw determinedly as she dragged herself out of the warm bath, her mind thinking a hundred thoughts. She hurried to change. Not sure what the appropriate outfit was for what she was about to do, she settled on a shorts jumpsuit made of a soft fabric with a bare left shoulder.

Her hair was still wet, so she shivered as she approached the intimidating double doors of the master bedroom. She knocked quickly, afraid she might lose her nerve if she stalled for too long.

For some reason, she expected Sebastian to be in a suit, the way he was dressed most times she had seen him. The man who opened the door had no shirt to obscure the view of his finely chiseled chest and abs, and he wore a pair of loose denim jeans that hung low from his hips.

He didn't look happy.

"What are you doing?" he demanded.

Victoria took a deep breath, and held up a twenty-dollar bill.

Life is short.

"Does the offer still stand, Mr. Chase?" she asked softly. Her nervousness gave her voice a slight shake, but she steadied her nerves as best she could.

Sebastian didn't say a word. He stood staring at her, his expression indecipherable.

She stepped closer until she was near enough to feel his breath on her forehead.

He didn't move.

Looking down, her eyes glancing over the magnificence of his stomach muscles, Victoria tucked the twenty-dollar bill inside his jeans pocket.

His hand gripped her wrist before she could pull her hand away. He yanked her roughly through the open door, and pushed her hard against the wall.

She had half a second to breathe before Sebastian's lips came crashing down on hers.

CHAPTER 21

Losing Control

It was the longest shower Sebastian had ever taken in his life. It was also the coldest.

Despite the steady spray of the icy water, the memory of Victoria's rain-soaked body in his arms still lingered. The way she trembled even as she clung to him, hurt and vulnerable. He had wanted to do more to her than just tend to her wounds. He had ached to touch every inch of her skin, to warm her body with his own until she burned with the same desire he felt.

He closed his eyes briefly, letting the water run over his heated body. It had to end. He needed to stop thinking about her. Stop fantasizing about her.

Victoria was off-limits. She was his employee, and he didn't have affairs with his employees.

He reminded himself that there were other women. It had always been easy for him to find a willing, beautiful woman to take to bed. He just needed to get back to his regular, healthy sexual routines to get over whatever obsession he had for his son's tutor.

He stepped out of the shower and wrapped a towel around his waist, neglecting to dry himself off. He picked up his personal cellphone and went through his messages.

Perhaps it would be best if he just took Erika up on that dinner. She had been texting him all afternoon, as though she knew he was flying back to L.A. that day. Most of her messages were mildly suggestive.

Will you be hungry when you get back, babe? I got something special planned for dessert. Call me.

Or if you have something you want me to do with my mouth, I'm always open to suggestions.

Sebastian had not replied to any of her texts. But he knew now that he needed some release from his current state of restlessness. He'd been without a woman for so long. However, he knew Erika was completely out of the question: the woman was a scandal waiting to happen. But if not her, then it had to be someone else.

He had received invitations from three other female acquaintances since Saturday. The most interesting one was from Liskta Doubek, a 24-

year-old blonde Czech-Hungarian model. She had sent him nothing more than a single cellphone photo taken from under her short skirt, revealing her slim thighs and the white lace thong she was wearing, and a caption that said, "I be in L.A. up till Friday." She and Sebastian had gone out three or four times sporadically the past year, whenever she was in town. She was not very good in English, was incredibly smart, and liked having sex in cars.

His lip curled in amusement as he remembered how embarrassed his driver Connor had been the first time he drove them. Liskta had been playfully rubbing Sebastian's crotch for a few minutes before suddenly straddling his lap, undoing his pants and taking out his already hard dick. They had been so caught up in the heat of the moment that they had forgotten to close the window between them and the driver's seat of the limousine. It was only when Liskta had started moaning well into her orgasm that Connor realized what they were doing and hastily closed the window.

Would Liskta be free tonight? he wondered.

He texted her back: *Be ready in twenty minutes.*

Sebastian already knew she'd be staying at the Four Seasons, as she was never booked anywhere else. And even if she wasn't, one text from him and she'd go anywhere he wanted her to be.

Her reply came ten seconds after: *Waiting, baby. Hope you hard when you come here. No panties now.*

After he called Connor to get ready, he rang up his assistant to have him book them the penthouse. He was in no mood to fuck Liskta in a car tonight.

He was putting on a pair of jeans when someone knocked on his bedroom door.

Who the hell in his household would be calling on him at this hour? Was it Benson? He'd checked on his son as soon as he arrived, the boy should already be in bed by now. Unless something was wrong. He hurried to answer the door.

It was Victoria.

She had changed her clothes - a short, emerald green jumpsuit that bared one delicate shoulder. She looked cold. Her hair was still wet from the bath, and he could see the outline of her nipples through the silky material of her outfit. Her bare face was pale and beautiful, her skin freshly washed and glowing.

Was this woman trying to drive him crazy? "What are you doing?" he demanded.

Victoria held up her hand, a paper bill between her thumb and forefinger. "Does the offer still stand, Mr. Chase?" she said.

Sebastian stared at her, unsure of what she was saying. Was she paying him for something?

She stepped closer, until he could feel her breath on his bare neck. He felt her hand tug at his jeans pocket. He grabbed her wrist, intending to push her away.

But the touch of her skin lit a fire inside him, and he lost control.

He dragged her through the door, and pinned her against the wall before taking her mouth in his.

Sebastian felt her lips yield almost immediately. She kissed him back with an eagerness that took his breath away. Her tongue entered his mouth, exploring it in deep, firm strokes, sending all his blood rushing down to his cock.

He tugged at her clothes, desperate to remove anything that stood in the way between his body and hers.

"Mr. Chase..." Victoria gasped as the sound of her clothes ripping broke the silence.

"Come in a nightie next time," he growled against her mouth. He thrust his tongue inside her parted lips as he pulled down what was left of the torn fabric, leaving her naked above her waist. He felt her bare bosoms press against his chest. No bra. "Jesus Christ," he swore, and bent down to fill his mouth with her right breast.

She ran her fingers through his hair with one hand, encouraging him to savor the sweetness and heat of her flesh. Her other hand caressed his back, her fingers tracing slow circles on his skin.

He sucked hard, his tongue flicking over her sensitive tips. God she tasted so good. He wanted to devour every inch of her like a hungry animal.

She whimpered softly, her fingers tightening their grip in his hair. "Yes ... Oh God yes," she moaned. "Oh!" she cried out when he wrapped his lips around her other breast, sucking and licking furiously.

Mine, Sebastian thought as he kissed her body. *My woman. My Victoria.*

Tonight he would give her the most exquisite pleasure she could ever experience. He would possess her so thoroughly that the touch of any other man after him would leave her cold.

He licked her swollen tip one last time, before raising his head to kiss her hard on her lips. His tongue ravished the inside of her mouth roughly, as his hands caressed her back, pushing her harder against him. Her soft moans of pleasure only made him thrust his tongue deeper inside her.

Finally, he could no longer ignore the demands of his raging erection. His lips left her mouth and moved down the side of her neck, his tongue flicking her skin. "Hold on to me," he whispered.

Victoria put her arms around his neck. Nuzzling the spot under her ear, Sebastian moved his hands under her backside and lifted her up. Almost immediately, she wrapped her legs tightly around his waist. Her mouth found his once again and she kissed him with wild abandon as he carried her to his bed.

It took all that was left of Sebastian's self-control to keep from spreading her wide and taking her as soon as he laid her down across the width of his bed.

Standing in front of her, he dragged her torn jumpsuit down her legs, cursing under his breath. "Would it have killed you to wear a skirt?" he muttered, throwing the ruined outfit to the floor.

Naked except for her thong, she propped herself up by her elbows and looked up at him, a smile playing on her lips. "Are you going to be this bossy in bed, Mr. Chase?"

Sebastian didn't reply. Holding her gaze, he unbuckled his belt. "Are you going to be this infuriating while I fuck you, Victoria?" He tossed his belt aside, and it fell on the floor with a loud thud.

Her smile faded. She lowered her eyes to watch his hands as he unzipped his jeans.

He took them off, watching her eyes as she stared at the bulge in his boxers. She licked her lower lip, and slowly looked up into his eyes.

He crawled on top of her, his knees prodding her thighs apart. His eyes were dark with desire as he took in the sight of her body beneath him. She was more beautiful than in any fantasy he had ever had.

"Yes," she said. Her breathing was shallow and ragged. "You like it, don't you?"

Swallowing hard, he touched her jawline with his fingers. "God, yes," he groaned, and covered her mouth with his.

Sebastian would never tire of her lips. The way he craved the taste of her was unlike anything he had felt before. It was an addiction he had been fighting even before he had even kissed her. He probed her deeper with his tongue, desperate to satisfy his desire for her mouth, her body.

Victoria wanted him too. He knew this now. The way her mouth melted into his kiss. The way she pressed her body eagerly against his. The way she rubbed her bare legs against his as he lay on top of her.

He felt her hands gingerly tugging at the waist of his boxers.

"Are you ready for me, Victoria?" he said, guiding her hand inside to grasp his swollen cock. He caught his breath when she began to move her hand.

"Yes." She caught his lower lip in her mouth, and sucked it gently for a second. Her hand was still stroking him. "I'm ready."

He pulled her hand away reluctantly as he got off her. He knelt down to pull off her panties in one swift motion. "Christ," he growled, his eyes drinking in her complete nakedness. He grabbed the back of her knees to bend her legs upward, and his mouth came down between her thighs.

"Ohhhh!" Victoria cried out in shock as his tongue made its way up and down her slit. "Mr. Chase ..."

"Say my name," Sebastian ordered, his breath hot on the most intimate part of her body. He swirled his tongue around her heat.

"Mr. Chase," she moaned. "Oh God, please..."

"My *name*, Victoria."

"Sebastian ... " she gasped. "Oh fuck ... Sebastian..."

Her hips bucked furiously, and he had to hold her thighs firmly in place as he continued pleasuring her with his tongue.

"Your phone," she moaned.

What?

"Your phone," she repeated. "Ringing..."

He could hear it now. Swearing, he reached over to the nightstand beside the bed to grab his phone. He hurled it across the room.

Victoria gave a startled yelp when it shattered against the wall with a loud crash. "W-w-what did you do that for?"

He opened a drawer in the nightstand and grabbed a condom and ripped open the plastic with his teeth. He crawled back on top of her, yanking his boxers down his knees.

Her eyes grew wide as she watched him sheath his manhood, rolling the condom up the length of his shaft.

"Come here," he growled, grabbing her thighs.

She gasped as he entered her. "Sebastian," she whispered. "Oh God."

Sebastian buried himself inside her in one motion.

Victoria arched her back instinctively, feeling every part of her hum with the delicious sensation of his thickness filling her up, pressing against every nerve of her existence. His barely restrained shaft stayed throbbing, motionless inside her. She waited in breathless anticipation for him to begin his thrusts, the primal rhythm of beasts and men.

"Does that feel good?" he said softly. He lay still on top of her, looking into her eyes so intently she almost forgot to breathe.

She bit her lip, and nodded. She tried to move, eager for him to take his plow to her field, but his hips held her in place.

"Please, Sebastian," she said. "I want..."

"Tell me what you want, Victoria." He shifted his weight ever so slightly.

The movement sent a wave of pleasure shooting up her spine. She inhaled sharply, her hands fisting the duvet. "You. I want you."

He bent his head to nip her earlobe lightly. "Do you?" He rocked his hips against her thighs.

"Yes..." She threw her head back, relishing the friction of their bodies. "Oh God yes..."

He hooked his arm under her left leg, spreading her wide under him. "Victoria ..." he said. He stared at her face as he moved in and out of her in excruciatingly slow thrusts.

She looked up at him, waiting for what he was going to say. But he stayed quiet —his face calm, his gaze never leaving her.

He was so beautiful.

More than that, the way Sebastian looked at her made Victoria feel beautiful. The naked tenderness in his blue eyes. The raw desire lurking behind his gaze. Not even in her wildest, guiltiest fantasies about him did she imagine he would ever look at her this way.

It wasn't a dream this time. She was in his bed. His strong, powerful body possessing her with every surge of his hips. This beautiful man was on top of her, and inside her. Filling her up. Making her whole.

Victoria ran her hands up and down his chest, exploring the splendid perfection of his body, feeling every ripple of muscle under her fingers.

She felt him start to move with more urgency. "Ohhhh," she gasped. "Oh God ..."

"You like that?" he whispered, his breath heavy on her face. His hips ground into her faster, harder.

"Yes ... oh yes..."

Their bodies moved in rhythm, rubbing against each other. Skin crashing against skin, their sweat meeting in heat.

"Sebastian ... oh fuck..." She closed her eyes for a second, feeling her orgasm begin to surge.

He stopped.

"Please," she begged. "Sebastian ..."

He unhooked his arm from under her leg, and pressed his hand on her bent knee, bending her thigh back as far as it would go. He shifted his weight.

"Victoria ... baby ..." he panted. He moved his hips again. "Let me make you feel good."

He fucked her. Fast. Hard.

The currents of pleasure that blazed through her was almost too much to bear. "Sebastian ... yes ... yes ... yes ..." she cried out.

"Come for me, Victoria," he moaned. "Baby ..."

A shudder went through Victoria. And then she felt the universe explode.

Her body arched and writhed underneath him. She heard a voice crying out his name over and over, and realized it was hers.

Sebastian covered her mouth in a kiss. "Victoria," he murmured against her lips as his body bucked and shuddered through his own release.

Victoria wrapped her arms tight around his neck. She plowed his open mouth with her tongue, hungry for the taste of him.

"That was unbelievable," he said, breathless. He kissed her one last time before reluctantly pulling out of her. Kneeling, he peeled off the condom and threw it in the wooden trash bin beside the bed.

"Wait," she said, getting on her knees. She put her arms around him and straddled his thighs.

"Victoria—"

She cut him off with a kiss.

His hands moved over her back, caressing her skin with slow, gentle strokes. He released her mouth to kiss her neck. "Christ, you taste good," he muttered.

She arched her back, letting him run his tongue from her throat down to the valley between her breasts. "So good," he said, and captured her right breast in his mouth.

Victoria closed her eyes, savoring the warm sensations of his mouth on her body. Her hands cradled the back of his head, urging him to keep going.

"Are you trying to get me hard again, Victoria?" He took her other breast in his mouth, sucking on it gently.

She could already feel him grow stiff under her. She moved her hips to press down on his hardening member.

"Mr. Chase," she moaned. "You got another condom?"

CHAPTER 22

All Night

It was dark.

Sebastian felt Victoria move against him, and instinctively tightened his arms around her.

She stirred again.

"Are you awake?"

"Yes," she said.

He pulled up the duvet over their shoulders. "Are you cold?"

"N-n-no... Mr. Chase?"

He sighed, his hand caressing her bare chest. "You're lying naked in bed with me, Victoria. I think you don't have to call me that now."

"Sorry. Sebastian."

"What is it?" He kissed the back of her neck.

"I should have brought this up before ... you know." She paused. "Erika Daniels — is she your girlfriend?"

"I told you no. I don't do relationships." He moved his hand down her stomach, and pressed her closer against him. He was unable to stop nuzzling her neck, and realized he was getting hard again.

"Oh."

She sounded odd. "Ms. Slade," he said. "Did you perhaps think you and I—"

"No!" she said quickly. "I mean, this was just a ... business transaction, right?"

So that's what the money was for. He had made a clumsy attempt to get her to fuck him without any strings attached, and she actually called him on it.

"Mmmm. Yes." He licked her earlobe. It didn't matter. All he knew was that she was here in his bed, her body willing and responsive to him. He couldn't get enough of her. They had gone through almost half a box of condoms before practically passing out from exhaustion. "Anything else?"

"N-n-no. I just thought I'd check." There was a long silence. "I got cheated on a couple of times."

"I'm sorry." He felt her sadness, somehow. It was almost like the closeness of their bodies allowed them to share something more than just physical intimacy. "No one deserves that." He pressed another kiss lower down her back.

"I don't know. I think maybe Hitler would totally deserve getting cheated on. Or Torquemada."

His chuckle was muffled against her skin. "You're not Hitler. And technically, Torquemada should have been celibate to begin with."

Victoria giggled.

"How are you feeling?" He squeezed her breast softly.

Her breathing quickened. "What do you mean?"

Sebastian encircled his arm all the way around her waist. "I'd like to make another transaction, if you're up for it." He ran his fingers up and down her side.

There was silence for a few moments, and then she moved his arm and pulled away. The space she left beside him felt cold and empty.

Shit.

He started to roll over to turn on a lamp, but paused when he heard a drawer pull open and then the rustling sound of plastic. He felt the duvet peeled off him. Her knees came down either side of him.

Her hands found his erection and began stroking it. "You like that?" she said.

"Yes. Fuck yes." He ran his hands up her thighs and waist until they touched her breasts. He rolled her nipples under his palms, feeling them grow hard. He cupped her firm bosoms, rubbing her tips with his thumbs. He felt her tremble under his touch.

"G-g-good." Her breath was heavy and ragged, but her hands kept moving up and down his now spectacularly stiff member.

"Turn on the lights," he said. "Let me see you, baby."

"Not now." He heard plastic wrapper ripping, and felt her hands encase his cock with the latex.

She moved quickly, impaling herself on him. She rocked her hips, letting him slide in and out of her, soft moans escaping her throat.

"Fuck yes," Sebastian gasped. He ran his hands down to her backside. Gripping her firmly, he let her ride him to the edge.

"Could I borrow a shirt?" Victoria asked, twenty minutes later. They were both lying in bed, trying to catch their breath.

"Are we doing sexy roleplaying now?" He dragged a finger lazily over her forehead, brushing a few strands of her hair away from her face. "Because I'm not putting on a dress."

"I have to get back to my room. And you ruined my clothes."

"I'll get you another one," he said. "It's only three a.m. Go to sleep." He pulled her closer to him.

"I'd really rather not have the household staff see me walk back to my room in your clothes, Mr. Chase."

He didn't reply for a long time. Finally, he let his arms relax their hold, and she moved away and slipped out of his bed.

***

Victoria moved the pasta around her plate with her fork aimlessly.

"So... you're seeing someone else, then?" Ardan said.

"No, not really. It's ..." she said, then paused. "Things just got really complicated since Sunday."

I slept with my boss on a dare and it was incredible and I don't think I'll be emotionally available to any other man for the next ten years. Oh, and he doesn't have time for a relationship because he's too busy banging a country singer and God knows how many other women.

"Do you want to talk about it?" Ardan said.

"I'd rather not. But thank you so much for meeting me for lunch. This is on me."

"You don't have to do that."

"No." She smiled sheepishly. "But I dragged you all the way here on your lunch break, so it's the least I could do."

"You could have told me over dinner, you know. Although this is a really great place."

"It's not," she said, laughing. "I'm pretty sure your ravioli is terrible. I think they wash the tablecloth here once a year." She paused. "And I thought canceling dinner would be best. I don't want to be unfair to you."

"It doesn't have to be a date, you know. Dinner, I mean." He took a bite of his food and chewed thoughtfully. "And I don't know what you're talking about. This ravioli is... not terrible. Flavorless, maybe."

"But not terrible."

"I like to look at the bright side of things." He shrugged. "So. Do we have a non-date tonight?" he said, nonchalantly picking up another piece of ravioli with his fork.

She looked at him, trying to figure out what to say.

"We could invite Nicolette, if you like," he added. "She and I are friends you know. It won't be weird if the three of us hung out."

He didn't seem too devastated, or at least it seemed that way to Victoria. She felt guilty about canceling so close to the dinner date, but he seemed to understand.

She wondered what was really wrong with Ardan. No one could be this perfect.

He was fun, too. He made her laugh.

Maybe a night out with friends would take her mind off Sebastian. She was distracted all morning, going over what happened that night. Remembering the sound of his voice, thick with need, when he said her name. The way his mouth moved on hers ...

"I'll ask her," she said.

"Great. It's not a date, okay?" Ardan said, and grinned. "Don't try to kiss me."

She laughed. "I'll try to control myself."

***

"You were very naughty man, Sebastian Chase."

The tall, slim blonde who answered the door put a hand on her hip, pushing open her sheer white lace robe. Underneath, she was wearing a white satin teddy with a deep neckline that barely covered her ample bosom. Sebastian found her Slavic accent one of the sexiest things about her, but there was a great many other aspects of the woman he admired.

"Liskta, I've come to apologize," he said. His eyes fixed on her long legs and moved up to her heaving chest appreciatively. "May I come in?"

"You know I give up date with Orlando for you," she said as he entered her hotel suite. She shut the door and faced him. She crossed her arms on her chest and pouted. "And you stand me up."

"Forgive me, something urgent came up."

She smiled and threw her arms around him. "That ok. You come with big apology yes? Hard also?"

Sebastian felt his manhood twitch as she pressed up against him. He kept his eyes on her face, although it was difficult to tear his eyes away from her cleavage. "Just an apology, I'm afraid." He had a dinner appointment at Culina in five minutes, he barely had time for this.

The sad look on Liskta's face tugged at his chest. "And dinner tomorrow night to make up for it," he added smoothly. "Anywhere you want. Paris, perhaps?"

"No. I go Paris anytime I want." She shook her head. "You want to make up, you cook for me."

"Liskta —"

"Tomorrow night Leonardo take me on his yacht," she said. "You cook for me, I cancel with him."

Victoria would be at the house tomorrow night to study with Benson. He was not sure why this worried him. It was not the ideal situation, but Victoria knew he was free to see other women.

Furthermore, it was difficult to think when inches away from such delectable breasts.

He sighed. "Very well. I'll send a car for you at six."

"You no pick me up?" She caressed the back of his neck.

If he got into a car with Liskta, she'd have him pantsless and grunting under her in less than five minutes. "I have work till six," he said regretfully. "And I would have to cancel a conference call so we can have dinner."

"Serve you right." She brought her right hand down to his crotch, enjoying the feel of his manhood grow stiff to her touch. "After that?"

"I'm all yours."

Chapter 23

Waiting

Elton Lowry lifted his wine glass. "To China," he said.

"Cheers!" Everyone raised their glass in the toast.

The contracts had been signed. Mattheson Banking Corporation was now partners with one of the biggest banks in China. It was a coup, and Sebastian had taken his top people out to dinner to celebrate. There were about twenty of them around a long table, enjoying the fine Italian food and champagne.

"Congratulations, Callie," he said, leaning over to refill her wine glass. He was sitting at the head of the table, Callie on his right. "We couldn't have done it without you."

"Damn straight," she said. She raised her glass to him before taking a long sip. "Of course Elton decides he gets to take most of the spotlight."

"I think he was not very pleased you're sitting next to me."

"No, he's not. Maybe we could send him over to Beijing for a while."

"Hmmmm." Sebastian mulled over the thought. "That's not a bad idea."

"Hey, what are you two whispering about?" Elton said. He sat across the table, a fake smile on his face.

Callie smirked. "Just talking about you, Elton," she said. "Great work."

Elton nodded, but he looked at them suspiciously. "Thanks. Will you excuse me," he said, pulling out his phone from his pocket.

"He won't be happy, will he?" Sebastian whispered.

"He's been banging some eighteen-year-old UCLA freshman on the side for a couple of months now," Callie said. "He won't be happy."

"I hear your father will be flying over next week for the party," David Lee said. He sat beside Callie, enjoying the prosciutto cups.

"Has he come around to the Beijing deal, then?" Henry McCade said. He was sitting on Sebastian's left.

Sebastian nodded. He was not at all excited at the prospect of seeing his father again, but his face did not betray his feelings. "The board of directors will be there, of course."

"Will *she* be there?" Callie said.

He looked at her, uncomprehending. She nodded to his left.

Erika Daniels was walking toward their table. She was wearing a short, tight black dress and a smile on her face.

"Darling, so sorry I'm late," she said. She put her hand on his shoulder, rubbing it sensually, and bent over, her lips lingering on his mouth.

He let her kiss him. It was not unpleasant. She smelled like honey and roses, and her lips were soft and warm and eager. He felt her tongue briefly touch his lower lip.

When she straightened up, Sebastian turned to see everyone at the table gaping at them.

"Ms. Daniels, please take my seat," Henry said, standing up and pulling up his chair for her. "I'm such a big fan."

"Why thank you. What's your name, sweetie?" She sat down, smiling up at him.

"Henry McCade," he said, grinning from ear to ear.

"Thank you, Henry." She beamed at everyone at the table, they nodded back excitedly.

"Don't say it," Sebastian muttered under his breath.

"I didn't say anything," Callie whispered. She saw him clench his jaw. "You didn't invite her, did you?" she added. "Should I call security?"

"No, I'll take care of it."

"Sebastian, sweetie," Erika purred. She slipped her hand under the table to rub his thigh. "I'm so glad things went well in Beijing. Did you miss me?"

He looked at her amusedly for a few moments. "As much as can be expected," he said. He picked up a bottle of Pinot Grigio. "Would you like some wine, darling?" He held her eyes in a smoldering gaze.

"Uh, yes," she said, flustered. She picked up Henry's glass and held it next to the bottle Sebastian held up over the edge of the table. "Oh wait, oh!" she cried out, standing up and pushing her chair backwards.

"I'm so sorry," he said, handing her a white cloth napkin. "Will you be all right?"

She took the napkin. "I'm soaked," she said, trying to mop off the wine that had spilled on her dress. Everyone at the table had looked up to see what was going on.

A waiter had rushed over to her side. "The bathroom is over there, Ms. Daniels," a waiter said. "Would you like a towel?"

"Yes," Erika said, throwing the napkin on the table in frustration. She grabbed her purse and turned to Sebastian, her red lips pressed in a thin line. "I'll be right back."

After she left, Sebastian called for the manager.

"How did she know you'd be here?" Callie said. "Are you on Instagram?"

"What?"

"Never mind. Maybe she has a friend who works here."

"Maybe." Erika knew about the China trip as well. This was not good.

Soon the restaurant manager came over, and she and Sebastian exchanged a few words.

"Isn't Ms. Daniels coming back?" Henry asked half an hour later, looking around. Everyone was tucking into their steaks and pastas.

"No, Henry," Callie said. She took a bite of her grilled octopus with relish. "I don't think she is."

***

"Nicolette just got home," Victoria said, looking up from her cellphone. "She says she's sorry she couldn't join us for dinner, but she's got the bluray all set up. And popcorn."

Ardan shook his head. "I don't know why I let you guys talk me into watching *Oldboy* again," he said. "It's really depressing."

They were driving from the Japanese restaurant to Victoria's apartment. Dinner was perfect. After a grueling 10-hour shift at the coffee shop, dinner at a nice elegant place with seafood and no smell of coffee engulfing her every minute was a refreshing change. Not to mention Ardan had been a perfect dinner companion. He was funny and interesting, and he never brought up the subject of dating once.

A message notification appeared on her screen. It was a text from Sebastian.

Are you home?

"You know, we could maybe convince her to watch something else," Victoria said absently, staring at the text. "She just got a copy of *Snowpiercer* last month." After some hesitation, she texted back.

Almost. What's up?

What did he want? She wasn't having her next session with Benson till tomorrow. And she really didn't want to think about Sebastian tonight. It was hard enough getting through the day distracted, thinking about what he had said last night.

"I don't do relationships."

That she had misread his intentions was an understatement. Sebastian did want her, but only just as any red-blooded man would want any reasonably attractive woman. He didn't have romantic feelings for her - or anybody for that matter, if she were to make a guess. He had offered her sex as a dare, and she called him on it. Nothing more.

"Is that a Korean film too?" Ardan asked.

"Kind of. I think it's a British-Korean production. Park Chan Wook produced it." Victoria put her phone back in her purse. She'd check for a reply when she got home. Sebastian had occupied too much of her thoughts since she left his bed last night. Over and over, she recalled the way he said her name as she was wrapped around his body. The way he kissed her. The way he touched her, exploring all her intimate places with his fingers, his tongue, his ...

"It's depressing, isn't it?"

"Huh?" she said, staring at Ardan blankly. "I'm sorry, you were saying?"

"Never mind." He grinned. "You've been a little distracted all night."

"I was?" Jesus, what was wrong with her. *Get a grip, Slade.* "I'm sorry. It's work stuff."

"The writing's not going well?"

"Uh, yeah." She hoped she wasn't blushing from the white lie she just told. She hated lying.

"Did you have fun tonight?" Ardan's voice softened. "Even just a little?"

"I had a lot of fun. Thank you." She did. Well, she managed to enjoy herself until halfway through dinner when she began imagining Sebastian kissing her again.

He parked on their block. "Good," he said, unbuckling his seatbelt. "Now let's see what new emotional damage Korea has in store for me."

She laughed as they got out of the car.

They walked to the apartment, and Victoria slowed down to trail behind him. "Hey Ardan," she said.

He turned around. "Something wrong?"

She walked toward him slowly. "Nothing. I just ... Thank you for tonight. I'm sorry I couldn't be better company."

"I understand. You did say you had things on your mind. I'm just glad you let me take you out tonight." He held out his hand. "Let's go?"

***

Connor didn't say anything the entire half hour they were parked.

Sebastian sat in the backseat of the Lincoln, restlessly fingering his cellphone. He had left Culina intending to go straight home, but some madness made him tell Connor to bring him here instead. He wasn't sure why. What exactly would he say to her? *Let's see other people, but please feel free to come up to my room whenever you feel like getting naked.*

He thought she knew the conditions under which they had gotten intimate. That offer of sex for pay was his ridiculous plan to get her in his bed without him feeling guilty, a loophole to get around his policy of not sleeping with his employees.

He'd been tempted before, many times. But there had been no temptation quite like Victoria. He couldn't understand it. She was by no means any more beautiful than all the other women in his life. She was quite average, objectively speaking. Except for the way she smiled that always managed to knock the wind out of him. And the way her body curved in places that forced his eyes to pay attention no matter what he was doing. And the way her voice called out his name in the dark, as her body moved under him ...

"Would you like me to turn up the air conditioning, sir?"

Sebastian took out his handkerchief to mop up the sweat on his forehead. "Thank you, Connor," he said.

Damn it, why was he waiting outside Victoria's apartment like a lovesick idiot? He didn't even know if she was home.

Biting the bullet, he sent her a message: *Are you home?*

It took a full minute for her to reply.

Almost. What's up?

He stared at her text for a long time. He wanted to reply

I am. Would you like to take care of it?

Jesus, what was he, fourteen? He shifted uncomfortably in his seat, thankful there was no one else in the car with him. He looked out the front. They were parked across the street from her building. If she was on her way home, he would see her.

This was probably the lowest he'd ever sunk to: stalking his son's tutor.

Maybe if he told her he was here, it would seem less creepy. However, just as soon as he'd composed a text, he looked out the window and saw her.

Victoria and a familiar-looking man got out of silver Audi parked in front of her building. They were laughing and talking as they walked toward's her front door. They went inside her apartment building holding hands.

They were too far away for him to be certain, but Sebastian knew it was the man she was with at Sophie's party. The knot in his stomach twisted as he recalled the way they had been kissing in the hallway.

Why would he think that Victoria would happily dump her boyfriend after one night in Sebastian's bed? He'd not made her any promises. She was perfectly free to see other men. Free to take them to her home and do whatever she wanted with them. She could screw her boyfriend all night long for all he cared.

"Let's go home, Connor." He was surprised by the raw anger in his voice. He took a deep breath and tried to calm down.

Sleeping with Victoria was supposed to fix whatever obsession he had with her. While he sometimes went out with a woman more than once, he'd never really *needed* a woman for more than a night. Now that he'd satisfied his lust for her, they should be able to get back to their professional relationship.

He had met with Liskta today to apologize, with no intention of making plans. Maybe it was good that they did. She was coming over to his place tomorrow night, and if her eagerness today were any indication, the sensual buxom blonde would be sure to *vigorously* dispel whatever lingering ... interest he had in Victoria.

CHAPTER 24

Study Habits

"Nice move!" Victoria said, nodding at the huge TV screen. "Keep him busy while I go get Nic off that wall."

"You can try, babe," Nicolette's voice taunted her over her earphones.

Benson chewed his lower lip in concentration, his thumbs rapidly pressing on his controller. "Hurry, Victoria! I don't know how long I can hold him off."

"Kid, you don't stand a chance," Julian said, his voice also coming through their headsets. He'd barely spoken during the half hour they'd been playing Kusunoki Blade VI on the PS4, except to grunt and offer a few choice Spanish curse words.

Victoria leaned toward Benson beside her. "Try the *Dai-Nankō* maneuver," she whispered.

"I'll try," the boy replied, nodding, his eyes transfixed on the screen.

***

"That smell heavenly," Liskta said. "I cannot wait to put in my mouth." She had her hand on Sebastian's shoulder, leaning over him as she watched the stew cook.

"I hope you're hungry," Sebastian said. He dropped a few bay leaves in the pot and stirred. "You're getting authentic Texan-Mexican menudo."

"Mmmm. I always hungry for you baby." She nipped his earlobe.

"Liskta, if you don't stop that, I won't be able to finish this."

"I'm sorry." She pouted. "You know I cannot resist man who cook." She snaked her arms around his waist. "You know, I move to California soon."

"Really?"

"I get accepted in Stanford." She smiled proudly. "I become neurosurgeon. Make Mama proud."

"That's so great, Liskta. You're giving up modeling then?"

She shrugged. "I guess. I want to be racecar driver, but Mama and Papa freak out."

"I'm not surprised. That's pretty dangerous."

"What to say? I love the cars. But being doctor, next best thing." She glanced to the side. "Oh hello!"

Sebastian turned to see Victoria standing by the door. She was carrying a big empty bowl and gaping at them. It took her a moment to speak. "I'm so sorry, I didn't know—"

"What are you doing here, Ms. Slade?" he said.

"I was going to refill the popcorn." Victoria swallowed. "Benson and I were —"

"There's a kitchen in the South wing. I would appreciate it if you would use that for the rest of the evening."

Liskta rubbed his lower back, her arms still around his waist. "Now Sebastian, you being rude. She is your staff?"

"Victoria is Benson's tutor," he said.

"Oh, you are tutor to dear Benson!" Liskta said. "So nice to meet you. I am Liskta. Please to join us for dinner. Sebastian cook for me." She leaned on his chest. "He is very good cook."

"Victoria will be having dinner with Benson tonight," Sebastian said, looking pointedly at Victoria.

"Y-y-yes," Victoria said. "Thank you. Again, I'm so sorry. I didn't mean ..." She looked up at Sebastian. "I should go."

"Nice to meet you," Liskta said.

"Likewise," said Victoria. She smiled hesitantly, and left.

"If you take me to bedroom, darling," Liskta said, "will pretty tutor disturb us while we ... having fun?" She ran her tongue over his lower lip.

"I don't think so."

***

"Victoria, you missed the gate again!" Benson said. "We're gonna get destroyed!"

"Sorry," Victoria said, blinking. For the past hour, it had been difficult for her to concentrate on the game: her mind was on Sebastian downstairs in the kitchen with the blonde supermodel. Well, she didn't really know she was a supermodel, but the woman had an almost unearthly beauty and ridiculously long legs that Victoria was almost sure she was.

Get back in the game, Slade, she ordered herself. "Watch this," she said, gripping her controller.

"*Chingg*—" Julian started to say, as his character lost both his swords from Victoria's attack.

"Language!" Nicolette and Victoria both yelled at him in unison.

"It's in Spanish," he protested. "Benson—"

"I'm from Texas, Julian," Benson said, grinning.

"Oh cr— I mean, darn it. *Perdón, hijo.*"

"*No es nada.*" He looked toward his left. "Oh hey, Uncle Sebastian!"

"What's this?" Sebastian said, his eyebrows raised.

Victoria swallowed. She hadn't noticed him coming in. "Playstation?" she said meekly. "I thought Benson and I could play a little after we studied. His homework is all done."

"Watch your back, Victoria," Benson said, his eyes back on the screen. "Sorry, there's no pause on this game, Uncle Sebastian. Did you have dinner? Mrs. Sellers made us hotdogs and finikia."

"I see," Sebastian said, eyeing the trays of food on the coffee table. "Yes, I had dinner. I just wanted to say goodnight."

"Good night." Benson looked up at him and smiled.

Sebastian ruffled his hair and kissed his forehead. "I'll be taking you to school tomorrow. Good night, see you at breakfast." He nodded at Victoria. "Good night, Ms. Slade. I'll be working in my study if you need anything."

"All right," she said, her game controller forgotten on her lap. "Good night."

His study? What happened to his date? It had only been about an hour since she saw him cooking.

"Victoria, the gate!" Benson said.

"Oh, right, sorry." She picked up her controller, her heart pounding in her chest.

***

Victoria stood outside the doors of Sebastian's study. Ten minutes ago, it had seemed like a good idea to come here. Now she wasn't sure. It was nine o'clock. Surely Sebastian was still up, right? What if he was busy?

She wanted to ask him about his text the previous night, the one asking if she was home. After her last reply, he never texted back. It had been bothering her all day. Now she wondered if she should just let that go.

Stupid. You just want to see him.

She had just turned to walk away and go back to her room when his voice made her nearly jump out of her skin.

"Ms. Slade, are you planning to stand outside the door all night? Come inside."

Victoria squinted and looked closer at the spot where the voice seemed to be coming from. It was a small speaker in burnished chrome next to the door. She hadn't noticed it before.

Wait, how did he know she was there?

She looked around her, and spotted a CCTV camera just below the ceiling.

Oh crap.

That meant he knew she had been standing outside his study for ten minutes, agonizing over whether to knock or run back upstairs. There was simply no dignified way out of this. After mentally kicking herself, she opened the door.

Sebastian was at his desk, pen in hand, writing. His laptop was open in front of him. "What can I do for you, Ms. Slade?" he said, not looking up.

The distance between the door and his desk seemed like a mile. She approached him hesitantly, furiously thinking of what to say. "I, uh," she stammered.

He looked up, his piercing blue eyes unreadable. "Yes?"

"Well..."

Why did you text me yesterday?

That just sounded demanding.

I was home. Did you want to see me?

Wow, desperate much?

Victoria swallowed hard. She should have just gone to bed. Instead, she was standing nervously in front of her boss like a silly schoolgirl about to be scolded by the principal.

A really sexy, hot principal.

He was wearing the grey cotton tee and jeans from earlier when he was cooking. It showed off his toned arms, and she could barely keep her eyes off his biceps. Or the outline of his chest.

"You know ... It's nothing, really. I can see you're busy, so I'll just go —"

His chair slid back silently as Sebastian stood up. He walked around his desk, to stand in front of her. "I'm not that busy," he said. "There's no need to be nervous, Ms. Slade. Just give it to me."

"What?" she said, staring at his hand. He had his palm up like he was expecting her to hand him something.

"It's twenty dollars, I believe?"

"Oh, no," she said, horrified. Good grief, he thought she had come here to ... She shook her head. "That's —"

"Did you want to negotiate the price?"

"I didn't mean that. It's just that ... I, uh..." Dear lord, did his mouth always look that amazingly kissable?

"What is it then?" He moved closer.

Oh God, he smelled so good.

"I, uhm... left my wallet in my room."

Sebastian took another step closer. "I'll send you the bill." He slid his hand over the back of her neck.

"Okay... " she murmured, before his mouth found hers.

He ran his tongue all around her parted lips, and her knees buckled. She felt his arm pull her firmly against him, keeping her from falling. She moaned when she felt the entire length of his tongue plow into her mouth.

His hand slid down her back to grasp her bottom, squeezing it, pressing her body against him. She felt something hard prod her stomach.

That's not his belt buckle.

Victoria clung to him, her hands on his back, as he kissed her deeply, ravenously. She rubbed her fingers on the fabric of his shirt, aching to feel his hard muscles. It wasn't enough. She fisted the fabric and pulled until the hem was free. She slid her hand under his shirt and explored the taut skin of his back.

She felt the skirt of her dress hike up. His hand was now under it, rubbing her ass. *That's what a thong is for*, she thought dreamily. She surrendered herself to his hands, his fervent exploration of her skin.

She nearly groaned in dismay when he broke of his kiss. "Victoria," he whispered, his mouth against her cheek.

"Don't stop." She moved her head to cover his lips in another kiss. She wanted the taste of him on her tongue again. They could talk later. Tomorrow.

Sebastian moaned against her mouth. He released his hold on her neck. With both hands, he grasped her waist to lift her up and put her down to sit on the edge of his desk. He wedged himself between her parted legs, running his hands up her thighs to push up her skirt.

She leaned back as he kissed her neck. "Ow," she said, feeling something hard on her back.

He lifted his head and bent forward to push something off the table. Something fell on the carpeted floor with a loud thud and a crack.

"What was that?" Victoria said, alarmed.

"Doesn't matter," he murmured, kissing her neck again.

She rolled her head back, letting him take her with his mouth as he wished. She dropped her hands behind her, palms against the top of the desk for support. His tongue darted over her skin as he kissed her. His hands were still on her parted thighs stroking them roughly.

With eyes shut, Victoria bit her lip to hold back her moans. The pleasure of his mouth and hands on her body was more than she could bear.

"What took you so long?" he growled. He nipped her earlobe lightly before licking the spot below her ear.

Her eyes flew open and her back arched involuntarily at the surge of electricity that shot up her spine. Christ, this man was going to kill her with that tongue. "I w-w-wasn't sure you were free," she said, gasping.

The truth was, Victoria didn't know if she would once again find herself in his arms after the other night. Know the taste of his lips, feel his hands on her again.

"Were you maybe expecting a bat signal?" His mouth was on her throat now, and he slipped his fingers inside her thong.

"That would have been really h-h-helpful— Jesus Christ!" she cried out when his fingers found her mound.

Sebastian pressed firmly on her sensitive spot, rubbing it in slow circles. "You're so wet, my darling," he murmured against her throat. "So goddamn wet ... for me ..."

She closed her eyes again, and forced herself to breathe. Her arms were buckling under her, every muscle in her body turning to jelly. "Sebastian!" she gasped. "I can't ... oh fuck..."

"Come for me, my darling."

CHAPTER 25

Sleep Over

Sebastian pressed harder on Victoria's clit. Her eyes were half-closed, and he watched, transfixed, as her eyelids fluttered and her lips parted, small moans escaping her throat as he pleasured her with his fingers.

Does your boyfriend make you feel like this? Do you cry out his name as loud and hard as you scream mine when I fuck you?

He kept his thoughts to himself. Victoria didn't belong to him. He had no right to either her loyalty or her affections. Whatever intimacies she allowed him meant nothing more than the satisfaction of their mutual lust. He had no right to ask for anything of her; all he could do was wait.

As he covered her mouth with his lips once again, he slipped a finger inside her folds. He had the satisfaction of hearing her whimper into his mouth. His tongue stroked hers furiously, tasting her sweetness and heat before pulling away to nibble on her lower lip.

"Does this feel good, baby?" he said, and slipped another finger inside her.

Her shoes banged against the front of the desk, as her hips bucked against his hand. "Oh, Christ ..." she cried out. "Sebastian ... "

"Tell me," he muttered, and kissed her throat.

"Good ... yes..."

His moved his fingers faster, making her writhe violently under him. Her moans turned to screams of ecstasy, but he only stroked her harder until he felt her clench around his fingers. He watched her face as she climaxed, and felt his erection straining through his jeans.

Sebastian ached to be inside her. But at that moment, nothing mattered but her pleasure. He kept stroking her pussy as she came, until her moans died down and the only sound was of their heavy breathing.

He grabbed her behind with both hands and kissed her mouth, thrusting his tongue as deep as he could. His hand moved up to undo the buttons on the front of her dress. He slid his hand inside and felt around her chest until he found the clasp of her bra. He unhooked it, and pushed aside the cups of the bra to fondle her breast.

Still kissing her, he rolled her nipple under his palm. Victoria moaned softly into his mouth. It was more than enough to push him to the edge of his self-control. He broke off the kiss and pushed her down to lie on the desk.

She looked up at him, breathing heavily. Her mouth was parted slightly as if about to ask him a question.

He covered her breasts with his hands, rubbing his palms roughly over her nipples. She closed her eyes and let him touch her, stir her to arousal.

"Sebastian ..." she moaned. "That's ... oh!"

He was done. Swearing under his breath, he unbuckled his belt.

***

Victoria lay on the desk, eyes closed. She felt his hands all over her body. Undressing her. Caressing her. Driving her crazy with need.

God help her, she wanted more.

Her eyes flew open when she felt him remove her panties.

She lifted her head slightly to see Sebastian's pants down, and his beautiful cock standing in attention. She watched him in silent anticipation as he tore open a condom wrapper and rolled the latex over his engorged member.

She raised her thighs, pressing them on either side of his hips in invitation. "I'm not even going to ask where you got that condom," she said, breathless.

He didn't respond. His eyes locked into hers as he slung her thighs over his arms. "Would you rather do this upstairs?" he asked as he gripped her waist.

"No." Her eyes were pleading. "Now. Please, Sebastian."

He pushed inside her with a grunt of satisfaction.

Victoria caught her breath, feeling the entire length of his cock fill her. She closed her eyes, submitting eagerly to his thrusts.

God, how she wanted him.

She wanted *this*.

The naked desire in his eyes. The way he took possession of her body, making her feel things she'd never felt from any other man's touch.

The way he kissed her, fucked her — like she was his world, and he was hers.

"Victoria..."

The way he said her name.

She opened her eyes. "Don't stop," she said, gasping. Her hand moved unconsciously to her chest, and she noticed his eyes flicker down to where she touched her breast.

He caught his breath when she rolled her nipple under her fingers. "Fuck, baby," he muttered, eyes dark, staring down at her hard pink tips. His thrusts quickened, spurred on by the sight of her touching herself.

"Yes! Oh God yes..." Victoria cried out, arching her back violently as his shaft plowed deeper inside her. The pleasure was so incredible she thought she would pass out.

"Don't stop," Sebastian growled, his eyes fixed on her chest.

She moved her hand to her other breast, fondling it while moving her other hand up to her mouth. She touched her index finger to her tongue. While rolling her nipple with her other hand, she kept her mouth slightly open and stroked her tongue with her finger.

"Fuck, baby .... Christ ..Jesus Christ... Fuck..." Sebastian panted.

She dragged her wet finger from inside her mouth down over her lower lip. "You like that?" She lowered her finger to her breasts, drawing wet circles around her nipple.

"Yes ... God yes..."

He was fucking her so hard, she thought she felt the earth move under her. Her orgasm came in shockwaves. She moaned so loudly her throat hurt. Her legs thrashed as she bucked against his hips. Her hands gripped her breasts, squeezing them as his cock pounded her into a mind-shattering climax.

She lay on her back, gasping for air. Her fingers kept stroking her breasts, her eyes on his face. Sebastian watched her, grunting as he came, hard.

After a while she sat up, pulling down the skirt of her dress that had been bunched up over her hips. His arms went around her waist and his mouth fell on hers in a soft, lazy kiss.

Even after everything they'd just done, the touch of his lips still made Victoria shiver. She put her arms around his neck, clinging to him as she kissed him back.

He kissed her mouth, and moved his lips down her throat. "Now that we've defiled my work desk," he said, "maybe we should move upstairs."

She rolled her head back, letting him take his pleasure with her. He flicked his tongue on her throat between kisses. He moved a hand up to her breast and began to knead it, his thumb rubbing her nipple. Her body was on fire again, her senses lit up like fireworks.

"Too far ..." she whispered. She didn't want to move.

"With what I'm planning on doing to you, Victoria..." He sucked the skin on her neck softly. "I'm going to need a very large bed." Reluctantly, he pulled away from her to pull up his boxers and jeans. "Come."

She let him take her by the hand across the room, wondering if she should even bother looking for her thong. He pressed a button beside a door.

"Where are we going?" she said.

The doors slid open. It was an elevator.

"My bedroom." Sebastian went inside, turning to face her. He pulled his shirt off him and tossed it in the corner. "Are you coming?"

Victoria's eyes dropped to stare at his naked torso.

In two seconds she was inside the lift with him. He grabbed her dress and pulled it over her head, and yanked her bra off her shoulders.

"Better," he murmured, kissing her against the wall as the doors of the elevator closed.

***

Four hours later, Victoria tried to disengage herself from Sebastian's arms without waking him up.

"What are you doing?"

Darn it.

"Sorry," she said. "I have to go. Your staff is coming in a few hours."

He moved his hand over her breasts, sighing in satisfaction. "And?"

She bit her lip, remembering where his hands had been a couple of hours earlier. She blushed at the memory, grateful he couldn't see her in the dark. "I'd really rather they didn't know ... uhm..."

"That I'm fucking my son's tutor?" He pulled her closer to him and kissed her shoulder. "They've seen me take a great number of different women into my bedroom before, Victoria. This will hardly be a shock to anyone."

"Oh."

They lay still for a long time, neither of them speaking.

Sebastian sighed. "Don't move."

She felt him roll over, away from her. His phone lit up in the darkness of the room as he dialed a number.

"Mrs. Sellers, no one is to come in before noon today . And have Connor bring the car around at seven. Thank you." He hung up.

"Is Mrs. Sellers still up?" Victoria said.

"Voice mail." His arms were around her again. "I gave everyone the morning off. Happy?"

She giggled. "Who's making breakfast?"

"I suppose I am. Do you like crepes?"

"I don't think I've ever had crepes." She paused. "Were you ... with Liskta earlier last night?"

"We had dinner, yes."

She swallowed. "Was it just dinner?"

"Does it matter? You knew she had been here, yet you came to me, willingly."

She bit her lip. He was right. She knew he was with another woman last night, yet she didn't hesitate to fall into his arms as soon as he kissed her. What did she expect him to do? Apologize for bringing home a date?

He's not your boyfriend, she reminded herself.

"I guess not."

"Go to sleep, Victoria."

***

Breakfast is at six. Don't be late.

Victoria couldn't stop smiling as she read Sebastian's text. She couldn't remember the last time a boyfriend made her breakfast.

Okay, he was *not* her boyfriend, she reminded herself sternly as she dried her hair with a towel. But he was still making her breakfast. Crepes. She couldn't wait.

She hurried to finish getting dressed.

The television was turned on to one of the entertainment channels. It was the standard background noise back in her apartment, as Nicolette needed to keep tabs on what was going on in the industry. Victoria had gotten into it as a habit now.

She was putting on her shoes when the host was announcing the morning's breaking news.

"Looks like rumors of Erika Daniels and her new boyfriend may be true."

Victoria froze.

"The country star and the hot young billionaire have been spotted Wednesday night in an intimate lip lock over dinner."

She turned to look at the TV. A photo of Sebastian and Erika kissing in a restaurant flashed on the screen. It wasn't a peck on the cheek, either. He was kissing her full on the mouth. It looked like there was tongue.

Her throat felt dry. That was two days ago. He was with her on Tuesday, Erika on Wednesday, and Liskta last night.

Was Sebastian some kind of sex addict? she thought. It made sense now. All those women. His insatiable appetite in bed — and on his desk. They had gone through an entire box of condoms in just two nights.

No wonder he couldn't commit.

Part of her had hoped that maybe there was some chance that what they had could be more than just physical. She liked him more than she cared to admit. But while they were so good together in bed, she felt there was some part of him he was still holding back.

Maybe she should just get out before she got her heart broken.

***

"Mango or strawberry?" Sebastian said, sliding a crepe from the pan onto a plate.

"Mango!" Benson said. He was sitting at the counter top, watching Sebastian cook. "And caramel sauce, please?"

"You got it, kid." Sebastian spooned cubes of fresh mango on the crepe before folding it up and drizzling caramel sauce over it. He set the plate in front of the boy.

"Isn't Victoria joining us for breakfast?" Benson said, cutting his crepe with a knife and fork.

"She's probably just running a bit late." Sebastian grinned at him as he made a crepe for himself.

"I like her," Benson said. "She's really smart."

"She is." Sebastian set his plate down, and took his seat beside Benson. "That's why I hired her."

The boy took another bite of crepe, chewing thoughtfully. "She never asks me about you. Not like the others."

"What do you mean?"

"Sandra used to ask me a lot of questions about you. And so did Ms. Keeler. Like, if you were dating anyone."

"Victoria only talks about your lessons, I take it?" Sebastian clenched his jaw in irritation.

"No. Sometimes she asks me about my friends. And stuff I like to do after school. I asked her if she could come to my violin recital tomorrow, but she said she had to work at the coffee shop."

"I see."

Where was she? It was almost seven. Sebastian picked up his phone to send her a text, but he saw she'd texted him first half an hour earlier.

They moved my shift to six-thirty, so I have to go. I left twenty dollars on your night stand. I'm so sorry about breakfast.

Chapter 26

Play

"So I may have slept with my boss," Victoria said, loudly. She was on the couch, legs crossed, typing on her laptop.

Nicolette stuck her head out her open bedroom door. "You're serious?" She narrowed her eyes. "Was it good?"

"Uh... yes."

"Huh."

"I may have paid him for it. Twice." She paused and rested her arms on her lap, looking up ruefully at her friend.

Nicolette crossed her arms and leaned against the door frame, frowning. She was wearing a light pink slip dress and her hair was up in curlers. "He's either the cheapest bazillionaire in L.A., or one kinky bastard. Which is it?"

Victoria shrugged. "He bought me a coat that costs more than what he pays me in a month. I don't think he's cheap."

"Hmmm. He *is* your boss. Maybe it's his way of giving you some control over the relationship."

"What relationship?" Victoria mumbled, leaning back on the couch. If she *had* a relationship, she wouldn't be at home on a Friday night, typing on her laptop. "I think he's suffering from some kind of sex addiction, Nic. It's almost like every time I see him, he's either making out with another girl, or ..."

Her roommate raised an eyebrow. "Trying to get you to bed?"

Victoria blushed. "Technically, I initiated it the first time."

"Fooling around with Erika Daniels's hot billionaire boyfriend," Nicolette mused. "I'm very impressed." She grinned. "Hey, after you're done with Chase, maybe you could steal Miranda Kerr's boyfriend too."

"Very funny." Victoria leaned forward and got back to her writing, but her friend's words hit her like a punch in her gut. Erika may not be Sebastian's girlfriend, as he claimed, but it didn't mean they weren't seeing each other. Or making out in restaurants.

They've seen me take a great number of different women into my bedroom before.

Just how many, exactly? Maybe he was just bragging, the way guys do? But he definitely knew his way around a bed — and a desk — so yeah, he was experienced. That much she knew. She bit her lower lip, remembering what it felt like having his tongue down there between her thighs. A delicious shiver crawled up her spine.

"Hey, Victoria!"

She looked up to see Nicolette standing in front of her. "Sorry! You were saying?" She'd completely zoned out.

Her friend was holding a pair of shoes in each hand. "Which one? Slutty?" she said, holding up the white slingbacks. "Or sluttier?" She held up the black strappy stilettos.

Victoria pointed to the black stilettos. "Sluttier, definitely."

"It's that good, huh?"

"What is?"

"Sex with your boss. You had a stupid, horny look on your face when I mentioned it." Nicolette gave her a knowing look and turned to go back to her room.

"I did not!" Victoria yelled after her. "I'm thinking about the plot of my story!"

"Liar."

***

"There you are!" Ed Taylor gave Victoria a wide smile as she approached the counter of the Foxhole. She'd just arrived for her shift.

It was odd. Her boss was never this cheerful, especially on a Saturday morning. A tall, well-built man in his forties wearing a black suit standing sideways in front of the counter turned to face her.

"Connor?" she said, recognizing Sebastian's chauffeur. "What's going on?"

"Mr. Chase is requesting your services today," Connor said. "Unfortunately, he's been called to a meeting and can't be at Benson's violin recital this morning. He'd like for you to be there in his place."

"Oh." She looked at Ed. There was no way he was going to let her take the day off on such short notice.

"Go on ahead, Victoria," the elderly man said. "You can come in tomorrow."

"Really?" Now Ed was *really* acting strange.

"This way, please, Ms. Slade," Connor said, gesturing toward the door.

"Thank you, Ed!" she called out to her employer as Connor hurried her to the door. "What did you say to him?" she whispered as they walked out the coffee shop.

"I explained the situation, and he was very understanding," Connor said.

"You didn't threaten him did you?" she asked half-jokingly. A former Navy Seal, Connor was first of all Sebastian's personal body guard. Chauffeuring — a job he was vastly overqualified for — was only part of his duties.

"I'm sure I don't know what you mean, Ms. Slade." He opened the car door for her. "The program will be only till noon, but Mr. Chase will compensate you for the whole day."

"Oh, that's not really necessary, Connor." She slid into the back seat. "I'm happy to do this."

"You'll have to take that up with Mr. Chase, I'm afraid."

It was a nice quiet drive to Benson's school. Riding at the back of the silver Mercedes was a different experience from her daily bus rides, that was for sure. The luxury car practically glided over concrete; she could barely feel a single bump on the road. And the soft leather seat was more comfortable than any bed she'd ever owned. She smoothed the skirt of her dark blue dress, thankful she decided to wear it that day instead of jeans. With short cropped sleeves and crisp lines, it was casual but elegant enough for a school affair. At least she hoped it was.

"We're not late, are we, Connor?" she said as they pulled up in front of the auditorium.

"No, Miss. It starts in..." He looked at his watch. "Twenty minutes. Benson's already backstage. I'll pick you both up here after the show."

Victoria couldn't help smiling as she walked through the lobby of the auditorium. When Benson had asked her the other day if she could be at the recital, she had to decline. It was difficult for her to get Saturdays off from the coffee shop. And after finding out that Sebastian was still seeing Erika, she wasn't ready to face him again, at least until her next tutoring session. She had no idea how Connor got Ed to give her the day off, but she was glad she would be able to see Benton's performance. And without having to see Sebastian, too. Thank goodness her boss was so busy.

She wondered why he wanted her to be there. Did Benson not have any aunts or other relatives who could attend in his uncle's place? Did the boy put Sebastian up to it?

"This way please, Miss," said the usher, a teenage girl in a dark maroon suit. She escorted Victoria to a seat in the second row.

She took her phone out to set it to vibrate. She looked up and saw she was seated next to an elegant woman in her forties who was deep in conversation with a man on her right who was probably her her husband. The seat on Victoria's left was empty.

"Oh hello," the woman said, smiling at her. "My husband and I were just talking about how well the music program has improved since last year. Bringing in Nikolaus Scherer as head of the department was quite inspired."

"I'm ... sure it was," Victoria said, putting her phone back in her purse. She had no idea who Nikolaus was. "I suppose he's really good with the kids?"

The woman rolled her eyes. "Ghastly manners, my dear. He shouts at them during rehearsals, and expects the other instructors to do the same. I suppose there are very few such talented musicians who aren't so temperamental. Especially when they're German."

"I suppose so." Victoria paused. "Although I don't think shouting at children would make them any better at music."

"Is that right?" The woman smiled at her. "Do you have a child in the program? I'm not sure you look old enough, my dear."

"Oh no," Victoria said. "Not mine. He's—"

"Ms. Slade is here to accompany me, Betty."

The woman looked over Victoria's shoulder, her eyes looking like they were ready to pop out of their sockets.

Victoria turned to see Sebastian beside her, unbuttoning his grey suit jacket as he settled in his seat. His eyes met hers, his expression neutral.

So much for avoiding her boss.

What was he even doing here? She stared at him, unsure of what to say.

"Oh, my," the woman exclaimed. "She and I have just been chatting about the new music department head, Sebastian. I had no idea she was your ... friend."

Victoria turned to look at her. She wasn't sure she was comfortable with the way Betty said the word "friend".

The older woman looked at her a little more closely, and held out her hand. "It's so nice to meet you. I'm Betty Van Drunen, and this is my husband Noah. Our Jensen is in the junior lacrosse team with Benson."

"Victoria Slade," Victoria said, shaking her hand. "Very nice to meet you."

"Delighted, I'm sure." She smiled and nodded to Sebastian before turning away to speak to her husband in low tones.

Victoria finally found her voice. "I thought you had a meeting," she said.

"Cancelled."

"Oh, then I guess I should —"

"Stay, please." The imploring way he looked at her made her knees weak. "I told Benson you'd be here."

She was quiet for a moment, then nodded her head. She leaned back in her seat and prayed for the program to begin.

"Thank you for coming," he said.

"You're welcome," she said, trying to sound casual.

Please don't ask me about what happened at-

"You ran out on me yesterday."

Crap.

"I'm sorry," she said, her eyes glued to the stage curtains.

"If you didn't like crepes, I could have made you something else."

"It's not that." She gripped the arm rest between them. "I had to get to work—"

"Shhh," he whispered, his hand closing over hers. "We'll talk later."

Victoria was vaguely aware that the lights had dimmed, and the curtain was beginning to rise. All she could think about was Sebastian holding her hand. His four fingers were curled under her palm, and his thumb caressed the top of her fingers in an occasional slow, gentle stroke as though it was the most natural thing in the world.

She felt her body temperature rise, the awareness of his touch coursing through every nerve in her body. The fluttering in her stomach melted into a hot pit of need in her core.

She pulled her hand away from his grasp. "I forgot to put my phone on silent mode," she whispered as she fumbled with her purse. She took her phone out and went through the motions of muting it.

After putting her phone away, Victoria rested her hands on her lap. She clutched her purse, hoping it would dissuade him from trying to take her hand again.

Sebastian kept his elbow on the arm rest but didn't say anything for a long time.

After a while, she relaxed and started to enjoy the program. Most of the young performers were quite talented, especially the older ones. They performed on the piano, the cello, the violin and the trumpet. The strings were the last to play, and during the cello and violin performances, she had sat up straight in her seat in eager anticipation of Benson's turn on the stage.

"To perform the minuet from George Frideric Handel's *Berenice* on the violin: Benedict Mattheson."

The young boy was in a dark blue suit and silver tie. Violin in hand, he took center stage and bowed. He tucked the instrument under his chin and began to play.

Victoria caught her breath.

The song was beautiful, and one she didn't remember ever hearing before. Benson's fingers glided confidently over the fingerboard, as his bow teased the haunting, sweeping melody from the strings.

She felt her heart soar in pride. Her hands flew up to cover her mouth that had dropped open in awe. Impulsively, she turned to look at Sebastian.

He was staring at her. They held each other's gaze for a tense, heated moment, before he turned his eyes back to the stage.

CHAPTER 27

A Fear of Flying

After the program ended, lights flooded the auditorium and people started to get on their feet.

"Shall we?"

Victoria glanced up to see Sebastian already standing. He was fastening the button of his suit jacket, looking at her expectantly. Nodding, she got up.

She didn't look at him as she smoothed the folds her dress and slung her purse over her shoulder. She sensed his eyes still fixed on her and she felt her cheeks warm under his stare.

Briefly, she wondered if he would try to take her hand again, and panic began to rise in the back of her throat. When Sebastian turned to make his way to the aisle, she breathed a sigh of relief and followed behind him, trying not to get too close.

Did that really happen? He was holding her hand ... looking at her in the way that made her unable to breathe.

Calm down. He's acting normal now. So should you.

As she stepped into the aisle, Victoria felt his hand fall on the small of her back. Gently, he guided her up the steps as they walked side by side toward the exit.

Her stomach fluttered again, her skin heating up to his touch. The urge to lean into his chest was overpowering. She gripped the strap of her purse and tried to steady her knees as she walked.

"Did you enjoy the program, Victoria?" His voice sounded almost like a caress.

"Yes, thank you. I never knew Benson was so talented."

"He takes after his mother. She is quite a gifted musician, and an artist."

"Does she ... ever come to see Benson perform?"

"Circumstances don't allow it."

"Oh." She had no idea what those circumstances were. While Benson did occasionally mention his mother, Victoria made it a point never to pry. She still had no idea why the boy had been adopted by his uncle, despite still having a living parent.

"Don't worry, Victoria. Benson sees his mother quite often. He's visiting her this weekend, in fact."

She felt a jolt of happiness in her chest. Benson still had a mother in his life after all. "That's ... wonderful," she said.

They had reached the lobby. Parents were milling around them as they waited for their children. Smartly dressed waiters were serving drinks and small dainty snacks on trays.

"I hope you don't think I'm being inappropriate with my questions," she said. "Your family situation is really none of my business."

"Corinne," he said.

"What?" *Who?*

"That's Benson's mother's name. Corinne Walker."

"Oh."

"Corinne lives in Austin. She paints — mostly landscapes and still lifes. She also teaches piano to adult beginners."

He smiled, and Victoria's breath caught in her throat. "She loves Benson very much," he added.

She smiled back at him. It was almost like he knew the question she most wanted to ask.

"Do you play an instrument?"

"No, I—" She paused when she noticed two women in their thirties wearing sundresses a few feet away. They were staring at Sebastian. She saw a woman in a suit behind them sipping a mimosa — she looked about forty, gorgeous and quite fit — also staring at him. She turned her eyes discretely to her left and scanned the room.

There it was. More women openly staring at him. Or glancing at him repeatedly. There were also two good-looking men in their thirties who looked like they were a couple, and they were also looking at Sebastian appreciatively.

Then she realized some of the women were looking at *her*. A few of them were staring at her with something akin to hostility.

Victoria grabbed a mimosa from a passing waiter. "Are you all right?" Sebastian said, watching her gulp down the drink.

"I'm fine." She wasn't. It was nerve-wracking to be the center of everyone's attention. Is this how it was going to be every time she was out in public with him? Not that she was expecting this to be a problem. It wasn't like they were together ...

"So, you don't play, then?"

"What? Oh, you mean an instrument." She smiled ruefully. "We could never afford music lessons. But I've always wanted to learn the piano."

"It's never too late."

Looking around for another waiter serving drinks, Victoria felt her heart start to beat very fast.

It wasn't that Sebastian was so... *attentive*. It was the realization that he'd always been that way with her since she started working for him that surprised her. It dawned on her that even when they argued, or when he was criticizing her clothes and her career, he was always paying attention.

She took another glass from a waiter and nodded her thanks. She took a long drink, careful to avoid his eyes.

"Victoria, you made it!"

Benson came in with a group of kids, his violin case in hand.

"Hey, sport," Sebastian said, pulling the boy in for a hug.

"Didn't I say she'd come, Uncle Sebastian?" Benson said.

"You did."

"Thank you for inviting me," Victoria said. "You were very good."

"You like Handel?" Benson asked her. The three of them walked to the exit side by side, the boy between the two adults.

"I do. Although I think I only know *Messiah*." She grinned sheepishly.

"That's okay. I did Bach last time. But I think I like Handel more." He turned to Sebastian. "Is Victoria having lunch with us?"

"I was just going to ask her," Sebastian said.

"Oh, it's okay," Victoria said. "I should really get going now."

"We would really like it if you joined us."

She looked at Benson, who didn't say a word. He just looked up at her and smiled.

***

Sebastian knew he ought to be ashamed of himself.

He'd never thought the day would come that he would leverage his own kid to get a woman to spend time with him. But then he never thought he needed to.

They were in the car on their way to lunch. Benson was showing Victoria his violin, explaining the different parts of the instrument and what they were for.

Sebastian watched her as she asked his son questions about the violin, and how he played it. He would have been jealous at being all but ignored by the both of them if he weren't so amused at how close the two had become. Besides, it gave him a chance to watch her smile and laugh without reservations.

She had a beautiful smile. When he wasn't kissing her, he wanted nothing more than to see her smile.

As she fingered the instrument gingerly, he saw Benson glance sideways at him as if asking a question.

Sebastian winked.

Benson grinned, and handed her the violin. "Here, hold it," he said. "See how it feels."

"Oh my. Are you sure?"

"It looks cool, yeah? It's a Stradivarius."

"That sounds expensive," Victoria said, admiring instrument in her hands.

"Uncle Sebastian bought it from an old lady in London. I only use it for dress rehearsals and performances. It's not a lot better than my other violins, but the sound of this one really fills the room."

What the boy didn't mention was that the Baroness Grey de Ruthyn wouldn't sell the violin to Sebastian until he had beaten her at poker. He won ten thousand pounds in the game, and paid one million pounds for the Stradivarius itself. Benson had enough sense to ask him discreetly if it was all right if he let Victoria handle the violin.

"Wow. Is it old?"

"Almost three hundred years old."

"Right. Uh, maybe you should put this back in the case now." She carefully handed the instrument back to him.

"Mr. Chase, we're here," Connor said.

"Are you flying somewhere?" Victoria asked, looking out the dashboard, puzzled. They were on an airport runway, parked near a private plane.

"We're having lunch on the plane," Sebastian said.

She saw that Connor had opened the car door on her side. She stepped out, her eyebrows furrowed in confusion.

"Why?" she said.

"Uncle Sebastian is taking me to visit my mom in Austin," Benson said as he followed her out of the car. "You'll like her, I promise."

Victoria looked at Sebastian who had gotten out the car as well. "Austin?"

"The flight is less than three hours. I promise to get you home by midnight, all right?"

"I don't know ..."

"C'mon, Victoria!" Benson shouted down from the top of the stairs of the plane. "Uncle Sebastian says he has a surprise for me. Come on!"

***

There was so much room in the cabin of Sebastian's private plane, especially since the three of them were the only ones in it. The chairs had rich cream-colored leather upholstery, and there were even fresh flowers in the corner. Everything in the cabin was beautiful and elegant.

Victoria's knuckles were white as she gripped her arm rests, praying she wouldn't throw up.

"Why didn't you tell me you were scared of flying?" Sebastian said gently, mopping her brow with a cool, wet towel. "I wouldn't have asked you to come."

They had taken off ten minutes ago. He noticed Victoria hadn't spoken a word since they left the runway, and saw that her lips were pale and she was hanging on to her seat like her life depended on it.

"I didn't know," she said. "I've never been on a plane before. I'm so sorry."

"It's okay, Victoria," Benson said. He was standing in front of her, holding up a bowl of water Sebastian used to wet the towel. "It's not your fault."

"I'm going to tell the captain to turn back." Sebastian said. He had taken off his suit jacket, and the sleeves of his shirt were rolled up. He pressed the towel once more on her forehead before dropping it in the bowl.

She grabbed his arm. "No, wait," she said. She took a deep breath. "I'll be fine. I need to do this." She smiled faintly and loosened her grip on him. "I don't want to be afraid for the rest of my life."

She said she didn't want to be afraid of flying, but as she looked into his eyes, she knew he realized she meant much more.

"I understand," he said, taking her hand and pressing it between his palms. "I'll be here for you no matter what."

"Me too," Benson said.

CHAPTER 28

Market Day

The sky was wide and almost clear. Where it embraced the land on the horizon ahead, there were none of the familiar skyscrapers to crowd the skyline.

The chauffeur who picked them up at the airport drove them past factories, warehouses, car dealerships and the wide empty spaces between them. Victoria thought she saw a McDonald's, and her stomach rumbled. She'd barely eaten anything on the plane, except for some tomato soup. It was all she could manage to eat in her state of nervousness and panic.

"Have you been here before?" Sebastian said.

She turned away from the window to look at him. "My first time," she said. "I haven't traveled much." Sebastian had changed into a white oxford shirt and blue jeans, and she tried very hard not to stare at the skin of his throat showing under his open collar.

Breathe, Slade. Just stop staring at his neck. And his face.

"Hey." He moved closer to look at her. "Are you feeling better?"

Benson was sitting between them, but she could smell the scent of the cologne on Sebastian's skin, faintly.

This is not helping.

"Yes, thank you. I'm just a little, uh..."

"Hungry?" He grinned.

"You ... could say that."

"When we get to the market, I promise to buy you the best grilled-cheese sandwich you've ever had."

The market turned out to be a series of stalls selling paintings, clothing, handmade jewelry and a lot of other interesting artwork. The entire street was vibrant with casual cafes, bohemian-inspired shops with unusual names, and restaurants of various cultural flavors. Bright, colorful murals decorated the walls of buildings, and hand-made crafts decked window sills of stores.

"Wow," Victoria said, stepping out of the SUV. "Does your mom live around here?" she asked Benson.

"She's over there," Benson said, tugging her hand. "C'mon."

"Ben!"

The dark-haired young woman who couldn't be more than a few years older than Victoria stepped out from behind a stall to gather the boy in her arms.

"Hey, Mom," Benson said, hugging her. "Missed me?"

"I did," she said. "How did the recital go, sweetie?"

"It was okay." He smiled bashfully.

"Will you play your piece for me later?"

Benson nodded. "I brought Tony with me."

"Awesome." She looked at Victoria and smiled. "Hi."

"Hello, Ms. Walker," Victoria said. She was surprised when Benson's mother hugged her.

"Call me Corinne," she said. "Victoria, right? Benson's told me so much about you."

"Yes. So nice to meet you."

Corinne was in a loose black tee shirt, a full-length print skirt, and sandals. Her dark hair was pulled up in a relaxed bun. "Thank you for coming. I've been dying to meet you." She turned to Sebastian. "Hey, gorgeous," she said, her eyes twinkling.

"Corinne, you look great," Sebastian said, hugging her tightly.

"You too, hon. Will you guys stay for dinner?"

"What do you think?" he said, looking at Victoria.

"Yes," she replied, surprised. The man who had used his boss card to drag her to Barneys and that Italian restaurant was actually asking her if she wanted to accept Corinne's invitation to dinner. "Thanks," she said to Corinne. "That's very kind of you."

"Great. Excuse me a sec," Corinne said. "Hi!" she greeted a woman who was looking at her paintings on display. "Are you looking for something for you or a friend?"

"I'm going to get us some sandwiches," Sebastian said. "There could be a line at the food trailer, so just wait here with Corinne, okay?"

"Okay," Victoria said. "You're not going to ask me what I want?"

"I think I know what you want."

"Really," she said, grinning.

He winked. "I'll take Benson with me." He turned to see Benson standing in front of the stall, talking to Corinne's customer.

"You should get that one," the boy said, pointing up at an abstract watercolor of what looked like a burning forest overlooking a lake.

"That one, huh?" said the woman, smiling. She looked like she was in her mid-forties, and had an air of confidence about her. She was dressed in khaki slacks, a white tee-shirt, and high-heeled sandals.

He nodded. "It's pretty, like you."

She laughed. "I think I'll take it then," she said to Corinne. "I think it will look good in my new office. I just got a VP position at Dell. Your son?"

"Yes, he is," Corinne said. "Shall I wrap it up for you? I can have it delivered, if you prefer."

After the customer had left with her new painting, Corinne put her hands on her hips and narrowed her eyes. "Sebastian Chase, what have you been teaching my son?" she demanded.

"I, uhm ..." he started to say, looking between Corinne and Benson. Finally, he put his hand on Benson's shoulder. "We're getting us some sandwiches. You want your usual, Cor?"

She crossed her arms over her chest.

"Did I say something wrong?" Benson said.

His mother laughed. "Nothing, sweetie. Go with your uncle. Just get a little snack, okay? Dinner is in a couple of hours."

"Your paintings are really good," Victoria said, after Sebastian and Benson left. She bent down to examine a watercolor. "Is this a local river?"

"It's the San Marcos River." Corinne looked at the painting lovingly. "The water there is like crystal."

"Sebastian did say you liked to paint nature. Have you ever painted Benson?"

"A few sketches. I tried when he was about two, but he wouldn't sit down long enough." She laughed.

"Could I see them sometime?"

"Yes, of course. I have a few sketches of Sebastian too, if you're interested."

"I wish I could paint," Victoria said, trying to change the subject.

"Sebastian said you're a writer. I think that's pretty cool."

"He did?" She thought back on what Sebastian said about her lack of ambition. She was surprised he even bothered to mention her writing aspirations to Corinne. "Well, I'm trying at least."

"Promise me you'll sign a copy of your first book for me, okay?"

"Sure." She smiled. "Benson's a really sweet kid. I think Sebastian's a good influence on him. You're not really mad at him are you?"

"No. Just keeping him on his toes." Corinne looked at her thoughtfully. "Is my idiot brother-in-law still playing around?"

Victoria felt her face redden. "I, uh ... It's really none of my business," she said.

Corinne sighed. "You know, he wasn't always like that. Did he tell you he was engaged once?"

Victoria felt the air leave her lungs. "It didn't come up, no."

"Two years ago. Her name was Alaina Maddock. Their families go way back. She was one of those annoyingly perfect girls. Rich, beautiful, elegant. And she was a doctor. Sebastian loved her to distraction." Corinne looked Victoria in the eye. "I'm only bringing this up because he doesn't exactly bring all Benson's tutors to visit me, you know?"

"Yeah," Victoria said. Corinne wasn't stupid, she knew something was going on. "But we're not really dating."

Corinne nodded. "Yes, well. That Maddock girl really did a number on him. I don't think he's ever trusted any woman since."

"It's hard to believe any woman could ... break his heart like that."

"It seems that way, doesn't it? But Sebastian has a weakness."

It was the unmistakable sadness and regret in the young mother's eyes that made Victoria realize what it was.

"Benson," she whispered. She felt a white-hot anger slowly crawl up her spine at the thought of anyone hurting the boy.

"I had Ben when I was nineteen.," Corinne said. "Eric and I didn't plan it, and I was young and scared. I'm also bipolar. I'd been suffering long bouts of depression since I was twelve, and I didn't think I was capable of taking care of another human being. He begged me to keep the baby and marry him, and for a while I thought we could make it somehow. The marriage didn't go well. A few months into our separation, he died in that accident. Ben was five."

"I'm so sorry," Victoria said.

"I couldn't take care of my son. Not by myself. I know a lot of people diagnosed with bipolar disorder or depression have raised kids really well, I just ... couldn't do it. I was afraid I might hurt my baby boy. When Sebastian offered to adopt him, I said yes. When Alaina came into the picture, she never let Sebastian know she didn't want Ben. Instead, she pretended to be my friend. Then made me feel guilty about giving up my son. She was so... manipulative. I didn't even realize what she was doing until it was almost too late."

"She wanted you to get Benson back from Sebastian?"

Corinne nodded. "He loves Ben so much. But he promised me he would return parental rights to me if I ever changed my mind. It would have destroyed him, but I know he'd do it. Alaina knew this. She counted on it. I was a mess, even with my medication and therapy. The guilt threw me down a horrible well of depression. But Sebastian found out what Alaina was trying to do."

"And they broke up." Victoria's chest felt tight, thinking about what Corinne went through. And Sebastian. She almost wished he was just a shallow playboy after all, if it meant that he hadn't suffered such heartbreak.

"Yes. She never apologized for what she'd done. He was so angry. And hurt. It was painful for me to see him like that, but he made sure I never blamed myself for what happened. And we both made sure Ben didn't find out.

"He still loves her, I think. Some days I wonder if he's just waiting for her to come back to him and tell him she was sorry. Most of the time, though, I think he just doesn't want any woman to get close enough to hurt him or me or Ben again."

***

Victoria's grilled cheese sandwich was drizzled with a sticky caramel-like sauce. She licked a few drops of it from her fingertip. "It's sweet," she said, frowning.

"It's dulce de leche," Sebastian said. "Try it. It's good, I promise." He grinned and took a bite of his own sandwich.

She took a bite, and chewed thoughtfully. Her eyes grew wide.

"See?" he said.

She nodded, smiling. After she swallowed her first bite, she said, "The emcee of the program earlier said Benson's piece was from Berenice. What is that?"

They were sitting on stools beside Corinne's stall. Benson was having his sandwich behind the table, where Corinne was busy talking to customers.

"It's an Italian opera," he said. "About Berenice, a queen of Egypt. She fell in love with a man who betrayed her."

"Did she ... get over it?"

"She ordered his beheading, and planned her suicide."

"What."

Sebastian chuckled. "Don't worry. It ends well. She falls in love with someone else more worthy."

"I think I like 'The Pirates of Penzance' better."

"Definitely fewer beheadings in that one."

"Right? Even the pirates were kind of pussies. I mean, they don't seem to have done a lot of *pirating*. How they managed to stay in business for so many years is a mystery."

Narrowing his eyes, he looked at her suspiciously. "What's going on?"

Victoria took another bite of her sandwich, and took her time chewing it. "Nothing. Why?" She looked at him quizzically.

Since he and Benson had gotten back with their sandwiches, Victoria's mood seemed to have changed. He couldn't put his finger on it, but she seemed a lot more ... *friendly* toward him for some reason.

"Never mind. Don't get too attached to that sandwich," he said. "I'm making us dinner."

Chapter 29

Blue Bird

Victoria found Sebastian in the kitchen.

"Hi," she said.

He looked up to see her standing in the kitchen door. "Hey," he said, smiling.

"Meatballs?"

"Meatball soup." He patted a lump of ground beef into shape. "Benson's favorite."

"Oh." Hesitantly, she walked over to where he was standing on the kitchen counter. "That looks good."

"You ever had *sopa de albóndigas* before?"

"Once, I think." She watched him shape another raw meatball with his hands. "A long time ago."

"I thought you and Corinne would be getting better acquainted right now."

"Benson's showing her his new Playstation. I set it up for him, and I thought I'd give them a moment to themselves." She smiled. "That was a really nice surprise. He never really asked you for one before?"

"He rarely asks me for anything, actually. The last thing he asked me for was permission to try out for lacrosse."

Vitoria sensed a slight sadness in his voice. "He's a good kid," she said.

"Sometimes I wonder..." He paused for a long time.

"Yes?"

"If he thinks I'm just the uncle he's staying with until his mom decides to take him back. If he thinks my home isn't his, and he has to be careful about the space he takes up." He smiled ruefully. "Sometimes I wish he'd break something. Or act out. Whatever it is kids do that make their parents crazy."

"I think he loves you," she said. "I think when we care about someone, that's all we need."

"I want more than that, Victoria," he said softly.

When he looked at her, it was as if she could feel the weight of his thoughts.

"He doesn't know, does he?" she said.

"Know what?"

"That you call him your son when he's not around."

"No." He put the last meatball on the platter. "I'm not sure either of us is ready for that."

She nodded. "So what's next?"

He raised an eyebrow.

She pointed at the plate of meatballs. "You put that in the pot?"

"Yeah. Help me?"

"Okay. Hang on." She moved to the sink to wash her hands.

Together, they dropped the meatballs carefully into the soup that was simmering on the stove. "It smells so good," she said.

"I hope you like it." He stirred the soup carefully with a wooden spoon. "We're having this with corn tortillas and salsa."

"Yum." She smiled. "You really like cooking, don't you?"

"You don't?"

"I can fry a doughnut. That's it."

"To be fair, you do make a good doughnut."

Sebastian took a fresh spoon and scooped a little of the broth. He blew on it and held it up to her. "Here, taste this for me," he said.

Victoria sipped the warm soup and let the taste settle in her mouth for a few moments. "It could use a little more salt," she said.

"Let me check."

He lowered his head and kissed her.

She closed her eyes, and felt his tongue gently caress her lips before slipping inside her mouth. She moaned softly as his tongue stroked the inside of her mouth languidly.

Reluctantly, she opened her eyes when he broke off the kiss.

He licked his lower lip. "You're right," he said. "Maybe a little more salt."

***

"I'm stuffed," Corinne said, dropping her spoon into her empty bowl. "Ben, sweetie, leave some room for dessert, okay?"

Benson nodded, and took another bite of tortilla.

"What do we have, Cor?" Sebastian said. "I could have William pick up some ice-cream." The driver had left for his house a few miles away, and would come back when they were ready to leave.

"No need. I made flan yesterday. Give me a hand, will you, Sebastian?" She got up.

"I'll help you," Victoria said, getting up too. "He already made us dinner. It's only fair."

"You like flan?" Corinne asked as they headed for the kitchen. "It's basically the only dessert I can make. I had to learn to make it, because Benson loves it."

"I've never had flan," Victoria admitted.

They served the custard dessert in the ramekins they were baked in. It was sweet and creamy, and light enough to be perfect after their heavy meal of meatball and rice soup. Benson had polished off two before the adults were halfway through theirs.

"You guys staying in town for the night?" Corinne said, wiping flan off Benson's cheek.

"I can do it, Mom," her son said, squirming away. He tried to get the napkin from her.

"We're flying back to L.A. tonight," Sebastian said.

It took him a moment to realize how much he regretted this fact. The day was going to be over too soon. He promised Victoria that she would be home by midnight.

In the corner of his eye, he watched her laughing at the sight of Benson trying to stop his mother from wiping his face. He felt his heart skip a beat. The overwhelming urge to reach up and touch Victoria's hair, to slide his fingers down the curve of her cheek was almost too much to resist.

"But not for a couple of hours," he added. "We'll just do the dishes and Victoria and I can get going."

Corinne waved him off. "Don't be silly. Benson and I can handle a few dishes. Go."

***

"Is this the way to the airport?" Victoria said, looking out the window of the SUV.

"We have a little time before our flight," Sebastian said. "I thought we could get a drink first."

She turned to him, eyebrows raised. "Where are we going?" She wasn't sure if she was ready for any more surprises today.

"You'll see."

They were dropped off in front of a white, two-story building with bright blue and grey striped awning. A large neon sign over the entrance read "Blue Bird". Yards of tiny serial lights hung around the entrance doorway.

She looked uncertain. It didn't seem like the kind of place Sebastian would actually go to. "Are you sure we're in the right place?"

"You'll like it, I promise." He took her hand.

She wrinkled her nose, but allowed him to lead her inside.

It was a dive bar. The interior was illuminated in red light. There was a heart-shaped mirror on the wall behind the bar above a shelf full of liquor bottles. It was surrounded by glowing light bulbs formed in the same shape. On the far corner of the room was a stage with a piano and a drum set, with a red glitter fringe curtain for a backdrop.

"Let's get a table." Sebastian spoke close to her ear. "The band should be starting any second now."

Victoria was staring at the silver disco ball that hung from the middle of the ceiling. She was too puzzled to do anything but let him lead her to a table near the side of the stage.

A waitress appeared by their table. She was petite, and looked like she was about twenty. "You folks thirsty?" she said.

"We'll have two Yellow Rose, please," Sebastian said. "Is the band playing tonight?"

"Sure. You two fixin' to dance tonight?"

"Maybe." He grinned.

Victoria could have sworn the young woman was blushing as she smiled back at him before leaving to get their drinks.

"I can't dance," she said. "Seriously."

"We'll find out, won't we?"

"How about you just take my word for it?"

"Not a chance." He chuckled. "How do you like the place?"

"It's ... different." She glanced around. "Hey, does that jukebox work?"

"I think so."

The waitress came back with their beers. Sebastian pulled out a couple of bills from his wallet. He handed it to her while whispering something in her ear. The woman giggled and nodded.

After she left, Victoria cleared her throat. "I didn't know beer costs a hundred dollars a bottle here," she said.

"That was for the band." Sebastian folded his arms, resting them on the table. "Why, Ms. Slade, are you jealous?"

"No." She took a sip of her beer.

He lifted his beer bottle. "Too bad," he said, and took a long pull of his drink.

She smiled, despite herself. He seemed a lot more relaxed tonight. There were very few times she'd seen him like this.

"What?" he said.

"You seem different here," Victoria said. "I mean, you're still bossy and all. You dragged me here without even asking."

"You're visiting. I'm just being a good host."

"I never in a million years would have guessed you'd take me to a place like this. The last one had Italian-speaking waiters."

"That's because they were Italian."

"Exactly. Wait, you live here, don't you? You have a house?"

"I have two."

"Why didn't we go there?"

"Are you asking me to take you to my place?" His glance swept downward from her face to her chest.

"That's ... " She turned red. "What I meant was—"

"Because that can be arranged."

"I'm saying," she continued, trying to change the subject, "that if I hadn't come, maybe you wouldn't have to fly back to L.A. right away."

"It's all right. I have an appointment in the morning."

"But it's a Sunday."

"It's an occupational hazard, I'm afraid. I can't afford to slack off."

"Because you're so young?"

He grinned wryly. "I didn't exactly have the full confidence of the board of directors when they appointed me. My father used his clout, but he did it grudgingly."

"But you're his son. Surely he wanted this for you?"

"Our relationship is rather ... complicated."

"How so?"

"I think he would have preferred a son who was more like him. Unfortunately, I was all he got."

"It's hard to believe he wouldn't be proud of you. You're ..."

"Yes?" The corner of his mouth lifted in a slow, teasing smile.

Victoria felt her knees go weak. She was thankful she was sitting down.

"You're pretty amazing," she said. "Running such a large company, and at such a young age. Most CEO's I know are old enough to be my dad."

"Thank you." He gestured to his side. "The band's about to start."

She turned toward the stage. A woman in a gold evening dress sat on the piano, fiddling with the mic stand. A woman in a pants suit sat behind the drums. They were joined by four men — one had a double bass, another had a saxophone, and the two others had guitars.

After they did a brief sound check, the woman on the piano started to sing. It was a song about freedom, and dreams of a better day. Her voice was soft but clear. A hush fell across the room.

Victoria realized she had been holding her breath.

The band began to play. She looked up to see Sebastian standing in front of her, his hand held out.

"I can't," she said.

"Trust me?"

Victoria felt a strange warm feeling in her chest as she looked at him. It was like she could decide then and there to make a fool out of herself, and everything would still be all right.

She stood up and took his hand.

"Be gentle," she whispered as he pulled her close.

"I promise." He slid his right hand down her back, pressing her hips against his. "Just keep close to me."

The closeness of their bodies sent her stomach fluttering, and she felt heady from the scent of his skin. She was afraid that if he would let go of her for one moment, there would be no strength in her to keep standing.

Sebastian navigated the turns slowly, allowing her to familiarize herself with the rhythm of the dance. After a while, Victoria felt a lightness in her step, a confidence she'd never experienced before.

"You asked them to play this song," she said, smiling up at him. "You like Nina Simone?"

"I do." He looked into her eyes. "Very much."

Chapter 30

Taking Flight

"Will you be all right?" Sebastian said, concern in his eyes. They were sitting across each other in the cabin of the plane waiting for takeoff.

Victoria fastened her seat belt, and tried to brave a smile. "I'll be fine."

"We could drive back to L.A. instead if you like."

"Oh, no." She shook her head. "That would take us too long —"

"About a day or so."

"Don't you have an appointment in the morning?"

"I can cancel it, Victoria. It's not a big deal."

"No, really, I'll be fine." She smiled wryly. "Maybe I should have had another drink back at the bar."

Sebastian didn't reply, although there was something odd about the way he looked at her.

"What is it?" she said.

The intercom bell sounded softly. "Mr. Chase, we're getting ready for takeoff now," said the plane captain's voice over the speakers.

Sebastian pressed a button on his armrest. "Thank you, Captain Moon. How's the weather looking?"

"Pretty good," Min Ah Moon replied, her girlish, cheerful voice making her sound considerably younger than her forty-five years. "Clear skies all the way. We should be landing in L.A. well before midnight."

"Thank you. Please advise the crew we'll need some privacy for an hour or so."

"Will do."

"Thank you," Victoria said.

"For what?" Sebastian said.

"Well, if I'm going to be a nervous wreck, at least I won't have an audience." She gave a shaky laugh, as the plane start to roll down the runway.

"Actually, there may be a way to help you overcome the fear of flying," he said.

"You mean talking? Okay." She took a deep breath. "I'll try anything."

"Anything?"

"Yeah. What are you doing tomorrow? Your appointment, I mean. Work?"

"Yes, you can say that." He looked amused. "You?"

"I have a 7 am shift at the coffee shop. Then a birthday dinner for a friend."

"I'm flying to New York in the afternoon."

"Oh." Disappointment formed a lump in her throat. "You travel so much. No wonder you need your own plane."

"I'm not allowed to fly commercial."

"You're not?"

"It's in the terms of my contract. As CEO of Mattheson, I can't take commercial flights. It's a security matter."

"And here I thought you were just being a jerk to the environment, using up all this jet fuel just to be fancy." She allowed herself a small nervous smile.

"Aren't you going to ask me when I'm coming back?"

Did she imagine it, or was he challenging her with his eyes?

"When are you coming back?" Victoria squeezed the armrests of her chair, her panic increasing as the plane accelerated down the runway.

"I'll be back on Tuesday. What's your favorite color?"

"What?"

"Don't think about the plane. Tell me what your favorite color is."

"Blue," she replied. Try as she might, she couldn't stop thinking about how this huge steel machine was about to take to the air and bring them all with it. Nothing between it and the hard ground but miles and miles of air.

Most of all, she thought of how much she wanted him to take her hand in his, and tell her it was going to be okay.

"What's yours?" she said, almost in a whisper.

"Red."

Is that a smirk on his face? she wondered through a haze of panic as the plane gently lifted off the runway and flew up into the sky.

***

Sebastian waited as long as he could.

To be precise, he waited until the seatbelt sign was off before he unbuckled his and got on his feet.

"What are you doing?" she murmured, her pale face looking up. He was bent over her, his hands on her armrests behind her elbows.

"I told you there was a way of overcoming your fear of flying." His breath felt warm on her forehead, and the touch of his wrists on her elbow was comforting.

"I thought ... talking would —"

"Shut up."

Her pale lips felt cold as he kissed her, but they parted immediately under the pressure of his mouth. He thrust his tongue in deep, hungry for the taste of her.

It had been what — two, three hours? It had been too long since he last kissed her. Too goddamn long since he last savored the sweetness of her on his tongue.

He could hear soft moans escape her throat. His manhood ached with the force of its sudden awakening.

Their tongues entwined in a slow, fierce dance of desperate desire. Her head pressed hard against the back of her chair under the weight of his kiss. He rested a hand on her shoulder, his thumb slowly rubbing the soft flesh below her throat.

When he felt her hands against his chest he stopped moving his lips for a breadth of a second. Was she pushing him away? But her hands didn't stop moving over his torso. He could feel her palms seeking out every muscle, every ridge of his abs as they moved downward.

With a growl, he reached up to run his fingers in her hair.

"Oh!" Victoria cried out, throwing her head back.

Keeping a firm grip of her hair, Sebastian licked her exposed throat. His mouth traveled down her neck, sucking, kissing, licking. He pressed the edges of his teeth lightly on the base of her neck, letting his tongue press hot, wet circles on her skin.

Victoria eagerly pushed her neck up harder against his mouth. Her legs parted to wrap themselves around his knees.

Her hands had moved down to massage the throbbing, aching bulge between his legs.

"Do you know what you're doing?" he whispered against her neck. At that moment, he was barely able to keep himself from wrestling her to the ground and tearing her clothes off.

If she tried anything else ...

He felt the button and zipper of his jeans come undone. Her hand slipped inside his boxers.

"Fuck," he swore as she stroked him.

"Yes," she gasped. "Please."

Sebastian fumbled blindly with her seat belt. Once she was unstrapped, he pulled her to her feet and turned her around.

Victoria grasped the back of her chair, positioning her trembling knees on the seat. He encircled one arm around her waist and pressed his body against her back.

"Tell me you want me," he whispered close to her ear.

"I want you." She leaned her head toward him until his lips brushed her forehead.

He kissed her temple as his free hand lifted the hem of her dress. He plunged his fingers inside her panties.

"Do you want this?" He rubbed his finger on her slit. She was soaking wet. "Tell me you want this."

"Yes ... Yes, please."

Keeping one arm around her waist, he reached into his back pocket and pulled out a packet of condoms. By the time he had torn open one plastic and sheathed himself, he was barely able to keep from exploding.

Swearing, he pulled her panties down roughly and bunched her dress up her waist.

"Oh!" she moaned as he pressed his tip against her.

It may have been the scent of her hair, or the way she felt so good in his arms, but an unexpected thought surfaced in his consciousness.

I love you.

The words burned behind his throat. Sebastian ached to say what he knew he had felt for such a long time.

He loved her.

This kind, beautiful, passionate creature in his arms who made him angry, who made him smile, who made him want to believe what he thought he never could again.

"Victoria, I—" he started to say, but she stopped him by slamming her hips back hard. He felt her folds surround the head of his shaft, and his one coherent thought splintered into a million pieces.

***

"Feel better?"

Sebastian's voice dragged Victoria out of her dreamy haze.

"Hmmm, yes," she said, smiling. She snuggled closer into his chest. "I think I'm over this fear of flying thing."

He brushed a lock of hair out of her face. "That's too bad," he said. "I was looking forward to helping you through it again."

"You horny man." She giggled.

"Woman, you were the one who practically assaulted me."

"Sorry about that."

"I didn't say I hated it."

"Okay, so I'm *not* sorry," Victoria said. "You know, there are, like, seven other seats in this cabin."

"And?"

"I don't understand why you're making me sit on your lap."

Sebastian patted the side of her rump. "I'm testing the seats."

"This one took quite a pounding earlier."

"It did. It's a very good seat."

"I hope you had a really good reason to wake me up, mister."

"Why, were you having a good dream?"

"Yeah. I dreamt my hot boss was kissing me."

He chuckled. "If you think you're getting a raise just because you called me hot, you're sadly mistaken, Ms. Slade."

"Cheapskate." She yawned.

"Don't fall asleep on me now. We're landing in five minutes."

***

"Who was your first?"

"My first what?"

"You know. The first time you made love. Or fucked. Whatever you old people call it."

Victoria had to bite her lip to keep from laughing at Sebastian's expression of fake outrage.

"Old, huh?" he said, narrowing his eyes at her.

"No, seriously. Who was she?"

The flight had landed just half an hour before midnight. They were driving to Victoria's flat, with Connor behind the wheel.

Sebastian leaned back in his seat. "Lupe Gomez," he said. He said her name slowly, deliberately. As if pulling it out of a long-buried memory. "She was the niece of our ranch foreman, Isidro." He grinned. "He practically raised me. He taught me to cook."

"Yeah?"

"I was fourteen, she was sixteen. She was gorgeous and smart. I worshipped her like a goddess. We dated in secret."

"You did not."

"I swear. My dad wouldn't have approved, and Isidro would have killed me. We dated for a year, until she left for college."

"She went to college at seventeen?"

"Lupe was accelerated in grade school."

"Impressive. Did you ever see her again?"

"Sometimes we're both at Isidro's place for the holidays. He's retired now. She works as an attorney in Austin. I heard she made senior partner this year."

"Wow."

"Your turn," he said, gently brushing a fingertip under her chin.

"Tommy Misner. We were seventeen. We'd been best friends since freshman year, before we started dating." Victoria wrinkled her nose. "After a couple of times, we decided we were better off as friends."

"That bad?"

"No, it was... good. I just didn't hear any angels singing, you know?" She yawned, feeling a deep peace settle around her.

***

Victoria felt something rough on her forehead. She opened her eyes and lifted her head, wondering why her pillow was —

"Sebastian?" she croaked. Looking down, she realized she had been leaning on his chest. Sleeping. She glanced around her. They were parked right in front of her apartment building. The morning sunlight filtered through the tinted windows of the Mercedes.

Morning.

"I promised you I'd get you home by midnight," Sebastian said. "It's not my fault you wouldn't get out of the car."

"Oh no. Did I fall asleep?" She vaguely registered the fact that he still had his arm around her. "We were in the car all night?"

He pulled her close. "You look so cute when you sleep. I didn't want to wake you."

"Sorry." She smiled, resting her head back on his chest. "Where's Connor?"

"I sent him to get coffee down the street. I tried to make him go home, but he refused. He takes his bodyguard duties quite seriously."

"Oh."

They let the silence stretch for a minute.

"I like you," she said. "Will you be my boyfriend?"

There was no reply for what seemed an eternity. Victoria wondered if there was any way she could bolt out of the car and sprint up her apartment before her embarrassment could catch up with her.

But she heard him exhale, and realized he'd been holding his breath.

"I'll be anything you want," Sebastian said, and kissed her forehead.

"Really?" she said, blinking. "I thought you didn't do relationships?"

"Are you trying to make me change my mind?"

"No." She smiled.

"My flight to New York is at 2pm. We can have lunch before we leave."

"I can't go."

"Has anyone ever told you you're a terrible girlfriend?"

She slapped his chest lightly. "I have work, remember? And it's my friend Casey's birthday dinner tonight. He just broke up with his boyfriend. We're trying to cheer him up."

"Fine." He kissed her lightly on the lips. "There's a company party on Tuesday night. It will be mostly boring bankers, and my father whom I'd barely spoken to in five years. Be my date?"

Chapter 31

Making Friends

"This better be good, Sebastian," said Elton as he entered the office. "I don't appreciate being called here on a Sunday. My wife and kids —"

"Frannie thinks you're in New York," Sebastian said, not looking up. He was sitting at his desk, studying a sheaf of photographs in his hand. "Would you care to explain?"

"What my wife thinks I'm doing is none of your business." The balding, middle-aged man looked around the enormous office, as if to ascertain there was no one else around. "Are you two talking behind my back now?"

"She and I had a long chat this morning. Lovely woman. She feels quite neglected, what with all those late nights at work, and frequent trips out of town." The pile of photographs fell from his hands to scatter on his desk. "I suppose she doesn't know anything about this."

The pictures were of Elton and a very young woman, apparently taken in different days in various locations: holding hands while walking out of hotels, holding hands in restaurants, sipping champagne at an evening party, kissing as they lay on lounge chairs at the beach.

"What's this?" Elton's face turned red with indignation. "You spying on my private life, Sebastian? Are your whores not keeping things interesting enough for you?"

"I don't pay my dates, Elton." The younger man looked at him in the eyes. "I sure as hell don't give them confidential information about the activities of officers of this company. Something I'm sure you're well aware of constitutes a breach of contract."

"What the fuck are you talking about?" Elton's voice was still angry, yet he had turned visibly pale.

"Lindy Mulligan, the young lady whose company you've been sharing the past few months or so. Film major at UCLA. Also the first cousin to one Erika Daniels."

"So?"

"Did you think I could have chalked it all up to sheer coincidence, Elton? All those times Erika just happened to know where I was. Even that trip to Beijing?"

"It could have been—"

"You just don't see it. The monumental stupidity of what you've done. Because you're *still* thinking with your cock. You've compromised your job — your life — for a girl. Your career is over, Elton. Finished."

"Listen, boy," Elton said. He leaned over, his hands curled up in fists pressed down on the desk. "The only reason you're even here is because your rich daddy owns most of this company. You're a fucking kid. You don't know shit. If it weren't for me, you'd be nothing."

"We'll see, won't we?" Sebastian pulled out a piece of paper from a drawer and dropped it in front of him. "This is your resignation letter. Sign it and I won't send over every photo my private investigator had been taking of you and your mistress for the past week to your wife's lawyer. Between your alimony payments to your first wife and another divorce, I'd be surprised if you had any money left to pay for dates with college girls."

"You're threatening me?" The quiver in his voice betrayed his bravado, and his eyes looked nervously down at the letter.

"I'm giving you a chance to leave while you still have your dignity."

Tight-lipped, Elton picked up a pen and signed the letter. "It's so easy for you, isn't it?" he muttered. "Dad hands you his company on a silver platter. Sluts throwing themselves at you."

Sebastian's eyes narrowed. "Don't call them that."

"You're not always going to win, you know." Elton straightened his tie. "One day, you'll know what it feels like to lose."

Sebastian didn't reply, and merely watched as the other man strode out of the room. As soon as the door closed, he reached out and pressed a button on his desk. "Frank, go ahead and send those photos to Mrs. Lowry's attorney."

"Right away, sir."

***

"I really should have taken it as a sign," said Casey Stewart, before gulping down a shot glass of tequila. His eyes widened with joy as he saw Nicolette and Victoria. "You guys made it! Thank you."

"Of course, sweetie," Nicolette said, giving him a kiss on the cheek. "Happy birthday." She handed him a gift wrapped in white paper and silver ribbon. "What sign?"

"Awww, you didn't have to. But thank you." He and Victoria air-kissed, and he happily took her present as well. "Thanks, Vic." He put the presents on the chair beside him. It was nine in the evening, and a good-sized crowd was amassing around them in the 20's-themed bistro.

"Casey here thinks Bill's Elena Ferrante obsession meant they couldn't be together," said Shane Harlow. Glass of wine in hand, he stood up to kiss Victoria on the cheek.

"No disrespect, but her books read like a B-movie." Casey put his hands up and shrugged. "Just saying."

"Hey, what's wrong with B-movies?" Nicolette demanded.

Casey laughed. "I've missed you, lady. And *you* ..." He wagged a finger at Victoria, who smiled sheepishly. "I haven't seen you in *years*."

"Sorry, I got another job," Victoria said. "So, did you move out or did Bill?"

"He moved." Casey picked up another glass of the amber liquid. "Somewhere closer to downtown, I think. Thank God, I can finally put my Pennie Smith photographs back on the wall."

"Bill didn't like them?" Victoria said. "But they're so awesome."

"I know right?" Casey lifted a hand and waved. "Hey guys, over here!"

Sandi Chang and Oscar Fuentes, who had just entered the bar, waved back, and carefully began making their way through the throng to their table.

"You guys didn't bring dates?" Casey said, after giving Sandi a peck on the cheek.

"No," Oscar said. "Nicolette told us — Ow!" he yelped, rubbing the spot on his elbow where Nicolette had pinched him lightly.

"What?" Casey asked, puzzled.

Victoria and Nicolette looked at each other. "Uhm," Nicolette said. "We thought that since you and Bill just broke up, it was better if we all just went stag tonight."

"I can't believe it." Casey shook his head. "You think I'm such a delicate flower that I can't take seeing couples being ridiculously happy together on my birthday?" He pouted, then pulled Nicolette in for a hug. "You know me so well."

"There, there," Nicolette said, patting his back as they hugged. She looked up at Oscar and mouthed the words, "Sorry about that."

"Oh God, we're hugging now?" Sandi said, making a face. "I'm gonna need some tequila first." She hailed a waiter. "Maybe some pizza too or Casey here will be drunk-dialing Bill in half an hour. What's your poison, Vic?"

"Vodka tonic, please," Victoria said. "More wine, Shane?"

"Yes, please," Shane said. "Hey, you haven't told us what your new job is yet. Did you get that staff writer gig over at the Tribune?"

"No," Victoria said. "I didn't even get an interview. I'm tutoring a fifth grader now. It's part time, but the pay's pretty good." She wrinkled her nose. "Although I may have to find another job soon."

"They fired you already?" Oscar said, raising his eyebrows.

"Uh. It's not that." She didn't want to bring up Sebastian at Casey's birthday dinner. "But I may have to quit."

"Why?" Sandi asked, looking at her suspiciously.

"Yes, Vic," Nicolette said. The blonde was smiling evilly. "Tell us why you need to quit your job tutoring the hot billionaire's kid?"

"What?!?" Casey, Oscar, Sandi and Shane exclaimed in unison.

"What billionaire?" Shane said.

"It's not the CEO of Twitter, is it?" Sandi said.

"Ewww!" Oscar said. "Jack Dorsey is totally not hot."

"Please tell me it's Eduardo Saverin," Casey said. "Because that man is *fine*."

"But you hate Facebook," Shane pointed out.

"Who cares. Eduardo is hot."

"I can't really say," Victoria said, giving Nicolette a dirty look. "Security reasons." She'd told her best friend about the weekend in Austin. And also about Sebastian and her being together. But for the purposes of tonight's birthday celebration, they both decided they were not going to mention it.

"Vic, I think you can tell them now," Nicolette said.

"No, really, I shouldn't." Victoria shot her best friend a look. *What are you doing?*

Nicolette sighed. "I think you're going to have to, babe."

"Why?"

"Because, sweetie," Nicolette said, nodding her head towards the entrance. "Your boss-slash-boyfriend just walked in ten seconds ago."

"What?"

They all turned to find Sebastian walking toward their table, a blue gift-wrapped box in his hand. He was dressed casually in a crisp, long-sleeved black shirt and dark grey pants.

Victoria stood up, but before she could say a word, he kissed her softly on the lips.

"Am I late?" he said.

"No. Uhm ... Casey?" She turned to her friends. They were staring up at Sebastian wordlessly. "This is Sebastian. My, uh ... "

"Boyfriend," Sebastian said. "Happy birthday." He handed Casey the gift.

"Oh, my," Casey said. "Thanks. You didn't have to." He put down the present next to his water glass. "Please, sit down."

"I thought you were flying to New York?" Victoria whispered as Sebastian took the seat next to hers.

"I had them change my schedule," he said. "Something wrong?"

She smiled and shook her head. It looked like Nicolette's no-date rule was out the window.

"I hope you don't mind me crashing your party," he said to Casey.

"Oh no. Crash away," Casey said. He looked positively giddy. "We were all excited to meet Vic's new man."

"This is Nicolette, my roommate," Victoria said. "And that's Sandi, Oscar and Shane."

"Very nice to meet you," Sebastian said. "Nicolette, I believe I saw your short at a film festival in New York last year."

"Really," said Nicolette. She eyed him with amusement. "Which one?"

"*Crushed*. The one where a girl stalks her teacher."

"Did you like it?"

"I did. It was ... very interesting."

"You mean depressing, don't you?" Casey said. "Because I'd never seen anything Nic's done that doesn't want to make me kill myself."

"I think it's safe to say I won't be doing any rom coms anytime soon," Nicolette said.

"A romantic comedy that makes you want to kill yourself," Sandi said. "I'd totally pay to watch that."

"I think you already did," Shane said. "Didn't Oscar drag you to see *How to Lose A Guy in 10 Days*?"

"Ough. Two hours of my life I'm never getting back." Sandi crossed her arms. "And the worst part was, I thought this idiot and I were on a date."

"In my defense, the fact that I asked you to watch a rom com with me should have been the first clue I was gay, Sandi," Oscar said.

"I was thirteen! What the hell did I know?"

"Am I the only straight guy at this table?" Sebastian whispered to Victoria.

"Yup," she whispered back. "They'll each probably picture you naked, at some point in the evening. Are you okay with that?"

"Well, I did come here to make a good impression." He grinned.

***

"It was terrible wasn't it?" Nicolette said. At Sebastian's raised eyebrows, she added, "*Crushed*, I mean. I made it when I was nineteen. It's hardly Oscar material."

He glanced at Victoria, who was sitting between him and Nicolette. It was past midnight and they were riding in the back of the Lincoln, with Connor at the wheel, on their way home.

Victoria looked as if she was trying to keep from laughing. She shrugged as if to say, *You're on your own, buddy.*

"Well. I was of course trying to suck up to you," he said finally.

"Not bad." Nicolette smiled.

It was a real smile, and it took him by surprise considering she'd only ever looked at him with either suspicion or amusement all evening.

"I did think the camerawork was good. Did you shoot it yourself?"

She looked surprised. "I did. You really think so? One of the judges said it was messy."

"You did that on purpose, I thought. It's what I would imagine recovering from a nervous breakdown would feel like."

"Or maybe I was just clumsy." She shrugged.

"Maybe."

He felt Victoria squeeze his hand. "You sure you can't stay over?" she whispered.

"My flight leaves in forty-five minutes," he said. "Come with me. You don't need to pack, we'll find you everything you need when we get there."

"I have to be at the coffee shop at eight a.m. Sorry."

"I'll miss you."

"Me too."

When they got to the apartment, Nicolette said, "Okay, lovebirds, I'm going in first. Say your goodbyes quick, Victoria has to be up in six hours." She waved at Sebastian. "Nice to meet you."

"You too," he replied.

"Goodnight, Nic!" Victoria called out.

"She's scary," he said, as soon as Nicolette disappeared into the building.

Victoria laughed. "I know. I think all my boyfriends avoided her as much as they could."

"I can see why you like her, though." He brushed a lock of hair off her forehead.

She closed her eyes briefly, enjoying the tenderness of the gesture. "Why did you reschedule your flight?"

"I missed you, obviously. Also, it's been a while, but I do remember I'm supposed to meet your friends at some point. You think they like me?"

"Do you really care?"

"I do." It surprised him that it genuinely mattered to him.

"You didn't care I had a boyfriend when you and I ... you know."

"You're never going to let me live that down, are you?" All that time he thought she was with another man. It was only this morning when she asked him to be hers that he realized he may have been mistaken all along.

She shook her head. "Nope. That was just way too funny." She wrinkled her nose. "Except maybe the part where you thought I was cheating on my boyfriend."

"You've never done that?"

"No, of course not." She was still smiling, but her eyes looked wistful. "You won't cheat on me will you, Sebastian?" she asked softly.

He hesitated. "No," he said, wondering if he imagined the way her smile faltered for a split second. He pulled her close and kissed her. "Now go inside and go straight to bed. I don't want to get on Nicolette's bad side."

Chapter 32

Distances

"I love him."

Victoria moved her cellphone to her left hand and lifted the coffee pot with her right. "You just met him, Casey."

"He gave me a Blancpain Fifty Fathoms Bathyscaphe Titanium."

She grimaced. "I have no idea what that is."

"It's a watch. It's gorgeous. It's twelve grand a pop."

"Wow." She put the coffee pot back on the warmer. "Sebastian can be pretty generous," she added, remembering her pimped-out bedroom and wardrobe.

"He's not overcompensating for anything, is he?"

"What? Uh, no, I don't think so."

"How big is he?"

"Casey!"

"Hey, I had to ask."

"No you didn't. That is not a thing you ask your friends."

"Don't be silly. Of course it is."

"I never asked you how big—" Victoria looked around furtively then dropped her voice. "... how big Bill was," she whispered.

"I told you anyway."

"I begged you not to."

"Oh yeah, you did. Sorry about that."

***

Casey loved your gift. Thank you.

You're both welcome.

He says he's thinking of scuba diving now. And he hates sports.

We can do a diving trip together. You don't get nervous on yachts too, do you?

I'll be fine. That sounds like fun.

No, really. I'm always ready to calm all your fears.

I'm going to pretend I don't know what you mean by that.

:-)

You don't have to overdo it, you know. A tie would have been fine.

I thought we were trying to cheer him up.

Are you trying to impress my friends?

Yes.

Is it working?

I think Casey likes you even more than he likes me right now.

:@)

Did you just text me a pig emoji?

Damn it.

Hang on.

O:)

Awww. You're adorable.

How's your day?

Good. But you're busy, and I don't want to keep you. We can catch up later tonight.

I'm fine.

Don't you have work?

Yes.

O:)

LOL. How's New York?

Boring. Cold. Quit your job at the coffee shop and come join me.

Victoria?

Hey, I wasn't serious. I'm not really asking you to quit.

I know.

But now that you brought it up— any luck finding a new tutor for Benson?

No.

Are you even trying?

No.

Sebastian.

Yes, dear.

I can't keep working for you.

You still can. If you want.

We both know it will get weird pretty soon.

Not for me. I thought you needed this job.

I do. But I can find something else.

Do you want my help?

No. But thank you for offering.

You can stay. At least until you find something else. Benson really likes you.

You think so?

Yeah. I have no idea why.

Hey!

:(

You have to admit, you spend more time with his uncle than you do with him.

We could have him tag along sometime.

Out of the question. Let him find his own girlfriend.

***

Victoria had just fired up her Macbook when the doorbell rang. She'd just had a quick shower after getting home from work, and was about to get back to her writing.

"Hang on, there's someone at the door," she said, standing up.

A young man in a delivery guy uniform held up a large paper bag. "Delivery for Victoria," he said, sounding bored.

"Oh, I'm sorry. I didn't order this."

The man read the bill taped to the paper bag. "Victoria Slade. Apartment 4E. 23 Calista."

"Yes, that's me, but—"

"Look, ma'am, we already got paid for this. You want it or not?"

She smelled *mole* sauce, and she suddenly felt very hungry. "Yeah, sure. Thanks."

After tipping the delivery guy, she dropped the paper bag beside her macbook.

"What was that?" Sebastian said over her cellphone speaker.

She opened the bag and found warm, foil-wrapped packets. "Someone just dropped off some take-out. Funny, I was just about to heat something up for dinner."

"Try the grilled chicken."

She smiled. "Did you have this sent over?"

"Well, I couldn't let my assistants do nothing all day."

"There's enough food here for five people." She frowned. "Are you implying something about how much I eat?"

"I saw you stuff an entire meatball in your mouth. It was horrifying."

Victoria stuck her tongue out as she unwrapped the chicken. "I'm making a face at you right now, in case you're wondering," she said.

"So immature. The *mole* is really spicy, be careful."

"Oh my God," she said, her mouth full of chicken. She chewed and swallowed. "This has to be the best thing I've ever had in my mouth."

"I resent that."

"Why would you..." Then it hit her. "Oh." She smiled, her cheeks turning pink. "Second best thing then."

"That's better."

"What time is it over there?"

"It's 11 p.m."

"Don't you banker types have to be up early or something?"

"I need to be up by five."

"Wow that's really early."

"I need an hour for the gym before a breakfast meeting at seven."

"Maybe you should go to bed now. It's only eight o'clock here, I'll be up for hours."

"I'm fine. Pretend we're having dinner together."

Victoria couldn't help smiling. "So romantic."

"Will you stay over tomorrow night?"

"I'd love to." She paused, her smile fading. "Does Benson know about us? We moved our study session to Wednesday. He'll wonder why I'm spending Tuesday night at your place."

"I'll talk to him before the party. This isn't something I can explain over the phone."

"I suppose you're right. I'm a little nervous." None of the men she had dated had kids. What if Benson didn't like the idea of her dating Sebastian?

"Don't be. He likes you."

"As his tutor, maybe. Not sure about the other thing."

"You mean as my girlfriend?"

"Yes." She felt giddy. She wondered how long it would take before she got used to hearing him call her that. "What will you tell him?"

"That I was helpless against your feminine wiles."

"Very funny."

"You showed up in my office in that rumpled shirt smelling like doughnuts and stale coffee. I couldn't resist."

"I'm serious."

"So am I."

"Oh God, what if he thinks I was just after you all along."

"He's ten, Victoria. That's not something that would cross his mind."

"Oh. Right. Sorry."

"Did you try the grilled salmon? There should be some mushrooms too."

"I love the mushrooms, thank you." She took another bite. "This is bad. I'm supposed to be writing."

"You need to eat first. Tell me about your novel."

"Well, it's science fiction. In the future, there's a war between a human colony in the other side of the galaxy and their alien neighbors. The protagonist is a young woman who pilots a mecha."

"What's a mecha?"

Victoria licked some sauce off her thumb thoughtfully. "Hmmmm. It's like a plane that needs a pilot. Except instead of a plane it's a huge humanoid robot-like thing."

"Does it fly?"

"Yes, but it has to transform into a specific mode first. Then it's basically a jet plane. Oh, and it's aided by a built-in AI."

"Artificial intelligence?"

"Yeah, that's right." She grinned. It was nice being able to talk to someone other than Nicolette about her work. "Her mecha's IA is the computerized mind of her sister who passed away when she was a kid."

"So it's like they're flying together. Like Jarvis."

She laughed. "Yes. Only the robot's as big as a small building. But yeah. Flying together. Fighting side by side. Most of her inner conflict centers on her forgetting that her mecha isn't really her sister. Sometimes she forgets her sister is gone."

"That's a pretty good story."

"Thank you." She was grinning like an idiot.

"Can I read it?"

"Sure. When it's done. Nicolette says never show someone an unfinished draft."

"That's good advice. She's like a sister to you, isn't she?"

"She'll roll her eyes if I tell her that, but yeah, she is."

"Did you ever wish you had a sister?"

"I do. Even a brother would have been great. My parents had me really late in life. My Mom was, like, forty. It would have been difficult for her to have any more children after me." She paused. "You were really lucky to have a brother. It must have been so hard for you when he passed away. And your mom too."

"It was. I miss them every day. Benson is all I have now."

And me. She blinked, surprised at how much she wanted to say it out loud. She cleared her throat. "What about your Dad?"

"We're not very close."

"You think you and he will ever... I dunno — have a real relationship?"

"I doubt it. I don't think he likes me very much."

"Isn't he lonely?"

"I don't know. You'll meet him tomorrow. Maybe he'll tell you."

"It's going to be awkward, isn't it?"

"Excruciatingly. You'll need to hold my hand through it."

"I will. I promise." She reached out and lightly touched the corner of her phone, as if somehow a slight physical connection to the device that carried his voice from so far away could lessen her longing to be with him.

"I can't wait to see you," Sebastian said.

"Me too. Did you just yawn?"

"No."

"Sebastian."

"Yes, dear."

"You're falling asleep. Get to bed."

"I am in bed."

"Alone?"

"Of course I'm alone. No, wait, there's a couple of supermodels here I forgot about."

"No kidding."

"They fell asleep while you were talking about the flying robots."

Victoria frowned. "Did I bore them?"

"They say you need a bit more social commentary in your novel."

She swallowed the lump in her throat. "I'll make a note of it."

"Hey. Vi, I was kidding."

"You're not very funny."

"I know. But you don't have to worry about you and me. We're solid."

"You didn't seem sure."

"About what?"

"Last night when I asked you if you were going to be faithful. It seemed like you weren't sure." She wiped her mouth with a napkin and tossed it in an empty paper bag. "Look, I get it. You're probably used to sleeping with a different girl every night—"

"Victoria, I —"

"I know being in a relationship is a big change. But if it's too much for you, maybe you should tell me now."

"It's not."

"We can go back to the way things used to be."

There was a silence that was much longer than Victoria could bear.

"I don't want that," he said. "Even if we wanted to go back the way things were, I wouldn't be able to do it."

"I don't understand."

"You make me happy."

"Oh."

"No one's ever done that in a long time."

"Sebastian ..."

"Stick around, okay? I promise not to make any more bad jokes."

Victoria had to laugh at that. "Okay." She wrapped her arms around her legs that were folded against her chest.

"Thank you. Now tell me what you want."

"What I want?"

"From me. Is there something I'm not doing that I should be doing?"

"I don't know. Will you cook for me again sometime?"

"Yes. Anything else?"

"Well ... Wait, did you just call me Vi?"

"I did. Do you like it?"

"I think I do." She smiled. "Should I have a nickname for you? Bash?"

"Not if you want me to answer."

"Seb?"

"I'm going to bed now."

"No, wait!" She laughed. "Did anyone ever call you something other than Sebastian?"

"No."

"Seriously."

"It's always just been Sebastian."

"Fine. Sebastian." *My Sebastian*, she thought. "I'll wait for you to go to sleep before I end this call, okay?"

"Don't hang up. I want to hear you wake up."

"Do I snore? Nicolette says I do but I'm not sure she was serious."

"Sometimes. You sound like an emphysemic bullfrog."

"You're my boyfriend. You're supposed to think my snoring is cute."

"You sound like a cute bullfrog with respiratory problems."

"Hey."

Sebastian chuckled. "Good night, Vi."

"Good night."

She sighed contentedly, and rested her finger on the side of her phone as she waited for him to fall asleep.

Chapter 33

Family

Sebastian knocked on Benson's door.

"Come in."

"Hey, buddy," he said, entering the room. "I thought you might need help with that tie."

Benson grinned. "It's okay, I got this," the boy said. He was standing in front of a full-length mirror dressed in a white shirt and dark trousers. He tugged at his bow tie, trying to make sure it was fastened properly. "Why can't I wear a tie like yours?" He looked wistfully at his uncle's charcoal grey tailored evening suit and black shirt and tie.

"Your mom likes you in a bow tie." Sebastian sat down on the side of the bed. He smiled as he watched Benson pick up his suit jacket and stare at it uncertainly.

"You can wear one, too," Benson said.

"Maybe next time." Sebastian rested his upper arms on his lap and linked his fingers together. "Victoria will be joining us tonight," he said. "You don't mind, do you?"

The boy frowned as he put on the jacket. "Why? Isn't she your girlfriend?"

"She is." Sebastian stared at him in surprise. "How did you know?"

"You keep staring at her when you think I'm not looking."

"Oh."

"And Mom told me."

"How did *she* know?"

Benson shrugged. "She's Mom. I think she knows everything."

"How do you feel about it?"

The boy sat on the bed beside Sebastian. "I'm used to it, I think. It's just weird, like when I tell her I don't mind so much that Mr. Holland in Math class is not very good even though I'm pretty sure she knows I do."

"I mean, what do you think about Victoria and me being togeth —" Sebastian crossed his arms. "You're messing with me, aren't you?"

"Yes. Sorry." Benson tried not to laugh.

"Your Mom and Dad used to do the same thing to me all the time." Sebastian shook his head. "Your Mom still does, actually. And now you."

"Mom says you need to lighten up."

"Someone just told me recently that I'm not very funny."

"I think Victoria likes you anyway."

"You think so?"

"She stares at you when she thinks I'm not looking."

Sebastian tried not to grin. "She does?"

"Yeah." Benson ran his finger over the crease of his trousers on his knee, not looking up.

"Things aren't going to change between us, all right?" Sebastian said. "It's just that Victoria will be around a bit more from now on. You okay with that?"

Benson nodded, still staring at his knee. "Okay." He slowly looked up to meet Sebastian's eyes and gave him a small smile.

"We're seeing Grandpa tonight." Sebastian paused, reluctant to continue. "He says he misses you."

The boy looked thoughtful. "He asked me if I wanted to move to Fort Worth," he said. "I don't have to, do I?"

Sebastian jaw clenched. His father had tried many times to convince him to send the boy back to Texas to live with him. He'd been uninterested in Benson until the day Eric passed away, probably realizing it was a chance to have an heir he could groom into his own image. "No." Sebastian pretended to look at his nephew sternly. "You're stuck with me, buddy."

Benson wrinkled his nose. "He said I could have a pony."

"I can get you a pony," Sebastian said. "I'll get you two."

The boy laughed. "Where do we put them?"

"I think we could hide them behind the gazebo." Sebastian's forehead furrowed. "You think Mrs. Sellers will notice?"

"Probably."

***

Sebastian was waiting for her in the main hallway as she entered the front door with tentative steps. Her champagne-colored cocktail dress glinted under the chandelier lights, but it was her smile that took his breath away.

"Hey," Victoria said shyly, tucking a lock of hair behind her ear. Her hair was up in a loose chignon, with small strands left loose to curl around her face.

He kept his hands in the pockets of his trousers as he waited for her, resisting the urge to close the distance between them himself. His eyes swept over her from head to toe.

"What's wrong?" she said. She stopped a few feet away from him.

He moved toward her. "That dress is hideous," he said.

"Hey! Deborah sent it over." She frowned. "I like it."

"I hate it." His arms went around her waist and he pulled her snugly against him. He moved his mouth down to brush against her ear. "I'm afraid I'm going to have to tear it off you later tonight," he whispered.

"Oh." She suppressed a smile, and instead put on a hurt expression. "I don't know. Then maybe I'll sleep somewhere else tonight." She looked up at him. "I really don't want this dress damaged."

"I'll buy you another one?" He slid his hands down her backside, and fought the urge to press her harder against him. Already he felt a familiar stirring in his pants, but it was the furious beating of his heart that reminded him of how much he had missed her.

"Why do you keep buying me clothes if you're just going to rip them up?" she said.

"Everyone needs a hobby." He pressed his lips on her forehead. "This is my new favorite thing to do."

"You're terrible." She leaned on his chest.

Sebastian allowed himself the luxury of a few moments of having her in his arms until the reality of their having to be somewhere else in a few minutes became a concern. "I have something for you," he said.

She looked up at him suspiciously. "What is it?"

He led her over to the coffee table a few feet away and picked up a black velvet box the size of a small book. He opened it carefully.

"Oh my. That's ... " Victoria stared at the gold cuff bracelet resting in the cream satin lining.

"Is the style too old for you?" He sounded odd to himself, and he realized he was nervous.

"No! It's beautiful. It's just that ... wow." She bit her lip. "It looks expensive."

"Do you like it?"

"I do." She smiled. "You really shouldn't have. You've already given me so many nice things."

"May I?"

She nodded.

He lifted the gold band and put the box back on the table. Lifting her right arm, he fitted the bracelet carefully on her wrist.

"This is made to go on the right arm," he said.

The gold cuff molded on her wrist perfectly. "I can't believe how well it fits," she said. "Did you..."

"I had it adjusted to your size, yes."

"Thank you." She winced. "Now I feel bad about my drugstore earrings."

Sebastian gently cupped her face with his hand, and ran his thumb on the tiny pale pink crystal stud on her earlobe. "Don't be," he said. "You make everything beautiful."

She blushed. "Thank you. But I don't really—"

He interrupted her with a kiss to her forehead. "You realize it only turns me on when you argue with me, don't you?"

"Horrible man." She giggled. "Oh Benson, hi!" She pulled away from Sebastian.

"Hi," the boy said, stopping midway down the staircase across the hall. He looked at them uncertainly. "Should I go back upstairs?"

"It's okay Ben," Sebastian said, smiling up at him. "We were just about to call for you. You ready?"

Benson nodded, and continued walking down the steps.

Sebastian took Victoria's hand. "Let's go."

***

George Mattheson was a great many things: oil tycoon, shrewd businessman, neglectful father, unfaithful husband. He was the distant parental figure of Sebastian's childhood, and later on, his mentor. The man who looked at his son always with disapproving eyes no matter how hard the younger man tried to live up to his expectations.

Right now he was the VIP guest of the party. He arrived flanked by his bodyguards, another director of the board, and two company VPs. Nearly everyone stood up to greet him as he passed by their tables.

"Benson, my boy," he said as he neared Sebastian's table. "Let your Grandpa take a look at you." He smiled warmly as Benson stood up dutifully to go to him and shake his outstretched hand.

"Good to see you, sir," the boy said.

George ruffled his grandson's hair. "You're taller than I remember. Why don't you ever come visit your poor old grandpa?"

"Sorry." Benson ventured a look toward Sebastian, who had stood up as well.

"Dad," Sebastian said, walking over. He held out his hand. "Ben and I were thinking of coming to see you in the spring. How have you been?"

His father stared at his son's offer of a handshake for a moment, his lips curling up in amusement, before taking it. "I suppose congratulations are in order. Even Elizabeth was quite pleased with how things turned out."

Sebastian nodded. Elizabeth Beal was his father's second cousin. A retired CEO of one of the biggest food manufacturing companies in Arizona, she was never a big supporter of his appointment to run Mattheson. She was by far the hardest to please of anyone in the board of directors.

"I guess she couldn't make it tonight?" he said. "What a pity."

"She has a couple of new thoroughbreds at the ranch this week, I hear. Can't tear her away from her horses these days."

"No, I suppose we can't." Sebastian turned to Victoria and held out his hand, palm up.

Her eyes grew wide as she set down her water glass. She sat frozen in her seat.

He smiled encouragingly. Nodding nervously, she stood up.

"Dad," Sebastian said. "I'd like you to meet—"

"You made it, my dear," said George, smiling at a young blonde woman who had just joined them. He took her hand and patted it affectionately. "You remember Brooke, don't you son?" he asked Sebastian.

"Hello, Baz," she said. "It's been a while."

It took Sebastian all of five seconds to recover from the shock of seeing Brooke Hildebrand. Tall, blonde and unnervingly elegant in a short white dress, she was a far cry from the skinny, gangly girl in a ponytail and glasses he remembered.

"Bree," he said, almost in a whisper.

She smiled when she heard him call her by the nickname he gave her years ago. "I was afraid you'd forgotten."

"How are you? Your glasses..."

"I got LASIK after college," she said. "Pretty vain, huh?"

"No, no." He swallowed. "You look good."

"You look amazing." She averted her gaze downward for a moment. "But then you always did." She looked back up to stare him in the eyes. They were the same beautiful shade of hazel he remembered.

It was then that Sebastian remembered. He looked back at the table.

Victoria was preoccupied with her salad. Or at least she tried to look like all her attention was focused on the arugula and lettuce she was busily moving around on her plate.

"Excuse me," he mumbled.

When he reached Victoria, she smiled up at him. "Hi," she said.

"Sorry about that. My father is rather ..." He rested his hand on her shoulder. "Let me introduce you, all right?"

"No, really, it's not necessary." She shook her head. "I'm sure you two have a lot of catching up to do."

"Aren't you going to introduce me to your date, son?" George Mattheson said, sitting down beside Victoria.

"Dad," Sebastian said, surprised. After a brief moment, he said, "This is Victoria Slade. Vi, my father, George Mattheson."

"Very nice to meet you, Mr. Mattheson," she said, shaking his hand.

"Charmed," George said. "What's a nice girl like you doing with my boy here?"

"Oh, Sebastian, he's ..." She swallowed. "He's been great."

"If he ever gives you any trouble, you just come to me, all right?"

"Yes, sir." She smiled, at ease with the older man's friendliness.

"Call me George, sweetheart. Now tell me." He raised a hand to signal a waiter. "How'd you two meet?"

With his father having taken his seat, Sebastian sat beside Benson. He turned to see Brooke take the empty seat next to him.

"Your dad's been telling me about you," she said.

"Has he?"

She laughed at his expression. "Don't worry, Baz. It was all good. You've done really well for the company, I hear."

"I do my best." It was difficult for him to believe his father was anything but critical of him and his work. But he supposed George wouldn't bore Brooke with details about his concerns with the way Sebastian had been running his company. "And what about you?"

"I'm helping my Mom run her campaign. She's running for Governor in the next primary." She narrowed her eyes. "You didn't know, did you?"

"I didn't, no." He hesitated. "You quit your job then?"

"I've always worked for her."

"Oh, I'm sorry. I just—"

"It's fine." She shook her head. "I didn't really expect you to be keeping tabs on an old girlfriend you hadn't seen in more than a decade."

"Actually, I'm surprised you even remember me." It just occurred to him he hadn't expected their meeting again to be this congenial. Considering the way he had ended things between them.

"How could I forget you, Sebastian?" Brooke gently touched his hand that had been resting on his lap. "You were my first."

Chapter 34

Trust

"Benson, sweetie, slow down," said Victoria. She slid a glass of water toward him. "You'll make yourself sick."

The boy nodded, his mouth full of fruit.

She ventured a slight brush of her thumb against his cheek and smiled. She tried to not look directly at the strikingly pretty blonde woman across the table who seemed to be monopolizing her boyfriend's attention. She'd been waiting for Sebastian to look her way at least once. Just so she could assure herself he hadn't completely forgotten about her.

"I keep telling my son that Ben here ought to have a proper nanny to keep an eye on him," said George beside her.

She turned to him. "Maybe Sebastian thinks Ben is old enough to not need a nanny," she said carefully.

"Well, good thing he has you then."

There it was again.

Victoria tried to quell the suspicions that had been edging their way into her consciousness, ever since George Mattheson showed up — and the blonde whom Sebastian didn't see fit to introduce her to. While Sebastian's father seemed outwardly cordial, she could sense an underlying animosity in the way he spoke to her. Were his statements heavily-veiled implications or entirely well-meaning remarks? Her good nature wanted her to believe he was merely trying to make her feel at ease, but she could not entirely ignore the nagging thought that he was trying to get her out of the way of whatever terribly important matter Sebastian was discussing with the attractive woman.

"I don't think I've been introduced to your guest," she said, throwing a less-than-subtle glance at the woman. "Does she work for you?"

"Brooke's mother is an old friend," said George. "Soon to be the next governor of Texas. Brooke was Sebastian's college sweetheart."

"I see." She tried not to sound too surprised. "Why ... How do you ... Uhm, governor?"

He seemed oblivious to her discomfort. "I admit, I may be too optimistic," he said, "but it would be a mighty fine thing if things go our way in the next elections."

"I suppose it would." The tightening in her chest was almost unbearable. "I imagine it would put your company at an advantage. You being old friends and all."

"You can say that." He nodded. "Although the company will be in pretty fine shape, either way. Like I always tell my boy: it takes a bad businessman to need so many friends in high places."

"He works so hard. It's difficult to imagine Sebastian relying on favors to achieve anything."

"True, true. Of course," George said, and paused to grin, "Sebastian was never one to take chances when it comes to business. In personal matters, he's more likely to be — how shall I say it — flexible."

Victoria tightened her grip on her napkin to keep her hand from shaking. "So long as it doesn't interfere with business, you mean?" She felt an almost physical ache in the pit of her stomach.

"No." He gave her a look of sympathy, and she was was almost sure it was entirely sincere.

"I see." She nodded. "You must be very... proud, Mr. Matheson," she added, fighting to keep her voice from trembling.

"That remains to be seen, Vicky." He tilted his head and regarded her curiously. "You don't mind if I call you Vicky, do you? And call me George, please. You are Benson's tutor after all; I don't see why we have to be so formal with each other."

Benson's tutor. That was all she was now. Somehow she managed a smile, if only because she didn't want the humiliation of letting him know how she really felt. "I don't mind." She paused. "George."

"There, that wasn't so hard was it?" His eyes twinkled as he smiled back.

She shook her head. In the corner of her eye, she could see Sebastian was no longer in his seat. She tried to look casual as she glanced around her.

Brooke was nowhere to be found either.

After he was done in the men's room, Sebastian found Brooke standing in the hallway on his way back to the ballroom.

"Waiting for someone?" he teased.

"I need to tell you something," she said. Her hands were clutched together, a mannerism which he knew meant she was nervous. "Could we talk in private?"

"Brooke, I have to make a speech in fifteen minutes," he said. "What is it? Could we talk after?"

"It won't take long, I promise." She moved closer and looked up at him imploringly. "Please, Baz?"

"I suppose I could—"

"There's a balcony down there," she said, taking his hand and leading him down the corridor.

"If I'm late for my speech, you'll have to do the explaining to my father."

"Oh God." She laughed. "Remember that time I had to explain to your mom that it wasn't your fault your car crashed through the gate of the Harveys' ranch?"

"I do. My parents would have taken my car away if it weren't for you. No one believed me when I said I tried to avoid a cow that got loose."

"Maybe because you've used that excuse before? Like, twice? Just a thought."

"They believed you." His eyes softened as he looked at her, remembering the sweet teenage girl who had harbored a crush on him for years before fate stepped in. He'd barely noticed her until the day their families went on a skiing trip together. At the end of that week, they were officially dating.

"They did. Your mom used to tell me stories of the crazy things you did growing up." She squeezed his hand. "I miss her."

"I do too," he said as they stepped out to the balcony.

Victoria sat numbly as around her guests chatted and dined. Thankfully, George had excused himself from the table to speak to some party guests. A classic string band played Mozart, but she could barely appreciate the music as she found herself turning back to her thoughts.

Where was Sebastian?

The image of the lovely Brooke — her perfect hair and fine jewelry and dress — kept flashing in her mind.

Logically, she knew that just because Sebastian and Brooke were both gone, it didn't mean they had left together. It didn't mean they were together at that moment, while Victoria was left to look after Benson and make uncomfortable conversation with his father.

It doesn't mean anything, she told herself. But applying logic to the situation didn't make her feel any less uneasy.

She would have been less nervous if Sebastian had told her he'd be gone for a while. But he just left without a word.

"Uncle Sebastian has to give a speech and a toast," Benson said absently, pushing a piece of steak around with his fork. "He's not here."

"I'm sure he's on his way back now," Victoria assured him. "Do you want dessert?"

He shook his head. "I think I ate too much."

"Uh huh." She patted his shoulder as she scanned the room one more time.

As if on cue, Sebastian entered the ballroom. His expression was grim as he made his way toward the front of the room.

Victoria waited. Silently, she willed him to look her way. To give her even one glance. A sign that everything was all right.

He didn't look at her, and kept his eyes focused ahead.

It didn't surprise her to see Brooke enter the room a few seconds after. The woman's eyes were glued on him as he took his place behind the lectern.

Sebastian's serious expression disappeared as he flashed a heart-stopping smile. The room burst into applause. "Ladies and gentlemen, thank you for coming tonight," he said.

His speech was short and rousing. His charisma blanketed the room in a warm glow, and Victoria felt her pulse race as she listened to his voice.

Finally, someone handed Sebastian a glass of champagne. Everyone stood up and raised their glass with him. "To the future," he said.

Everyone around her echoed his toast enthusiastically. She, however, felt the words stick to her throat. She gulped down a glass of the bubbly drink, but the delicious liquid did nothing to lift her spirits.

When she sat back down, she noticed the odd look on Benson's face. "Are you okay, sweetie?" she said.

The boy started to nod, then paused before shaking his head. "I feel funny," he said, his hand pressed above his stomach.

"Are you going to be sick? Do you want to go to the bathroom? Here, let me take you." She stood up but he grabbed her hand and tugged at it.

"Not my tummy."

"Your chest?"

He nodded again.

She bent down to put her hand gently on his. "Have you had this pain before, Benson?"

"No." He swallowed. "My throat hurts too."

"I think we should get you to a doctor." She stood up and looked back to where she last saw Sebastian. He was gone.

Victoria sat back down and called his number only to get his voicemail. She hung up and tried again. After a few rings, she got his voicemail again. Biting her lip in frustration, she sent him a text telling him Benson wasn't feeling well.

"Is he coming?" the boy said.

"I'm trying to reach him, sweetie. Can you hang on? Just for a little while?" She smiled at him encouragingly.

"Okay." He leaned back in his seat.

She stood up again, and tried to call Sebastian one more time. He wasn't answering.

Desperate, she rang Connor's number.

"Ms. Slade?" The chauffeur's calm, deep voice on the other end of the line gave her some hope.

"Connor, hi! Look, Benson needs a doctor right now. Nothing too serious, I think, but he'll need to get looked at right away. I have no idea where Sebastian is, and I keep getting his voicemail."

"Ms. Slade, I'm sorry, but Mr. Chase requested me to drive the Singaporean ambassador's cousin back to his hotel. I'm afraid you'll have to get help from someone there. Frank is Mr. Chase's assistant, and he should know who might be able to assist you."

She wasn't sure if she remembered what Frank looked like, but maybe someone there could point him out. "I'll find him. Thank you, Connor."

Finding Sebastian's assistant wasn't difficult at all. She found him speaking to a wait staff near the bar. But the young man looked apprehensive when she told him the situation.

"How bad is it? Benson, I mean."

"He's in a bit of pain. But it's getting worse, I think. We really ought to get him to the hospital."

"Of course. This way, please." He gestured for her to follow him. "Mr. Chase is at a ... meeting right now and we're under strict instructions not to disturb him," he said as they made their way to the elevators, "but I'm sure in this case—"

"No, wait!" Victoria turned pale.

A meeting.

It couldn't be. Not Brooke. Sebastian wouldn't do this to her.

"A meeting?" she echoed weakly.

Frank nodded.

"No, I don't think we should ... " She swallowed. "Maybe I should just take Benson myself. Will that be all right?"

He looked visibly relieved. "Of course, Ms. Slade. Mr. Chase trusts you with Benson implicitly. How about you wait back there with Benson while I go call Mr. Chase? Even if he's not answering his mobile, the suite has a phone."

"I think we can manage, Frank. Thank you." More than anything, she didn't want her worst fears confirmed. Not right now. Benson needed her.

"That will probably be best." He paused. "The LAC-USC Medical Center is only a couple of miles away. You'll need a car."

"Yes, I suppose I do. I can drive, but Connor has the car."

"Mr. Chase has a couple of cars in the basement parking. They're in perfect condition, you can use one of them."

"Why does he have cars here?" she asked as they made their way back to the ballroom to fetch Benson.

"He owns part of the hotel, Ms. Slade."

Ten minutes later, Victoria pulled into the street in a black Chrysler. "I really think you should sit in the back," she said.

Beside her, Benson wrinkled his nose. "I'm old enough to sit up front."

"Okay then. We're just going to take a quick trip to the emergency room and have a doctor take a look at you, okay?"

"This is one of Uncle Sebastian's favorite cars," he said. "I haven't seen him drive it much."

She bit her lip at the mention of Sebastian's name. "He won't mind if we borrow it for a bit, will he?" she said, trying to keep her voice light.

"Nah. He says I can trust you with anything."

"He did, huh?" She felt tears gather behind her eyes, and a lump in her throat.

Trust.

"Do you have a car?"

"I did, but I had to give it up. I couldn't afford the insurance."

"What do you ride to work?"

"I take the bus."

"What's that like?"

"Don't you have buses in your school?"

"No. What are they for?"

Victoria laughed. "So parents don't have to take their kids to school if they're busy."

"Uncle Sebastian likes to drive me to school. We like to play a game where we— ow!"

"Benson?" She took her eyes off the road to glance at the boy. She put her hand on his chest. "Is it getting worse?"

He shook his head. "I'm okay."

"Hang on, all right? We're almost there."

The traffic light ahead turned red. "What the—" she said, panic tugging at her chest.

"What's wrong?" Benson said.

"Nothing," she said, trying to sound calm. The brakes weren't responding. She jammed her foot hard on the pedal but the car didn't slow down.

"Victoria?"

They sped through the red light. She looked over to Benson's window to see the headlights of an incoming SUV. She floored the gas, praying they'd outrun the vehicle before it hit them.

"Hang on, baby." She gripped the steering wheel with her left hand, and threw her right arm over Benson.

The last thing she heard was a loud crash before darkness overcame her.

Chapter 35

Decisions

"I expect you'll tell me why this can't wait till after the party," Sebastian said, entering the suite. Behind him, outside, the big burly bodyguard closed the door with a soft click.

George was pouring some scotch in two glasses. "Sit down, son," he said, not looking up. "I have a flight in two hours. I'm sure your fawning minions could do without you for a few minutes."

"They're called employees," Sebastian sat down on one of the two large leather chairs in the middle of the room. "I have to be getting back soon, so let's make this quick."

"Ah, yes, your date." George handed him a drink. "Funny, I never saw you as one to get friendly with the help."

"I would think you would be the last to object, seeing as you've been ... friendly with just about every assistant you've employed." The words felt bitter in Sebastian's mouth, but he kept his face impassive. The best way to deal with his father was to keep his emotions in check.

He took a sip of his drink and waited.

"True," George said. "However, I've never given them any of your mother's jewelry. Come now," he added, sensing the barely-concealed surprise in the younger man's face. "Did you assume I wouldn't notice?" George took a seat across from him. "I may not have been the most attentive husband, but I do remember giving her that bracelet for our first anniversary."

"You're right. I didn't think you'd remember," Sebastian conceded. "Nevertheless, my mother's jewelry was left to me. If I recall, you weren't interested in anything of hers. You'd already gotten majority shares of her family's real estate company, she had nothing else you were interested in." He looked around the large room, feigning boredom. "Is that all you came to tell me? Because I have a date waiting."

"She's very sweet, your son's tutor. A little too innocent, perhaps. Are you wary of leaving Benson in her care for just a few minutes?"

"Victoria is the one person I trust the most," Sebastian said, looking at him pointedly.

George chuckled. "You'd trust her with your life? How about your future, would you trust her with that? What about your son's future?"

Sebastian's fingers tightened around his glass. "Leave Ben out of this."

"You don't get to play babysitter for a few years and expect to know what's best for that boy," George said.

"You would know more than anyone, I suppose." Sebastian looked him in the eye. He didn't like where this conversation was going. When he was informed right after his speech that George wanted to see him urgently, he braced himself for the usual argument about how badly he was running the company. How it may have been a mistake for George to risk his reputation and his interest in the bank on an ungrateful son who refused to listen to his advice.

"Elizabeth is making her move soon," George said, not taking his bait. "She already has three other board members on her side. They're afraid the company isn't ready for the expansion in China, and they're rallying the rest to put a stop to it. That means getting rid of you."

"It's hardly an expansion. It's a partnership." Even as he spoke, Sebastian knew what his father said made perfect sense.

"Call it whatever you like. The truth is, all company resources will be geared towards fulfilling its part of this deal. And we're already in tenuous footing against the local competition."

"You said she was impressed we pulled off the Beijing deal."

"Only because they didn't expect you could do it. It's not your abilities they're doubting, it's the soundness of your decisions."

"I suppose you're here to give me advice on what decisions I should be making."

"No, but now that you brought it up, I'm here to tell you that firing Elton has gotten the board worked up. I don't suppose you'll tell me why you did that?"

"He couldn't be trusted."

"You know, I've pissed off a good many people in my time, son. But making an enemy of a man who's golf buddies with two state senators was astoundingly stupid."

"We'll manage without him." Sebastian tried not to show his discomfort toward the topic of Elton Lowry. Had he been too brash in getting rid of the man? On hindsight, conspiring with a jilted would-be lover sounded like a rather insubstantial reason for firing a senior vice president.

George leaned forward. "You and I may not see eye to eye on most things, Sebastian, but I'll be damned if I'll let that woman and her sniveling cohorts take away your control over your company."

"You mean *your* company, don't you, Dad?"

George shrugged. "I think in this case, you will agree we're on the same side." He leaned back in his seat and grinned wryly. "I'm not getting any younger, son. And you and Benson are all I have left. This company is our legacy. It's worth more than any amount of money you or I can leave that boy when we're dead. Years of hard work. Sacrifice. Your mother understood."

"Ah yes. I was wondering when you'd bring her up." It was only because of decades of practice that Sebastian was able to keep his anger in check. "Have you ever even loved her, Dad?"

"I did. In my own way, I did." George took a sip of his scotch. He swallowed the drink slowly, his eyes on his son. "And I think she loved me too. She loved you, and Eric. And do you know what? She loved the company. She knew what she had to give up for the Mattheson Corporation to achieve what it did. She did it for you." His gaze turned away. "She did it for you and Eric."

"This is all very touching, George, but get to the point."

"My point is, there's a beautiful woman downstairs who wants you, son." George smiled. "And it's not the one babysitting your nephew."

Sebastian was quiet for a few moments. He rested his elbow on the armrest and studied the side of his glass. "I guess the Texas governor's seat is a done deal, then?"

"Gov. Granger is going to take a shot at the White House, as you know. Clare Hildebrand's only real competition is a congressman who's waking up in a few days to the biggest sex scandal expose since Clinton and his interns."

"And you had nothing to do with that, I presume."

"Nothing I can admit to, no." George smiled smugly. "But it would be wise to take advantage of this opportunity."

"Brooke is vulnerable right now." Sebastian's anger felt cold in his chest. "But you knew that, didn't you?"

"So she's already told you." George shook his head. "Poor thing. I never gave it much thought, but it seems sometimes even smart, confident women get into abusive relationships. But her ex — well. The son of a bitch is out of the picture now." He lifted his drink slightly. "You and she were good together, even I could see that. You're just what she needs right now."

"What she needs right now," Sebastian said, trying to keep his voice calm, "is to not be manipulated into one of your schemes."

"I'd like to think I'm doing what's best for the young lady. Clare is a dear old friend, after all. Brooke is like a daughter to me. And for God's sake, Sebastian, she still loves you. You'll be good for her. And she'll be ..." He smiled. "She'll be the best decision you'll ever make in your life. You'll have everything. A beautiful, loving wife. A son. A family. Your position at the company will be uncontested. This is what I want for you, son."

"She's not what I want. And as for decisions," Sebastian added, setting down his drink. "I've already made mine." He stood up.

"That redhead?" George frowned. "My boy, no one is asking you to give her up. You like her well enough, even I can see that."

Sebastian's eyes narrowed. What was his father getting at?

George sighed. "I'm not the heartless monster you think I am," he continued. "If you like the girl, keep her. No one's expecting you to stay faithful, Sebastian. Not even Brooke."

"You don't know her," Sebastian said. "And you don't know me."

"I do, son. Hell, everyone knows about you and your women. Brooke was a sweet girl, but she's all grown up now. She's practical about these matters. You think Clare bothers to hide her lovers from her daughter? Who do you think makes restaurant and hotel reservations for them, for God's sake?"

Sebastian shook his head. "Unbelievable. You've really outdone yourself this time, dad."

"If Victoria is as smart as I think she is, then she probably doesn't expect you to be faithful either. I'm betting she knows about your women, eh? Everybody does. She won't have any delusions about you. She'll agree to whatever .. conditions you offer her. You won't lose her, I promise you that."

"What is wrong with you people?" Sebastian said, no longer bothering to hide his anger. "You live selfish lives. And you take your young and destroy whatever ... good they have left in them."

George stood up. "You're angry. That's fine, I understand," he said, nodding. "That's why we're giving you a few days to think about it." He cocked his head. "When you're done with this childish outburst of self-righteousness, come see me. I'm hosting a party in Fort Worth for Clare this weekend. It will be the perfect time and place to announce your and Brooke's engagement."

"Don't hold your breath," Sebastian said. He tried not to let his father's self-satisfied grin bother him. Without another word, he turned to leave.

The phone rang. He heard George pick it up.

"Hello," George said. His voice sounded cheerful, like nothing bothered him at all. "It's for you, son."

Sebastian frowned, but he closed the door. He walked slowly towards his father, who held out the phone to him.

"It sounds urgent," George added.

Sebastian took the phone. "Yes?" he said, wondering who would be calling him on this line.

"Mr. Chase?"

It was Frank. It was odd. His assistant would have called him on his cellphone. It was then that Sebastian realized he'd put his phone on mute right before his speech, and forgotten to turn the ringer back on.

"What is it, Frank?"

"Sir, I'm afraid there's been an accident."

***

Victoria opened her eyes. The fluorescent lights above her were blinding, and she turned her head to the side. She could hear familiar voices.

"Nicolette?" she said, her voice sounding weak to her ears.

"Babe!" Nicolette stood up from the table and rushed over to hug her. "What the hell, Vic," she said. "You scared the shit out of me."

"About time you woke up," said someone else.

"Sandi?" Victoria said, blinking. "You guys are here." When Nicolette let go of her, she found herself in another hug.

"Of course, we are, silly," Sandi said, squeezing her tight. "Casey's at work — some drawn-out libel case involving some Hollywood director — but he said to let him know when you're awake. He says after he finally makes partner, he'll be sure to be present for all your future hospital stays."

"That's good to know, I guess," Victoria said, still feeling disoriented. She struggled to sit up, and felt her body ache. "How long have I been out? Oh, God, where's Benson?"

Nicolette and Sandi exchanged looks. "Sweetie—" Nicolette started to say.

"Is Benson all right?" Victoria felt her tears spill down her cheeks. "Oh, God, please tell me he's all right."

Chapter 36

Moving On

"He's fine, Vic," Nicolette said. "It's just that ..."

"Benson's okay, really?" Victoria said, her voice shaking.

"According to the nurse, yeah." Nicolette paused, looking uncomfortable. "Uh, she also said Sebastian ... Well, he came and took Benson home as soon as the MRI and other tests were done."

"Sebastian? Did he..." Victoria looked down. "Did he say anything?"

"We didn't see him," Nicolette said. "Apparently, he got here before we did. He must have already checked on you." She handed Victoria a box of tissues. "You've had a slight concussion, and you've been out for a few hours, but it's nothing serious. The doctor will have another look at you now that you're awake."

"Right," Victoria said, but her words rang hollow in her ears. It wouldn't surprise her to know that Sebastian didn't bother to check if she was all right. Deep down, she knew she couldn't blame him if he didn't want anything more to do with her.

Why would he want to see her, the woman who nearly got his son killed?

"It was the cops who went through the car who found your purse, so I got the call a couple of hours after the accident," Nicolette said. "But they got Sebastian's contact information from the glove compartment. They called him almost immediately. He was here. I'm sure he came to see you."

"I must have been too passed out to hear him yelling at me," she added, wiping her tears and forcing herself to smile. "Was anyone else hurt?"

"Nah. Some other car hit you sideways, but the impact was mostly at the back of the car you were driving. The other driver was just a little shaken up. Insurance will take care of the damage to his car. And why would Sebastian yell at you? It was clearly an accident. " Nicolette took her hand in hers. "You weren't drunk or anything, were you?"

"No!" Victoria was horrified. "I had a glass of champagne, that's all. I would never have ..." She shook her head. "The brake didn't seem to be working. I tried slowing down so I could use the parking brake, but the car just seemed to go faster."

"It wasn't your fault."

"Yeah, wasn't it his crappy car in the first place?" Sandi said. "You should sue him."

"Sandi, you just want to sue everybody," Nicolette said. She turned to Victoria. "If he breaks up with you, then you can sue him."

***

"You don't have to stay, you know," Victoria said. She finally had her phone back, and she waited anxiously while it booted up.

"We're fine," Sandi said. She was sitting on the leather sofa, typing on her laptop. "This place is way nicer than my office."

"Yeah." Victoria looked around. "I didn't know my insurance could afford to give me a private room."

"The tutoring gig came with a nice insurance plan, I guess," Nicolette said. She was unloading cartons of Chinese food from a paper bag. "There must be some celebrity on this floor. There are security guys everywhere."

"As soon as I got off the elevator, they made me show them my ID and then frisked me to within an inch of my life," Sandi said, then grinned. "Not that I minded."

"I thought you said you looked horrible in your driver's license," Victoria said, puzzled. After a few seconds, what her friend said finally sank in. "Oh."

"Here," Nicolette said, handing Victoria a carton of dumplings. "Lunch."

"Uhm, in a second," Victoria said absently, going through her messages. There was one text from Nicolette, probably sent after she got the call from the hospital. She had voice mail from Casey and a couple other friends. And from one number she didn't recognize.

Sebastian?

She didn't bother checking the message, she just called the number back. With every ring, she felt her heart beating faster.

Please don't be angry. I'm so sorry. Sebastian, I'm so sorry.

"Hello. Morris Lamont speaking."

"Uh, hi," Victoria replied, her heart sinking. "This is Victoria. I'm returning a call you made early this morning to this number."

"Victoria Slade?"

"Yes."

"Hi, Ms. Slade, thank you for getting back to me. Are you free this afternoon? I have an opening at three o'clock."

"I'm sorry?"

"Oh. Did you not get my message?"

"No, I thought I'd just call you back. What is this about?"

"I'm the lifestyle editor here at the Tribune. I understand you sent in an application for a writing staff position a couple of months ago?"

"Yes, I did. I was told the position had been filled."

"It was. But my assistant editor just jumped ship last week, and I remembered getting a recommendation for you about, oh, three weeks ago."

"You did?"

"Yeah. Sebastian Chase called out of the blue, said he'd emailed me your resume and a bunch of articles you've written."

"I'm sorry, what? He did?" Three weeks ago. That didn't make sense. She'd only just met Sebastian three weeks ago.

"I barely knew the guy, to be honest. Kind of a snob. Never liked him, but his bank does a lot of advertising in our paper. It's funny, I got the impression you two were dating somehow."

"Why would you …"

"Sorry. It was just that he was practically gushing over your writing skills, Ms. Slade. He described your writing as a cross between Gloria Steinem and Chris Rock." Morris laughed. "He said you had more talent than the quote-unquote hacks in my staff."

"Oh, I'm sure he didn't mean that."

"I'm not sure he was wrong, though. That piece you did on the connection between climate change and the patriarchy was spot on."

"Thank you."

"Anyway, if you're interested in the job, I thought you might come by my office later today for a chat."

"Yes, of course. I mean, I'm interested, but I got into a little accident yesterday," she explained. "But I'll be free to come by tomorrow afternoon, if that works for you."

"Accident? Are you all right?"

"Yes, thank you. It was just a little thing last night. I'm perfectly fine."

"Good, good. Two o'clock?"

"Great. Thank you. And Mr. Lamont? Would you happen to remember the date Seb— Mr. Chase called you?" Victoria looked up to see Nicolette staring at her, eyebrows raised.

Sebastian? Nicolette mouthed.

Victoria shook her head.

"Let's see…" Morris said. "That was a Tuesday, I think. I got the call on my way to the press conference in the Mayor's office …" Finally, he figured it out and told her the date.

"Thank you," she said, trying to keep her voice from breaking. After she hung up, she stared at the phone, her eyes blurry with tears.

Sebastian had called Morris the evening after he'd interviewed her at his office. After he'd told her she didn't get the job, he called an editor at the Tribune and asked him to hire her.

"What's wrong, babe?" Nicolette said, handing her some tissue.

"Nothing," Victoria said, wiping her eyes. She felt emotionally spent — worrying about Benson, wondering if Sebastian would ever forgive her, and now this.

He had truly believed in her. Even when she was still practically a stranger to him, he'd done something for her few people would have made the effort to do.

It was all over now. She'd done the one thing Sebastian would never forgive her for.

She looked up to see Nicolette handing her a pair of chopsticks. "Give him some time, okay?" Nicolette said. "If things don't work out, well … You'll move on."

"Yeah." Victoria smiled, but her heart was so heavy she felt was going to collapse under the weight of her emotions. "It's not like I have a choice, do I?"

"No, sweetie. Because sometimes all we can do is love someone." She pushed a lock of hair out of Victoria's eyes. "It's their decision whether to love us back. And if we screw up, it's their decision to forgive us."

"I don't …" Victoria shook her head.

Love?

But she realized at that moment that no matter how much she denied it, it was as clear to her as day. She knew. Somehow, she'd always known.

She loved Sebastian.

"Have you tried calling him?" Nicolette said.

Victoria shook her head. "I should. But I'm … I'm not sure I can face him right now. Not yet."

"Give yourself a few days. You've been through a lot. If he breaks up with you because of this, then frankly he's not worth it."

***

"How are we doing on that vegan restaurant article?" Morris said, dropping a sheaf of magazine clippings on Victoria's desk.

Victoria looked up at him and smiled. "I just uploaded it now," she said. "Going over the European vacation piece now."

"Hey, Morris," Carmen Velez called out from across the room. "I have a few questions about some italicized words in the European vacation piece. You got a minute?"

"Be right there," Morris said, then turned back to Victoria. "So here are the articles I'd like you to take a look at. Don't forget we're meeting with the web team tomorrow about the redesign."

"Okay, thanks," Victoria said. "Are you sure you need me there? I don't really know anything about websites."

"I think maybe you ought to go check up on the layout team, sir," Clay Barton said, walking up behind Morris. "Amy and Greg are arguing again. Something about photo filters."

Morris sighed. "Be right there, Clay," he replied. "Anyway," he continued, "we have more readers online than those who read us on paper, Victoria. We have to keep that in mind when creating articles."

"I suppose that makes sense." She flipped through the clippings. "I'll take a look at these and I'll have the rest of the articles up on the server by five."

"Great. I really appreciate you getting on board today. As you can see, we're almost understaffed for the work that needs to be done."

"Honestly, I had no idea I'd be starting today," Victoria said. She'd interviewed with Morris right after lunch, and she agreed to start that afternoon. She glanced around her, taking in the chaos of the busy newsroom. In a way, it reminded her of breakfast hour at the Foxhole — all tables are full, and the wait staff had to juggle two or three tasks at a time trying to get everyone's order within the required 20 minutes. "But I'm just glad I got the job. I'd always wanted to work here."

"Let's hope you still feel that way after a week." Morris grinned. "If you need anything, I'll be back at my desk as soon as I get Greg and Amy off each other's throats."

***

Victoria couldn't remember the last time she was this exhausted. It was only eight in the evening, and all she wanted to do was crawl into bed for a week. She was hungry, too. The tiny sandwich she ate at her desk while going through proofs was not going to be enough for dinner, as evidenced by the grumbling in her stomach.

She wondered if she should get takeout. There was a two-block walk from the bus stop to her apartment, and there was an assortment of fast food places on the way. She was in the mood for a pizza, a really large one. But the idea of balancing a 24-inch pizza box while in heels was not appealing, so she decided to call for delivery instead.

Pepperoni and cheese, she thought. Or maybe something with anchovies. She remembered they had a bottle of pretty good red wine in the cupboard that Nicolette had brought home the week before. Was her roommate still home? She pulled her cellphone out of her bag and dialed Nicolette's number.

"Hey, Nic, you at work?"

"Yeah. You still at the office?"

"On my way home. Too bad. I was hoping we could get a pizza before you left. I wanted to celebrate."

"Let's have dinner tomorrow, okay? Faustino's maybe? What time are you getting off? Was your boss hot?"

Victoria laughed. "Yes, yes, around 8, and yes. He's married, though."

"Guess you can't have everything. Gotta go. I'll see you at breakfast, okay?"

"What are you talking about? I have to be out the door by seven thirty and you don't get up before …" Victoria looked up and stopped, feet frozen on the sidewalk.

There are few things in life more disconcerting than seeing the man you love standing in front of your apartment building. Especially when you've just spent the last 24 hours agonizing over whether or not to see him ever again, or wondering if he would ever want to see you again.

Sebastian didn't say a word. He put his hands in his pockets and waited, his eyes on her.

"You were saying?" Nicolette said.

"I'm, uh," Victoria stammered. "I'm going to have to call you back."

CHAPTER 37

On the Street Where You Live

Sebastian tapped his fingers on one knee. Where was she?

The large black Lincoln town car was parked in front of Victoria's apartment. He rang the doorbell thirty minutes ago but no one was answering.

"Have you tried her mobile, Mr. Chase?" Connor said. He was sitting in the driver's seat, his ramrod straight posture betraying neither restlessness nor impatience despite having been sitting in that same position for the past hour.

"I would really much rather deal with this in person, Connor," said Sebastian, staring outside his window at the apartment entrance. The door opened, and two elderly women stepped out into the sidewalk, chatting animatedly. "I'm sure she'll be home soon."

"Yes, sir."

Benson was on his knees looking through the rear window, his chest pushed up against the back of the seat. His right arm was in a cast. "Do you think maybe she moved away, Uncle Sebastian?" he said, squinting.

"No, Ben, I don't think she moved away," Sebastian said. "And be careful with your arm."

The boy smiled sheepishly and leaned away from the back of the seat, then turned back to look out the window.

Sebastian sighed. "Just remember our deal, okay?"

"Uh-huh." The boy nodded solemnly without looking at him. "There she is!"

"Stay here," Sebastian said, opening the car door before Connor could do it for him.

Victoria was on her mobile phone, completely oblivious to him as she walked. She was dressed in a cream-colored suit, and her hair was pulled up in a tight bun.

He stood there, unable to think of anything to say. On impulse, he put his hands in his pants pockets, and he realized he was nervous.

When she finally saw him, she paused, not moving an inch closer. After what seemed forever, she put the phone in her purse.

"Sebastian," she said. She spoke so softly he thought he'd imagined her voice.

"Vi." He moved closer. "Are you all right?"

The sadness in her face was almost too much for him to bear. For a nerve-wracking few moments he was afraid she was going to turn and run.

"I'm fine, I—"

He reached out to cup her face in his hands, covering her mouth with a kiss.

Don't go, he wanted to say to her. *I love you. Please forgive me.*

But he was lost in the sweetness of her lips. He clasped his fingers on the back of her neck, pulling her closer against him.

"I'm sorry, Sebastian," she whispered against his mouth.

"It was my fault," he said. He pressed a kiss against her forehead. "If something had happened to you, I could never forgive myself."

"But …" She looked up at him, puzzlement in her eyes. "I was driving. I put Benson in danger."

"Someone hacked the onboard system of that car." He put his arms around her shoulders and pulled her close. "It was due for a system patch, and no one was supposed to be driving it. Frank didn't know. It wasn't his fault."

"But who would do a thing like that?" Victoria's eyes swelled with tears.

"Someone who hated me. His name is Elton. I spent the last twenty-four hours with my best tech guys tracking the hacker who messed with the car, and then tracking Elton's bank activity to figure out where he was so the cops could arrest him."

She breathed a sigh of relief. "I thought you hated me. You didn't call. I waited for you to call."

"I know, I'm sorry." He pulled her chin up and kissed her, softly at first. But the desperate longing that had been tugging at his consciousness took over and he kissed her deeper.

Victoria moaned against his mouth. Her hands moved up his sides, gripping his waist as though it was the only thing keeping her from falling.

When he broke the kiss, they were both breathless.

Sebastian put his lips on her temple. "I was with my father when you and Ben left. Why did you not have Frank call me?" he said.

She bit her lip. "I thought that maybe … maybe you had run off with Brooke somewhere."

He sighed. "Why would I do that, you idiot?"

"I dunno!" She sniffed. "She was all beautiful and blonde and—"

"And she's not you." He squeezed her tighter. "I have a strict policy of only running off with women who are … you."

"But—"

"Look, I have never slept with anyone else since you and I…" He paused. *Since you and I met. I've never had sex with anyone else since I first laid eyes on you.* "Since you and I slept together."

"And you didn't call," she said, her voice almost breaking. "While I was at the hospital, I didn't hear a word from you."

"I didn't have a lot of time. Elton had a lot of friends, powerful ones. I knew we had to get hold of him before he tried anything else. Before he tried to hurt anyone else. Before he tried to hurt Ben, or you." Sebastian closed his eyes. "I was afraid if I heard your voice, I'd be a bigger emotional mess than I already was."

He opened his eyes to see her looking up at him anxiously. "But Benson is okay?" she said.

"Yes, we had him on lockdown in a safe house. I got two of the best security guys to watch him. He drove them nuts."

"But Benson's so quiet," Victoria said, smiling through her tears. "How could he—"

"That's exactly it. Ben just sat there reading. He even made them tea."

"Oh God." She laughed, laying her head on his chest. "That sounds just like him."

"I sent a few security professionals to keep watch over you at the hospital."

She looked up again, her eyes wide. "You mean those big, armed men were there to protect me? We thought Jennifer Lawrence was getting an appendectomy down the hall."

"Who?"

She laid her head back on his chest, chuckling. "Never mind."

Sebastian stroked her back. He felt a sense of peace come over him. It felt good having her back in his arms. There was one more thing he needed to do. One thing he needed to tell her.

"Vi," he said. "I need to tell you—"

He stopped, feeling her being pulled away from him. He looked down. "What the—" he said. "Ben, I thought we agreed you were to stay in the car until we called for you."

Benson shook his head stubbornly, and kept hugging Victoria with his one good arm.

"I'm sorry, Mr. Chase," said Connor. "I tried to keep him in the car, but he slipped right past me."

"Benson!" Victoria said. "Oh, my God, your arm."

"I'm okay," the boy said. He looked up. "I was worried about you."

Victoria hugged him back. "I'm great, sweetie. I was worried about you."

Sebastian patted Benson's shoulder. "I told you Victoria was okay, Ben." He put his other arm around her shoulders, and leaned close. "She's perfect."

And I love her, he thought.

"What happened to you the other night, Benson?" Victoria said. "Was it allergies?"

"Acid reflux," Benson said. "I'm okay now."

"We just need to keep him away from oranges from now on," Sebastian said.

"I love you, Victoria," said the boy.

"I love you, too," she said, stroking Benson's hair. She looked up into Sebastian's eyes.

Sebastian kissed her.

Was it too soon to tell her how he felt?

"Sebastian?"

"Yes, dear?"

"Is Connor crying?"

***

Two weeks later

"I don't even know why you're making me do this," Victoria said. She didn't bother to hide the frustration in her voice.

"Don't grab it too tightly, Vi," said Sebastian. "Are you trying to break it?"

"You've been making me hold this for hours. My arms are tired."

"Don't exaggerate, darling. We've only been doing this for twenty minutes."

"What do you mean 'we'? I'm the one getting finger cramps here. You're just sitting there telling me to move my hand faster."

"That's because you keep hesitating, baby." He sighed. "This won't work if you keep stopping."

"I don't think I'll ever get this right."

"You will. Just don't stop. There, that's good. Keep going."

"Is this better?"

"Hmmm ... Hold it properly, Vi. You'll poke yourself in the eye again."

"I'm trying. This is hard."

"You're doing fine, baby. Just keep your fingers firmly-- ow!" Sebastian winced.

"Sorry!" Victoria bit her lip. "Did that hurt?"

"No, no. It's fine. You just hit the wrong note." He rubbed his right ear gingerly.

"Okay, I give up," she said, taking the violin out from under her chin. "I sound like a cow being murdered." She placed the violin and bow on the stand. Frowning, she added, "What are you laughing at?"

"Nothing." He tried to stop chuckling, but he couldn't help it. "I'm sorry, baby." He forced a serious expression on his face. "I'm very sad about that cow." He patted the space on the sofa next to him. "Come here."

"Why?" She eyed him suspiciously. "More violin lessons?"

"Of course. You're a very bad student."

She bit her lip. "I don't think I want any more lessons. Not from you."

"You'll like this one."

Chapter 38

Confessions

Victoria leaned back on Sebastian's chest, letting him wrap his arms around her. "I've been meaning to ask you something," she said.

"Yes?"

"The board meeting is tomorrow, isn't it? Is your Dad going to get you fired?"

"He'll try." Sebastian pulled her closer to him. "I won't let him. The deal with Beijing is done. I can convince the board they're better off with me than with anyone else if the company is going to make it through. After all, I do have a business plan for this. I'll promise them that if they don't like the way things are going after a year, I'll resign."

"Yikes." She paused. "Are you sure you don't want to make this problem go away and just marry Brooke?"

"Who?"

She smiled. "You always this smooth, Mr. Chase?"

"I do my best." He took her hands in his, and began rubbing her fingers gently.

"I think I'm getting callouses on my fingertips now." Her voice trembled slightly; the heat from his body was making her dizzy with desire.

"Poor baby." Sebastian kissed the tips of her fingers before rubbing her hands. "Tired?"

Victoria bit back a moan rising in her throat. His lips were warm and soft, and left a delicious tingle on her fingers. She turned her head, brushing her mouth against his chin. "Not really," she whispered.

"Good." He covered her hands with one hand, while his other hand reached down to pull up the hem of her skirt.

She whimpered, feeling her body heat up as he caressed her thigh. "Sebastian, what are you doing?"

His lips were against her temple, his breath hot on her skin. "Do you think I'm behaving inappropriately with my son's tutor, Ms. Slade?"

"I quit, remember?" Her breath was coming in short gasps, her arousal quickly building. "You've been, uh, inappropriate with me for weeks."

"Is that so?" He moved his hand up her thigh. Slowly.

"Are you sure you wouldn't rather do this in your room?" she whispered.

"Says the woman who practically tore my clothes off in the car yesterday."

His fingers slipped inside her thong. She closed her eyes, savoring the pleasure of his hand stroking her between her thighs. "You were gone for two days on that business trip," she moaned. "I missed you."

"Is that your excuse for public indecency, Victoria?"

He tugged, pulling down her panties. After a moment's hesitation, she moved her legs to let him slip the underwear completely off her. She got on her knees on the sofa and turned to face him.

"You do know some of your staff haven't gone home yet, right?" she said, straddling his lap. She nipped his ear playfully with her teeth. "I can't promise to be quiet."

"We're in the music room." He grasped her ass cheeks and pulled her closer against him.

She gasped when she felt his rock-hard erection under her. "So?"

He brushed his mouth over her lips. "It's soundproof," he whispered.

"Oh." She blinked. "Completely ... soundproof?"

"Let's find out."

When he pulled her head back down to kiss her, she parted her lips instinctively. His tongue darted between her teeth to tease the edges of her tongue. Each lick sent a jolt of pleasure up her spine. She ground her hips down on his cock that was straining against his pants.

It felt good. The taste of him in on her lips. The hardness of his manhood against her bare pussy. The touch of his fingers as he gripped her naked buttocks. She could almost hear the air around them grow still to give way to the sounds of their breathing, the push of their bodies against each other. Her desire was a tightly bound spring slowly uncoiling with every kiss, every caress.

Victoria wrapped her arms tightly around his neck. She pressed her mouth harder against his, pushing his head against the back of the sofa. But their tongues kept up their feverish dance, only brushing at each other's edges. Licking, tasting.

Sebastian's fingers were on the buttons of her shirt, undoing them one by one. He pulled her shirt down her back, then tugged the straps of her bra down her arms. He moved his mouth down her throat, teasing her skin with little wet flicks of his tongue. He covered her breast with one hand, pressing and rubbing it.

"This is way better than violin lessons," she said, breathless as she reached down to undo his pants.

"Slow down a little, baby." He now had both hands on her breasts, fondling them with gentle but firm strokes. "We have all n—"

"Shut up." She pulled down his pants zipper and plunged one hand inside his boxers to wrap her fingers around his swollen shaft.

He met her eyes as she began to stroke his cock. "Are you bossing me around now, Ms. Slade?" he said, his voice heavy with arousal.

"You like it, don't you?" She kept one hand on the back of his neck while she moved her other hand up and down his stiff member in a steady rhythm.

"Always, my love."

She lowered her head to kiss him deeply. With one slow, firm push, he was inside her.

She pumped her hips, letting the length of his pulsating rod push and slide through her. No matter how many times they did this intimate dance, this frenzied, savage coupling, every moment of it still felt incredible. And every time, she was alive with a fire only he could create inside her.

He kept a firm grip on her waist, letting her take him again and again with every dip of her hips. His grunts of satisfaction were deep and loud, and — God help her — were the sexiest sounds she had ever heard in her life.

Her own cries of pleasure were becoming louder and sharper. Each slam of his turgid hammer against her inner walls brought a shiver of ecstasy through her more intense than the one before.

"Sebastian," she gasped.

She was coming. She could feel her flower clench involuntarily around his thick, slick branch. Her body was shaking. She had to grab his shoulders to steady her movements. Because she couldn't stop. At that moment, she needed this — her lover inside her, pulsing and rubbing and making all her senses fire up like guns on a battlefield — far more than she needed air to breathe.

"Victoria." He looked into her eyes. For the moments that followed, his gaze, thick with lust and longing, never left her face. They stayed locked into each other's eyes as she climbed, higher and higher until she found her peak.

"Fuck, yes … Oh, fuck," she gasped.

"So beautiful," he growled. "My beautiful woman … Victoria…"

She parted her lips, her head rolling back slightly. Her hips slowed their pace, but he tightened his grip.

"Keep going, baby," Sebastian said.

"But I'm … Oh fuck!" Victoria's eyes went wide for a moment as he began furiously pounding his ramrod up into her.

"That's right, baby … don't stop."

She gave out a long, loud cry as she climaxed once again.

He snaked an arm around her waist. Holding her fast against him, he came hard inside her with quick, short thrusts.

Victoria could hear nothing outside the sound of their heavy breathing and the deafening staccato of her heartbeat. Or was it his? He was still inside her. Her arms were locked around his neck, and his body pressed snugly against her chest.

Sebastian gently moved to pull out of her, but as soon as he did, he gathered her back into his arms.

"I told you," he whispered.

They were lying on the sofa. It was too small for his frame, let alone his and hers together, but somehow they managed. Mostly because Victoria was practically lying on top of him.

She didn't mind. And she guessed by the tightness of his embrace, he didn't either.

"Told me what?" The haze of sex was still all over her, and she was almost sure this was why her brain wasn't registering his question properly.

"That this room was completely soundproof."

"Oh. That." She chuckled. "I guess we'll find out when we see Mrs. Sellers tomorrow."

"Move in with me."

"What?" She lifted her head to stare at him. "But we haven't —"

"I love you." He brushed her cheek with his thumb. "I think I've loved you since that day you chased me into that elevator."

"Sebastian… I had no idea. Why didn't you say something sooner?"

"You worked for me, Vi. I didn't want to be that kind of man."

"I really did chase you, didn't I?" She winced. "Oh God. That was so embarrassing."

He raised his eyebrow. "And here I thought that's how you got men to fall in love with you."

"Nah. I think that only worked with you." She smiled. "I love you, Sebastian."

He cupped her face to pull her into a kiss. "So, you'll move in?" He took a quick nibble at her lower lip. "Today?"

"Have you spoken to Benson about this?"

"I did. Two weeks ago."

"What?"

"He's very excited. You're his favorite gaming partner. You don't mind, do you?"

"Mind?"

"Shacking up with a single dad."

Victoria smiled and shook her head. "I don't mind."

"Is that a yes?"

"Yes." She lay her head back on his chest, sighing contentedly.

END

About the Author

Ansela Corsino is a graphics artist living in the Philippines. When she was a child, she discovered classic science fiction books and her grandmother's old romance paperbacks. She has a weakness for hot men who can cook and fix things around the house. She once dumped a guy for not knowing what Star Trek was.

She wanted to grow up to be a spy, until she found out that writing was way more fun.

Facebook Page: http://facebook.com/authoransela
Twitter: http://twitter.com/anselacorsino
Instagram: http://instagram.com/ansela.corsino
Website: http://anselacorsino.com
Mailing list: http://anselacorsino.com/subscribe

Email: author@anselacorsino.com